For Andrea
Our Canadian s... ...

COURAGE
& COMPLICITY

by

Claudette Languedoc

Claudette Languedoc

*This book is dedicated
to Ray Kohut*

Tellwell Talent
www.tellwell.ca

ISBN
978-1-7750600-0-0 (Hardcover)
978-1-7750600-2-4 (Paperback)
978-1-7750600-1-7 (eBook)

FACT OR FICTION?

The places and people presented here are entirely fictional. The characters are not based on anyone, living or dead, there is no town of Bear Lake (that I'm aware of), and there is no Bear Lake Indian Residential School.

However, the stories told here are based on fact. Many of the children who attended residential school suffered terrible abuse at the hands of their guardians, many did not. But all lived in fear of punishment, all were forbidden to speak their language, and all were returned home with nothing but a basic education, and no idea of how to parent the next generation. As Mary says in the epilogue, "There were good and kind people at Bear Lake Indian Residential School. I'm sure there were good and kind people at every Indian residential school. But goodness and kindness can only go so far when your role is to make someone believe their history, culture and very DNA are something shameful."

What *is* shameful is our history of residential schools. We cannot change the past, but we can affect the future. The First People of Turtle Island have suffered much at the hands of the settlers. And the settlers have lost much in not working with, and learning from, the people who knew this land as intimately as they knew their own children. We need each other, and we are richer for knowing one another.

LABELS

Words are powerful tools, and never more so when we use them to label a person or group.

I am old enough to have seen a number of different labels attached to many of the Indigenous people in Canada. When I was growing up the label was "Indian." It changed to Canadian Indian, then North American Indian, then Native, Aboriginal, and First Nation. At the time of writing, Indigenous is the politically correct iteration. It seems, though, that there is a movement towards avoiding a general term at all, and referring instead, to the linguistic or cultural group, Haida, Anishinaabe, Cree etc..

Throughout this book, I use the term, "Indian" to describe the First People of this land as this was the term in use during the time in which the book was set.

PROLOGUE

AUGUST 2006

When the doorbell rang I was in the Happy Baby pose. It's supposed to be restorative, but as I struggled to stand, I worried that whoever was at the door would become impatient and leave before I managed to get up off the floor and answer their summons.

A delivery man in a neatly pressed uniform greeted me, handed me a book-sized package, shoved an electronic pad my way and asked for my signature. At a time when even a handwritten letter was a novelty, the package, wrapped in plain brown butcher paper, was almost anachronistic. I scratched my name on his pad which he took back before handing me the parcel. After pushing a few buttons, he gave me a polite thank you and bounded down my front porch stairs. A large circle of sweat on the back of his shirt was the last I saw of him before he disappeared into his truck.

I turned inside, impatient to find out what the mysterious package could hold. The return address was a lawyer's office in Winnipeg. Had some unknown uncle died and left me a treasure? That was unlikely, as I was eighty myself and most of my older relatives were long gone.

Closing the door on the bright sun that was bouncing off my linoleum floor, I ripped open the simple paper wrapping. The moment I saw the mottled red leather which bound the books inside, I knew exactly what I was holding. My hands went limp and the half-opened parcel dropped to the floor.

A few hours later, I kicked it under the hall table so I didn't have to look at it. Two days after that, it was still there.

You're being ridiculous, I told myself. It's just pen and paper. Pick it up, throw it out if you want to, but deal with it.

So I did.

I brought it into the living room and sat on the sofa. With the morning sun warm on my back, I stared at the soft red covers I remembered so well. Inside the wrapping, I discovered an envelope with the same lawyer's return address. I opened this first.

Dear Mrs. Morrison,

I am sorry to inform you of the passing of Brother Thomas, late of the parish of St. Albans in Winnipeg.

I understand that your relationship with Brother Thomas was short and occurred a long time ago, but in preparing his will he assured me that you would not have forgotten him. He asked that I send you these journals which he had saved from the period during which you knew him.

Brother Thomas died six years ago, on Thursday, March 9, 2000, of pneumonia. He was 97 years old. I apologize for the time it took for these books to reach you, but I'm sure you'll understand that we had some difficulty locating you after all these years.

If you have any questions regarding this bequest, or indeed anything at all about Brother Thomas I would be happy to tell you what I can.

He struck me as a simple, honest and kind man.

Sincerely yours,
Milton T. Harvey, LLB

Simple, yes, kind, maybe, honest, not so much, I thought. But Brother Thomas was right, I could never forget him. Even though I thought I had.

On the cover and the spine of each journal the year was stamped in gold leaf that still sparkled: 1947 and 1948. So very long ago.

So very long ago, I thought again, wistful, but still anxious. The anxiety won out and I procrastinated once more. It has waited this long, I thought, it can wait a little longer. I put the books on a shelf in my study. When I could look at them without a pounding heart, I would read them. I owed him that much.

Two years later the journals went down to the basement with some other books that were not being looked at but were loved too much to give away. They sat there, mostly forgotten, until one more year had passed, and another surprise arrived at my front door.

Later, I wondered if Brother Thomas had sent Emily to me. It wouldn't have surprised me one bit. He wasn't one to leave a job undone.

SEPTEMBER 2009

My family knows to come right in when they stop by for a visit. So when my granddaughter, Clarice, arrived with her university friend for a cup of tea, she shouted a loud "hello" from inside my front door and waited for me to appear. I was delighted to hear her voice and headed down the stairs from my study to greet her. A young woman stood beside Clarice on the black and white linoleum.

Slight of build and timid of demeanour, this young woman was as innocent of the shock waves she produced in me as the unexpected parcel had been a few years earlier. Yet the moment I set eyes on her, from my vantage point halfway down the stairs, my heart stopped and my hand clutched the wooden banister.

"Are you all right, Grandma?" Clarice asked.

"Fine, dear. How wonderful to see you."

I smiled reassuringly and continued on down the stairs, concentrating on moving my feet, feeling the tread and hearing the reassuring protest with each step.

The girl at the bottom of the stairs was not a ghost, but her resemblance to another young woman, someone I had known many years ago, was striking. I knew she could not be anyone other than a direct relative. I marvelled at how windows opened, even years after doors had closed.

When I reached the foot of the stairs I put out my hand, and my granddaughter introduced us, "Emily, this is my grandma, Mrs. Morrison—although most of my friends call her Grandma."

Emily looked a little uncertain.

"Grandma is fine with me," I said. "If it makes you uncomfortable though, 'Mrs. Morrison' works just as well. Let's go make some tea."

I led the way to the kitchen, anxious to have something to do while the girls' small talk filled the room. They spoke of their university courses and how they had met. They had found an instant connection despite their very different backgrounds. Emily was from Bear Lake, a small Northern Ontario community, Clarice from Toronto. They were both enrolled in Indigenous Studies. I always smiled when I heard my granddaughter say that. In my day, they weren't Indigenous, or First Nations, they were Indians, and no one was interested in studying them—just changing them.

Emily's fine black hair hung down her back, framing a soft oval face. Her eyes defied description as green, brown and black all vied for attention. Clarice, her counterpoint, looked as I did at her age. European stock, her blond hair was cut short in an attempt to tame her curls. Her grey-blue eyes were deeply set, and a surprising dimple showed up in her left cheek when she smiled.

As I set the steaming yellow teapot on its trivet, my mind turned to another table, and another kitchen, this one in a small cabin outside of Bear Lake, Emily's hometown. There, many years ago, two other young women had sat around that very same teapot. A casual onlooker could be forgiven for thinking nothing had changed but the décor.

The teapot was the first purchase I made from Johnson's General Store, in Bear Lake, Ontario. It was September 1947. I was a new teacher at the Bear Lake Indian Residential School, fresh out of teacher's college and ready for adventure.

In 1947 the war was over. My brothers had returned; my fiancé had not. I was a restless young woman, suffocating in the cocoon of my parents' upscale Toronto home. I was as sure of myself and my limitless potential as my granddaughter and her friend were that day. I was ready to take on the world without the faintest idea of, or the least bit of concern about the complicated mess I was willfully jumping into.

By the time I left Bear Lake, only ten months after my arrival, my ardour had cooled and I didn't think I'd done a particularly good job of changing the world. But this young lady at my kitchen table, drinking from my Bear Lake teapot, made me hope that perhaps my small bit had contributed to a larger whole. That, while it had taken longer than I had believed possible, maybe some of my naïve and idealistic dreams were going to see the light of day.

It was time to look at Brother Thomas's journals.

AUGUST
1947

FIRST IMPRESSIONS

Brother Thomas's Journal
August 15, 1947

A staff meeting today. One of the few I have to attend, thank the good Lord for that. It's hot enough outside, sitting in a stuffy room with a large group of stuffy people, sweating in their ridiculous habits is close enough to hell that I'm going to try extra hard to be saintly!

It seems that the rumours are true. We're getting two new teachers this year, both lay people, neither Catholic. They must have been desperate.

One is a young man from Montreal. Apparently, he is paddling his way to the school. Took him all summer! Quite the expedition, and no doubt good preparation for teaching here. He's expected next week, and I'm curious to meet him. The other one I'm not laying any bets on. A young lady from Toronto, who's only just finished Normal School. She's coming up on the train. Not that I hold the train ride against her, I'd be coming that way myself.

There are two tents outside the gate already. School is still a couple of weeks away, but students are starting to arrive. Simon and his brother are two of the early arrivals. They came in today. It's good for the students who have to stay all summer to have some old friends return; makes them feel less like orphans. I can use the extra hands as well.

It's been a strange summer for growing. All that rain and warm weather in July, and now this drought with no sign of relief. It's cooling down a bit, but it doesn't look much like rain. We've been trying to keep the vegetables watered, but it's a pathetic affair. I've sketched out some ideas for an irrigation ditch and I'll run them by B. Christopher, but I don't hold out much hope for anything to come of them this year. We can only pray that the big sprout in July will make up for this miserable August.

From the moment I spotted the small advertisement for a teacher in the paper—through my father's lectures on the dangers of life for a single girl in the rough North woods, my girlfriends' wide-eyed horror and my church minister's quiet warnings of a Spartan lifestyle—I never lost my resolve, or my enthusiasm, for the post I had accepted. I had spent the war in the safe and comfortable confines of a well-appointed home, and this was my chance for adventure. I turned a deaf ear to the warnings and built a wall around my own misgivings.

Besides, I was confident that I was not as unprepared as my detractors thought. My family and I spent every summer at our cottage on Bella Lake, near Huntsville, Ontario, and I also went to a summer camp for girls in the same area. Huntsville had started as a manufacturing and wood-milling centre, but by the forties it had become the commercial centre for thousands of summer visitors and hundreds of winter ones. Cottages dotted the shorelines of lakes large and small, too numerous to count. In addition, there were lodges, inns and camps. The more adventurous brought their own tents and canoes to nearby Algonquin Park. I was among them and lived for my August canoe trips: a week in Algonquin Park. I knew the North. Or so I thought.

When the day finally came for me to take the train to Bear Lake, any trepidation I had was lost in my excitement. In addition to a small suitcase that came with me in my first-class sleeper, I had two pieces of luggage—my big blue trunk, the one that always came with me to camp, and my father's suitcase, easily recognized by his initials, "JWB," which had been burned into the leather just below the sturdy handle. When I saw them disappear into the baggage car I knew I had reached the point of no return, and I couldn't wait to get on the train myself. My parents weren't as ready. My mother cried and my father pressed a hundred dollars into my hand with the whispered promise of train fare home when I changed my mind. I smiled and thanked him, then broke from their embraces to climb aboard.

It took two days on the train to get to Bear Lake. They were glorious days! Most of the passengers were young men going to work in the newly discovered oil fields of Alberta or even farther west to British Columbia's mines and forests. I was the belle of the ball, flirting shamelessly and loving every minute. It was an auspicious start to my grand adventure!

When we finally pulled into Bear Lake, we all looked eagerly out the windows to see my new home. For a long moment a sombre silence filled the car. It was broken when someone joked that I could stay aboard with them—oil fields and coal mines might be more to my liking. Gathering my things, I felt my first moment of hesitation. Maybe, just maybe, my parents were right.

Instead of Huntsville's freshly painted station with a restaurant and waiting room, there was a dusty wooden platform with a tin roof. Instead of harried attendants in the midst of a jostling, eager crowd dressed in summer linens and colourful hats, there were a few slouching men, their hands in the pockets of their dirty dungarees.

The man who had been sent to meet me would have been easy to spot, even in a Huntsville crowd. He stood out not only in his dress, but also his posture. Tall and straight backed, wearing an old fashioned black habit, he was a lanky man of indeterminate age. A few grey hairs topped an otherwise bald head, and his hands hung loosely at his sides. Despite these differences, he didn't look out of place. He was as sparse and dirty as the other men milling on the platform, grease stains competing with dust to see which could cover his habit completely.

As our train ground to a stop, I watched him walk, with slow deliberate steps, to the baggage car, which was just in front of the caboose. Apparently, he didn't feel it necessary to greet me first.

Stepping off the train and into my new world, I hurried to the baggage car myself to make sure that nothing would be left behind. I needn't have worried. By the time I got there, my worldly belongings were already at my host's feet and the train whistle was blasting into the hot August sky. Shouts followed and I turned to wave to the handsome faces blowing kisses out the windows. I watched with rising uneasiness as my old world pulled out of the station. Soon there was nothing to see but tracks and I stood alone in my new home.

Really alone. My host was obviously not one to waste time on pleasantries, either hellos or goodbyes. When I turned back to greet him, he was gone, along with my big blue trunk. I picked up the other suitcases and followed him to a pick-up truck, which, like everything else I had seen so far, was covered in dust.

It wasn't until we were finally seated next to each other in the cab of the pickup that I heard his voice for the first time.

"Hello," he said. "The name is Brother Samuel. I'm assuming you're Mary Brock."

I turned to smile at him. He reciprocated with a tight-lipped grin.

"That's me. Thank you for picking me up. I'm very excited about this coming year. I've never lived up North, and this will be my first year teaching, although I did do student teaching of course. I hope I live up to the trust placed in me."

Brother Samuel grunted and put the truck into gear.

"What do you do at the school?"

"I fix what needs fixing."

"What's it like there? Are there any students there yet?" I could have asked a million questions, but I got the feeling that two at a time was probably enough for Brother Samuel.

"You know little girl," he said, "this truck needs a lot of concentration. If you don't mind, Mother Magdalene'll be a much better person for your questions and I'll be a better driver if I can concentrate. Don't mean to be rude. I know you're just being friendly. Just how I am."

And so he was.

I didn't have to endure the silence for long. The dirt road took us past a few houses, and then a lumber mill. As we moved farther from town, the forest closed in, darker and denser, until the canopy closed over us completely. We drove under it for about ten minutes when, like a curtain pulled back to reveal the stage, the trees disappeared and the school came into view. Sitting on a small hill, it commanded attention. Four stories high, with arms spread wide, it sat like a misplaced apartment building in the middle of a wide and unnaturally empty space. Its immensity dwarfed the barn and the few visible outbuildings.

The forest had once held primacy here. Now it formed a dark circle around the perimeter, barely there in sections, where fields of vegetables and grains had replaced the trees, and tantalizingly close in others; a threat of what might be if vigilance were not kept.

Just outside the school's gates I saw a few canvas tents pitched on the grass. Children ran between them, a dog following close behind, and two women stood talking by a fire. One man was impossible to miss. Like the school, he too was immense and solid. He reminded me of the "Chief," the name my father had given to the wooden Indian that stood outside the tobacco shop he frequented when I was a child. He stood stock still, a tree embedded into the earth, roots running deep and far. As we passed he stared straight at me.

While trying to soften his cold stare with a smile, a realization shook me. This man was the first Indian I had ever seen.

Before applying for the job I was about to embark on, I had never even heard of an Indian residential school. If I had thought about it at all, I would have told you that Indians went to school wherever they lived, just like the rest of us. If you had asked me where they lived I would have told you that they lived like the rest of us, in town or in the country, or maybe in the bush.

I had never noticed the lack of Indian faces in my world. My life had been spent in Toronto, the largest city in Canada, and if Indians lived in cities, then surely a few lived in mine. But they must have lived somewhere else than I did, and they must have gone to different schools. I never saw an Indian in the stores I frequented, the restaurants or movie theatres. I had certainly heard of Indians. We had been taught a few bits and pieces in school, but when something, or in this case someone, is completely absent from your life, it's as though they hardly exist.

I didn't have long to ponder this new awareness as the Chief, and the quandary he presented me with, were quickly obscured with the dust of our passing and my attention was drawn back to the big brick building. With the roar of the poorly muffled engine announcing our arrival, we drove through the gates of Bear Lake Indian Residential School.

The entrance promised grandeur, with a regal, if dusty, driveway winding through expansive lawns to an imposing entrance. Promising to take care of my suitcases, Brother Samuel dropped me off at the bottom of the front steps. They were broad and solid, rising to meet two substantial wooden doors. The sheer size of the building, especially where it sat in the wide-open area carved out of the surrounding forest, made it as intimidating as a fortress. Smoothing my skirts, I tried to quell the feeling that I was a foreign interloper. Then I slowly climbed those ten stone steps into my new world.

Once through the heavy front doors the first thing I saw was an enormous crucifix. Hanging on the back wall of the semi-circular foyer, it was about six feet tall, with plaster blood dripping down Jesus's side and onto his nailed feet. A banner above the crown of thorns proclaimed, "Jesus Saves Us From Our Sins." Below it, a sign with the word "OFFICE" pointed to the left.

Despite this fearsome welcome, the institutional décor of the rest of the building soothed my rising insecurities. I had spent the last fifteen years of my life in school. Corridors stretched to the left and right, and the familiar sight of a clean tiled floor and numbered wooden doors was reassuring.

I gave my hair a quick pat, put a smile on my face and turned left. The first door opened on to a spacious room with a long counter.

"Mary Brock," said a soft-faced woman in a wilting wimple. "Welcome. I'm Sister Abigail. Mother Magdalene is expecting you."

Leaving her post behind the counter she led me by the elbow a little farther down the corridor, to a closed door. A brass plaque embossed with the word "PRINCIPAL" left me with no doubt as to who Mother Magdalene was.

"Here we are," she said, smiling broadly. Then, with a reassuring pat, she left me and padded back down the hall.

I knocked quietly and heard something that sounded like an invitation to come in, so I did.

The large room was sparsely furnished. A bookshelf and a filing cabinet sat along the wall beside Mother Magdalene's utilitarian wooden desk; two student chairs sat in front. The only concession to comfort was to my left, where two easy chairs bookended a wooden coffee table.

Mother Magdalene stood as I entered. Her statuesque frame was silhouetted by the window behind her, one of three that lined the wall, but her gesture to one of the student chairs was easy to see. Despite the August heat, her black habit and starched wimple looked crisp and cool. She sat when I did, put her hands into the wide sleeves of her habit, and our short interview began.

"Miss Mary Brock, I assume," she said.

"Yes, Mother Magdalene, I'm so happy to have finally arrived."

"And we are delighted to have you here. I won't keep you in my office for long. We have a few papers to deal with and then I'll take you to your classroom. I'm sure you're anxious to see the school for yourself."

"Yes, Mother Magdalene, I am."

Like Brother Samuel before her, Mother Magdalene was not given to excess.

Trying to resist the urge to meet her straight back and immaculate dress by straightening both my back and my clothes, I signed a few papers. She gave me a timetable for the first few days and a manual of the school's rules and regulations, exhorting me to read as much as I could. She would go over any questions I had tomorrow, after the staff meeting.

"You'll get more information at the meeting. I don't want to overwhelm you in your first five minutes. We've arranged for you to stay in town at the home of Mrs. Norton, but tonight you'll stay here with us. I hope you don't mind; we thought it would be easier and give you a chance to see the whole operation. We're not a full house as yet, but a few students are already here and most of the staff have returned. Dinner is at five."

I glanced at my watch; three hours.

She stood, and we were off to my classroom.

The elementary school, up to grade five, was on the first floor, to the right of the big front doors. As we walked down the hall from

Mother Magdalene's office, we passed many open classroom doors. The rooms were all set up in exactly the same way, with the teacher's desk visible from the door. In many, I saw nuns sitting quietly at work. We stopped at the end of the hall, next to the gymnasium.

"Here we are," said Mother Magdalene. She removed her hand from her sleeve to wave it in a grand gesture through the open door. "This is your classroom."

It was a simple statement of fact for Mother Magdalene, a momentous sentence of portent for me. "It has been given a thorough scrubbing in anticipation of your arrival. Teachers' supplies are in a closet beside the office and the students' supplies will be sorted out in a few days. Let me introduce you to Sister Beatrice."

With that we turned our back on my new classroom and I followed Mother Magdalene's perfect posture across the narrow hall.

Sister Beatrice was at her desk, chewing thoughtfully on a pencil. Her elbows rested on the desk's wood surface, revealing pale forearms. Her gaze rested somewhere in the middle distance. At our unexpected arrival, her pencil clattered to the floor and she jumped to her feet to greet us.

"Good afternoon, Mother Magdalene," she said. "Goodness, you startled me!"

Pulling her sleeves down, she reached out her hand to shake mine. "You must be the new recruit. Mary Brock, isn't it? Welcome to Bear Lake, I'm sure you'll like it here. The children are wonderful, as is the staff." This last said with her warm smile moving from me to Mother Magdalene, whose expression remained stern.

"Sister Beatrice teaches grade four. She's been with us for a few years and she'll be your guide these first few days. She'll help you get familiar with the school and our systems, and in any way she can, help you to get settled in."

"Of course, Mother Magdalene, I'm looking forward to it," said Sister Beatrice.

My shoulders loosened with the thought of being left in Sister Beatrice's care.

"Well then," said Mother Magdalene. "I'll leave you two to get better acquainted. I've shown Mary her classroom, but she hasn't had a chance to step inside it yet. She'll be having dinner with us today and she'll be staying in the girls' dorm tonight."

She gave a brief nod to each of us as she intoned our names, "Sister Beatrice, Mary." Then with a smooth turn of her long skirts, she was out the door.

I smiled shyly at Sister Beatrice, unsure how much I could share with her, but she put me at ease right away.

"She comes across as a battle-axe, and she has high standards, but her bark is worse than her bite. Don't take her seriousness too much to heart."

"Thank goodness," I said. "I was wondering what I would have to do to earn her respect."

Sister Beatrice laughed. "That," she said, "might be a long time coming. You'll have to earn her trust first. She'll be keeping an eye on you to be sure, but as long as you follow the rules and your students show some progress, she can be counted on to support you. Now, let's get you organized!"

We headed down the hall to the supply closet and Sister Bea, as she insisted on being called, filled me in on routines and gave me a few details about some of the children in my class.

"Most of the students here are quiet and obedient, although there are always a few who like to stir the pot. The worst one in your class is Billy. If there's any trouble you can be sure he'll be found nearby. His sister arrived last year. I had hoped that having her here might make him want to set a good example, but if anything, he's been worse since she's arrived. He's such a smart boy, I hate to see him lose out on an education because he can't follow rules."

She stopped for a moment to hand me a box of chalk. "A lot of them get like that," she continued. "They start off sweet and compliant; then as they get older they start to chafe against restrictions. I've seen it time and time again. Some even go so far as to run away. It's frustrating, and I haven't figured out what to do about it.

"On the positive side, let me tell you about Belinda. We each get a teacher's aide from the high school and we've given you Belinda. You'll love her. She's like the dorm mother for the girls—they all adore her—and the boys are at her feet. She'll be wonderful to have in your classroom. She'll need some time to get settled herself, but she should start in a month or so. There isn't a regular schedule. They have to make sure they can get their own work done too, and there's lots of extra work in the fall with the harvesting. But they usually come for an hour, one or two afternoons a week."

"Harvesting? They help with the harvesting?"

"Oh yes. Everyone pitches in this time of year. If you want to, I'm sure you can get your hands dirty too."

Finally, with my arms full of paper and pens, chalk and erasers, I returned to my classroom. Standing in the doorway, I gazed at my new home.

Four tall windows lined the outside wall, letting in warm bands of sunlight which streamed across the wooden desks. A long blackboard ran across the front of the room, and continued on the wall opposite the windows. Along the back wall an empty shelf sat above a row of hooks.

The desks were the kind with legs screwed into the floor. The lids lifted and each had a hole in the top right corner where an ink well used to sit. Putting down my armload of supplies, I ran my hand over the nearest desk. It was perfectly smooth. There were no names carved into the surface, no love notes or drawings to give an indication that someone had been there before. I lifted the lid, but there was nothing on the inside either. It was as though the desk had been purchased yesterday. Disappointed, I got down on my knees to check underneath. It was just the same.

Except for its size, the teacher's desk was not much different. The surface was bare of any hint of a previous owner, inside and out. I didn't bother to look underneath, but instead sat down and faced the vacant room. In a week's time I would be looking into thirty faces, all expecting me to be able to offer them an education. The butterflies fluttered.

I stood up to greet my imaginary charges. Reaching for the box of chalk Sister Bea and I had brought from the supply closet I took one out and wrote my name on the blackboard that stretched behind my desk. The scratch of chalk was loud in the empty space. My spectral students waited, wondering what I would write.

"Miss Brock," I said aloud. "My name is Miss Brock and I will be your teacher this year."

An hour later, Sister Beatrice stuck her head into my classroom. "I have to go to the chapel in a few minutes for vespers. Do you know where the dining room is?"

I didn't. So, with a promise to give me the full tour after dinner, Sister Bea led me down the hall, past the offices and on to the large dining room, then she hurried off to the chapel.

Young girls in navy blue tunics with white blouses, some with aprons tied around their waists, flitted about the big room setting the long tables efficiently and quietly. I could hear the light laughter of others coming from an open door, through which I could see the large stoves of an institutional kitchen. Dinner wasn't for another hour, but the smells of freshly baked bread made me realize how hungry I was. Lunch on the train seemed like a lifetime ago. I retraced my steps back to my classroom, taking in my surroundings as I went.

Except for the farm side of the school, most of the myriad areas needed to support the community were contained in this one enormous building. Walking past the main office, I saw a family with three children, all in school uniforms, waiting in front of the counter. Maybe one of them was a student of mine, I thought. Excitement started to replace the butterflies.

The butterflies were back just before five when I returned to the dining room. Like a new student, I wondered where I should sit, and who would sit with me. The room was filled with long tables, only a few of which were set. Benches were pulled up against them, but the girls I had seen earlier, and a few boys, were standing silently along the outer walls. At one end of the room, on a slightly raised platform were more long tables, except that these ones had chairs. No black or brown habits were in sight, so I stood silently as well, waiting for whatever would come next.

At five on the dot, a procession of men, some in habits, followed by women, all in habits, entered the room. They strode up to the large table on the raised dais. I spotted Sister Bea among them and I was eternally grateful to her when she motioned for me to come and join her. Mother Magdalene came in last, accompanied by a handsome priest, his white collar as stiff as her wimple. They marched to the head table, and the two seats that had stayed empty for them. Sister

Beatrice had to yank my arm as I started to sit, and we all stood for what felt like an eternity as grace was said.

"Amen" was the last word anyone spoke.

Good manners are important in my family and I was taught the rules from a young age. My mother instilled in me that it was part of one's job at the table to engage everyone in conversation, family and guests alike. My attempts to do so at Bear Lake were met with stony silence. It took a few minutes for me to realize that good manners here meant that not a word was spoken during meals. I was ignored by everyone, except Sister Beatrice, who glared meaningfully at me. It was an embarrassing initiation.

True to her word, after dinner, Sister Bea led me up four flights of stairs to start my grand tour of the school. On the top floor were the dormitories: boys at one end, girls at the other. The dorms were huge rooms with rows of beds, each one made up exactly like the one beside it. Cupboards for personal items lined one wall. It was remarkably neat and tidy. Despite the fact that some students had already arrived, there were no teddy bears sitting on pillows, no lost shoes in corners, no sloppily made beds. The third floor was where most of the nuns and brothers slept, with a small infirmary at one end. The lower two levels were the main part of the school. The second floor housed the high school, the middle school and a small library. The north wing of the first floor held the elementary school classrooms and the gym; in the south wing were the administration's offices, dining room and kitchen. On the lower level there were two recreation rooms, laundry facilities, the furnace, a coal bin and root cellar.

Outside was a busy place too. The school raised pigs and chickens and had a few head of dairy cows. There were fields of hay and corn, and plots of vegetable gardens. We left those for the next day, and the two of us headed back to Mother Magdalene's office so I could get organized for my night in the girls' dormitory.

My small suitcase was waiting for me there, and with it was Sister Maureen, who was in charge of the girls' dorm. I was excited to get a chance to meet some of the students, especially since dinner had not provided the opportunity I had expected.

Once again, I climbed the stairs to the top floor.

Sister Maureen, like Sister Bea, was warm and welcoming.

"I'm sorry you have to start in the dormitory," she said as we climbed the stairs, "but there are so few students here we thought that would be easiest."

"Oh no," I said. "I'm looking forward to meeting some of the students. Pillow talks are the best way to get to know someone."

Sister Maureen looked at me. "Pillow talks?"

"You know, conversations that happen when the lights go out."

"Oh, you won't find pillow talks here. When the lights go out the children are expected to go to sleep. Can you imagine the chaos if everyone was having pillow talks?" She laughed. "It would be like recess!"

I was disappointed, but I could see her point. "What's the bedtime routine like then?"

"Since we have so few students, we can relax the rules a bit, but normally, after dinner there are chores, then study hall, then bedtime. The regular sort of bedtime: wash up, pyjamas, prayers and then sleep. No pillow talks!" She chuckled again.

"Well then, since you're relaxing the rules a bit maybe we can have some pillow talk tonight."

"Not on your life! Mother Magdalene would have a fit."

"How would she ever know?"

"She'd know about it before midnight. I don't know how she does it, but she seems to know every infraction almost before it's committed."

When we finally reached the top floor we found a few girls already there.

The younger ones ran to Sister Maureen, grinning with delight. She reached down instinctively and wrapped her arms around the first two to reach her.

"Sharon! Marta! I didn't know you two were here already!"

As she listened to the two talking on top of each other, I looked around the big room. Some teenaged girls were sitting on a bed, deep in conversation. They barely looked up at our arrival. A group of five younger ones on another bed sat and stared. Big eyes watched my every move.

I walked over and introduced myself.

"Hello. My name is Miss Brock. What are your names?"

They hopped off the bed and there was a pause until the bravest said, "Shirley." The others followed suit and there was silence again.

"I'm going to be teaching grade five this year. Are any of you in grade five?"

They stared at each other as though this were a trick question and they were unsure how to answer it. Finally, one of them pointed to Shirley and said, "She is."

It was hard to maintain a friendly, relaxed conversation with these uncomfortable girls, but I pressed on, determined to win them over.

"Wonderful Shirley! Then you'll be in my class."

"Yes, Miss Brock."

The rest of my conversation with them was no better. I was finally rescued by Sister Maureen who, small children trailing after her, showed me the staff bathroom and where I was to sleep.

The older girls stayed where they were, making no effort to meet me, or to say hello to Sister Maureen, who finally went to talk to them, after which they unenthusiastically came over and introduced themselves.

Things changed when the lights went out.

When I first heard the sound of soft crying coming from the little girl in the bed closest to me, I thought the best thing to do would be to leave her alone. Homesickness was a common complaint at camp, and sometimes a little cry was all that was needed before sleep took over and a new day began with homesickness forgotten.

But it didn't stop, and I could hear others crying as well. I got up and went to the girl I had first heard to comfort her. At the sound of my approach, she curled up into a ball and wept even more loudly. I sat down beside her anyway, and rubbed her back, trying to reassure her with soft words and a soft touch. It didn't work. When I tried to touch her head, she crouched as far away from me as she could get and her plaintive cries continued. I didn't know what to do.

Sensing someone behind me, I thought perhaps Sister Maureen had come into the room, but when I looked up after a gentle tap on my shoulder I saw that it was one of the older girls. She motioned me away and sat in my place, speaking a few words in a language I didn't know. The little girl turned, and like a drowning victim reaching for a lifeline, grabbed hold of the teenager with everything she had, crying loudly. I watched as more girls got up to comfort the little ones. Someone started to sing, and soon they all joined in. It was a soft, quiet song, a lullaby I had never heard before with words I didn't understand, but it was the magic that was needed and soon all was quiet.

August 27, 1947
Mary Brock, the young lady from Toronto arrived today. I was walking from the cowshed to the barn when she pulled in with B. Samuel in that beat-up truck he loves so much. She stepped out in her big modern skirt with pleats all around, but she looked pretty in it, I have to admit. Warmed these old eyes after so many years of black habits! I watched as she stopped at the bottom of the steps and stared up at the school before straightening her back and her skirts and stepping resolutely up to the big front doors. I would have loved to have been a fly on the wall in Mother Magdalene's office this afternoon! The other lad, Jonathan, is due in a few days. It's as hot as Hades today. I hope we get some rain soon.

August 28, 1947
Well, Miss Brock gave us all a treat last night. She kept trying to get a conversation going during dinner. I've forgotten what a normal thing that is, talking during a meal. I felt a bit sorry for her, she was only doing what she had been raised to do. On the other hand, I hate to admit it, but I found a very uncharitable humour in seeing her discomfort. She's got spunk, that'll help her, but she's a fish out of water right now, and she'll need a lot of backbone to go with that spunk to make it past September.

NIPIGON STREET

The loud clanging of a bell woke me in the morning. When I opened my eyes, I saw that one of the teenaged girls was standing beside my bed.

The minute she saw I was awake, she said, "You can't tell anyone about last night."

Now my eyes were wide open.

"But why? It was wonderful. You girls were wonderful."

She looked at me, her face inscrutable.

"We're not allowed to speak our language here. If anyone hears about last night, we'll be punished."

I found it hard to believe that the kind sisters I had met would punish these girls for comforting the little ones, but I agreed to say nothing about it. Her look said she wasn't sure I could be trusted, but as there was nothing more she could do, she returned to her friends, mission accomplished.

Sister Maureen appeared moments later, prayers were said and the morning routine began. I was better behaved at breakfast. The rules were different than what I was used to, but I'm a quick study and I was eager to please.

The full teaching staff of about thirty people were at the morning meeting, held in the basement recreation room. Father James, the head of the school, introduced me and announced there was to be another lay teacher, Jonathan Jessop, due to arrive tomorrow, by canoe!

"He's a great outdoorsman, which is an asset we should make use of," Father James told us. I couldn't tell whether he was being generous, or if he really believed it. Jonathan sounded like an unusual person, especially for this place.

After the meeting, everyone was friendly, making a point of introducing themselves and welcoming me. While some seemed genuinely enthusiastic, most offered firm handshakes and expressionless faces. This was the first time there had been lay teachers at Bear Lake and there were bound to be mixed feelings about this change to the order of things. I was determined to prove my worth and win them over.

That afternoon, I was finally brought to my new home. The school had made arrangements for me to stay at the home of Mrs. Norton, the postmistress. She had taken over the position about ten years earlier, when the previous postmaster, her brother-in-law, had retired. At the time, she was a widow with four of her six children still at home and she had been grateful for the job. A few months before my arrival, her nest had emptied when her youngest left to get married. I was told she was looking forward to having me.

When I walked down the wide front steps of the school, Brother Christopher stood waiting in the driveway beside the same worn out truck I had arrived in the day before. With his dusty black habit and lanky frame, he looked indistinguishable from Brother Samuel and I prepared myself for another silent ride. But his broad smile at my approach was completely unlike my surly chauffeur of the previous day. When I was close enough, he took my hand in both of his sweaty ones for an enthusiastic shake, then opened the door of the same dirty truck as though it were a limousine. Behind the wheel his eyes sparkled along with his easy conversation. He told me that he taught high school geography and biology and was the resident gardener—both the vegetable and flower kind he said. He was full of observations about the places we passed—the types of trees and forest fire history, the kinds of rocks and their formations, the barely seen roads running off the highway and into the woods, where small lakes dotted the forest. Each had a story.

The town of Bear Lake was large by the standards of the area, one thousand souls counted it as home, about seven hundred white and three hundred Indian, Brother Christopher told me. Many of the Indians had moved into the area when their children had started at the school, then stayed on. Now there was a large part of town, dubbed "Indiantown" where they lived.

"Stay away from that side," Brother Christopher told me. "It's not a good place for a young woman." He looked meaningfully at me and added, "Especially a white woman."

It was the first time anyone had defined me by the colour of my skin, and I wasn't sure what to make of it.

Brother Christopher must have registered my surprise, because he hurried to reassure me.

"If you make sure to stay on your side of town," he said, "you shouldn't have to worry. In fact, the most dangerous activity around here is when some bear decides to check out the residential garbage cans."

"Really?" I asked. "Does that happen often?"

"Once is too often! It does happen every now and again. But the town dump has been moved about ten miles away, and most bears are content to stay out there. It's easier pickings."

"When I was a child we would go to the Huntsville dump just to watch the bears. Do they do that here?"

"Not that I've heard. It may not be as exciting as the city, but it's not that boring either." He smiled at me. "Most of the townsfolk are wonderful people and almost all of them are connected to the lumber trade." He hesitated a minute before continuing. "Well," he said, "there are a few people you may have to watch out for. A pretty young woman like yourself, you need to be careful about the intentions of the lumberjacks. They come into town en masse, when they have breaks from the bush, and they can be a force to be reckoned with. They generally stay in the corner of town you're unlikely to go to, but you're probably best to just stay home if you hear they've shown up." He chuckled, "I seem to be painting a pretty grim picture. I hope you don't find yourself at the dump for a little excitement!"

Mrs. Norton lived in a residential area with wide, tree-lined streets. Brother Christopher had to sound the horn twice at children who were playing kick-the-can, with home base in the middle of the road. As we drove past, adults waved from their wide front porches where they sat taking in the warm afternoon sunshine and watching the world go by.

The house at 54 Nipigon Street was like most of the others that lined the road. Two stories, it sat unpretentiously back from the street, a small patch of grass in front. A paved walkway, bordered with white and yellow chrysanthemums, led to the front porch. At our arrival, a middle-aged woman in a flowered housedress got up from the swing chair, plumped the bright cushion and stood waiting for us at the top of the porch steps.

"Mary Brock, I do declare! It's so nice to finally see your pretty face! I've been looking forward to your arrival for weeks! You must be exhausted after your long trip. Let's get you settled in right away!"

She took the smaller of my two suitcases from me and directed Brother Christopher, who was carrying the trunk, inside and up the stairs, "First door on the right!" We followed close behind, Mrs. Norton chattering the whole time.

"I've given you what used to be my bedroom," she said. "I've taken over the girls' room. We had four girls and two boys, so when everyone was growing up the girls got the biggest room. But when Evelyn, she's my second youngest, when she got married and moved out, the only one left was my baby, Jennifer. I was perfectly prepared to leave things as they were, but Jennifer wanted me to have the biggest room, so she and I switched. It's a joy to have such wonderful children! I feel a little guilty staying in it, with you coming, but I've been using it for a few years now. Anyway, alls to say, that Jennifer took over my old bedroom and decorated it herself. I think she did a wonderful job too. It's a real girl's room."

Her timing perfect, Mrs. Norton stood back to let me look into the first door on the right.

I was assaulted by pink. Pink walls, pink curtains, pink bedspread, pink carpet, even the dresser had been painted pink. My blue metal trunk stood out like a heron in a flock of flamingos.

I didn't know what to say, but Mrs. Norton was clearly waiting for something. "You're right, Mrs. Norton," I said. "It certainly is a girl's room."

Mrs. Norton beamed. "She said she'd dreamed of something like this since she was a little girl. She even had old notebooks she'd saved with drawings and magazine cut-outs in them! She tried a canopy too, but she didn't like feeling so closed in. We still have it in the attic if you'd like to use it."

"I think it's perfect just the way it is," I said, wondering how difficult it would be to find another place to live.

"The bathroom is down the hall, and we have a washing machine in the basement. I'm happy to do the meals, but you're welcome to cook too. I always like to try new dishes. I'd love to learn some big city gourmet recipes! Now you make yourself at home while I take Brother Christopher downstairs for a cup of coffee. We'll be in the kitchen."

As the sound of their steps receded down the wooden stairs, I sat on the flowered chenille bedspread and tried to contain my tears. My father's suitcase, with its shiny brown leather, looked as out of place as my trunk. I felt like a transplanted orchid, missing the soil I hadn't realized was as perfect for my tender sensibilities as it obviously was.

Mrs. Norton's and Brother Christopher's voices drifted up the stairs, and the child in me felt some comfort listening to the sounds of adults in quiet conversation. But the lilt and cadence were different, and I was no longer a child. Sitting in that pink bedroom, it hit me how far I was from everything and everyone I knew and loved. Instead of feeling thrilled at the endless possibilities of the unknown, I felt adrift.

But good manners dictated that this was not the time to indulge in homesickness. I wiped the fullness from my eyes, went down the hall to the bathroom, splashed some cold water on my face and walked down the stairs to join them in the kitchen.

"There you are my dear!"

Mrs. Norton smiled brightly as I entered and pointed to a chair opposite Brother Christopher at the round wooden table.

"Brother Christopher was just filling me in on your trip. You've come a long way my dear!"

She rambled on and on. Even the verbose Brother Christopher was limited to an occasional comment or two along the way as Mrs. Norton kept us entertained with stories from around town and from her life in the small house on Nipigon Street.

It was a gentle start. Not much was expected of me, and my mind could wander, which was not at all unpleasant. Mrs. Norton's kitchen was a lot like her—busy and warm. Her counters were loaded with jars and canisters filled with everything from flour to homemade pickles and jams. The calendar on the wall showed a life filled with church committees and bridge dates, and tacked to the length of the valance below the cupboards was a row of family photographs. The kitchen door opened onto a broad back yard dominated by an old maple tree, from which hung a single swing with a wide wooden seat.

Finally, Brother Christopher took his leave, with promises to come and get me at eight o'clock sharp the following morning. I left the kitchen too, pleading the need for a short nap before dinner. The smell of roasting chicken was already filling the cozy kitchen.

The next thing I knew there was a quiet rap on the door, and Mrs. Norton poked her head in to call me to eat.

With just the two of us, there was a bit more conversation, and less storytelling. She told me that the others, whoever they might be, were looking forward to meeting me.

"I thought I'd give you a few days to find your feet and then I'll host a tea. Everyone is dying to meet you and that way you can meet everyone at once." She looked at her hands for a moment, then at me, "Unless you'd rather go to everyone else's house and let them host you."

"A tea here sounds lovely, Mrs. Norton. It's very kind of you to put one on for me."

"Actually Mary," she touched my arm across the table, "I love to host a party. Tea party, dinner party, sweet sixteen. I know in the big cities they have people whose sole job is to plan parties for people. That would be my dream job!" She gazed briefly off into the distance then turned a sympathetic face towards me. "I spent a few years in Toronto myself, and I know that coming from the big city this place may seem a bit boring to you at first. At your age, you're looking for some excitement, I'm sure. Most of our young ones would give their eye teeth for a chance to live in Toronto."

"I guess you always want something different," I said. "The city can be exciting, but it can be dangerous too. I'm looking forward to living here. I'm not the type who likes to drive fast cars or stay out to watch the sun rise."

"Well, I'm glad to hear that, my dear! You won't find it as exciting as Toronto but, while there are a few rough areas, it's a friendly, God-fearing place where women can walk at night without being afraid and nobody locks their doors. You can count on your friends and neighbours here when things get tough and you can raise your children knowing that everyone is keeping an eye on things.

"Any trouble in town," she said, "is usually caused by some roughneck lumberjack. And they're usually fighting with another lumberjack. And now, I don't like to talk ill of anyone, but if there's a fight it's usually over one of those fast young women who tend to be drawn to wild men." She looked at me meaningfully and I responded with what I hoped was wide-eyed innocence.

"If you're worried about me and wild men, you needn't," I said. "I'll have enough to keep me busy with teaching. I doubt I'll have any free time for galavanting."

"I hope you're right," she said, eyeing me sternly. "I keep a proper house here."

"And I'm sure I'll be pleased you do."

This seemed to reassure her. She smiled broadly and patted my hand. "And I'm sure we'll get along just grand," she said. "There is one more thing I need to warn you about though. You're teaching at the Indian school and some of the parents live in Indiantown, across the tracks."

"Yes," I said. "Brother Christopher mentioned Indiantown."

"I don't know if they'll be wanting you to take presents up to their young ones, or otherwise make themselves a nuisance. But I'd suggest you find out what the rules are. This is the first time that anyone working at the school full time has lived in town. They might try to take advantage of it."

"I'll be sure to ask Mother Magdalene about it tomorrow," I said.

"Mostly the Indians keep to themselves," she said. "Every once in a while some drunk will come weaving and yelling down the street. Then we just call Stuart McBride, he's our local constable, and he gives the miscreant a night in jail to sober up. There's a few have jobs in town, but generally, we each stick to our own."

"It may take me a while to get used to things here but I'm sure I'll love it," I said.

Mrs. Norton nodded approvingly and I wondered what picture I had painted for her. I was too tired to try to make my golden girl description more realistic, however.

After my long trip and the dormitory sleepover, I wanted to get an early night. But it was not to be. Word of my arrival had spread and before we could get the dinner dishes done, three different groups of people had found their way to Mrs. Norton's kitchen door, "Just to stop by and say hello! We wanted to welcome you to the neighbourhood." Finally, when my yawns became too obvious to politely ignore, Mrs. Norton shooed the last one out with an admonition to let me get to bed.

By eight the next morning, I was fed, washed and dressed for business when Brother Christopher came to get me. I couldn't wait to begin my new life.

JONATHAN

August 30, 1947

The other teacher arrived today. Or at least arrived at our doorstep, who knows how long he's actually been here. He's to teach in the high school and he met with B. Peter this morning. I haven't met him yet, but Roger did, and during the milking he gave me the rundown. Apparently, Mr. Jessop is the best teacher ever; he lives in a tent, he knows how to skin a rabbit and he talks like a "normal" person. I'm not quite sure what that last comment means, but I'm curious to meet the man myself.

I know from my own life here that the rules of monastic life can sometimes feel like handcuffs, but there's a certain freedom as well, and space for the odd eccentric like myself, and, I assume, Jonathan. Mary Brock, the other teacher, seems to be settling in well. She's no eccentric, which may or may not make settling in easier. I still haven't officially met her, just a passing hello when S. Bea gave her the grand tour. I don't expect I'll have much to do with her anyway. I'm more curious to meet this Jonathan Jessop. I sense a kindred spirit.

The first time I saw him, he was coming up the hill behind the barn. Watching from the window of my classroom I knew right away he wasn't one of the brothers. It wasn't just the lack of long robes; many of the brothers didn't wear the traditional habit. Jonathan was different. He strode up the hill with long, unhesitant strides. His arms swung widely and he looked around as he walked. I wondered if any detail missed his scrutiny.

Jonathan was tall, and his body had the lean look of someone who only eats because he has to. He was wearing jeans and a t-shirt, much like most of the men in town, but on him it looked like a statement, instead of the only choice in his closet. His curly blonde hair was cut short and he had the dark complexion of someone who spends a lot of time outside, someone for whom physical work is refreshing.

I wondered how he would fit into the classroom routine and sleeping in a house. Would he be staying with Mrs. Norton too?

Deciding that confidence was best met with confidence, I went out of the classroom to meet him on the path.

He smiled as the gap closed between us. "You must be Mary," he said. "Welcome to education for the pagans."

My jaw dropped and he laughed.

"I don't mean to shock you, dear Mary. But I just left my first meeting with Brother Pete and it would appear that these people feel their job is to make Christians out of these boys and girls even if they don't teach them how to read or write."

"I'm sure that's not true!" I said. "Christianity is only part of it."

"Part of what, do you think?"

My brilliant response was a blank stare.

Jonathan grinned. "I apologize. I've barely said hello and already I'm ranting. Don't let me make a cynic out of you before you even start. I'm cynical enough for us both. Let's hope I make it past the first month, without putting my foot in it and getting fired."

He stopped and looked at me, his head cocked to one side, as though a different perspective might make me more interesting.

"That was not a pleasant start. I do want us to be friends. Let me try again.

"Hello! You must be Mary. I'm Jonathan. How has your time at Bear Lake Indian Residential School been thus far?"

He had looked so promising striding up the hill.

"I've been having a perfectly fine time, thus far, thank you very much. What are you doing here if you think it's such a terrible place?"

"'Know thine enemy.' It was Jesus who said that wasn't it? It's somewhere in the Bible I'm sure. I'm actually a secret agent for the Ojibwa, here on reconnaissance."

I stared at him.

"Ah Mary, so serious! Don't worry, I'm not really a secret agent. I just needed a job, wanted to stay up North, and this dropped in to my lap. Nothing like wading into the thick of things. Maybe I'll find out it's not as horrible as I think. I may be pleasantly surprised."

"You just might you know." I had been hoping for an ally. I found him disappointing. "All the people I've met so far have been very nice."

"I'm sure I'll discover that side to them at some point. So far, most of what I've gotten are complaints. For example, Brother Pete, my illustrious principal, doesn't want me sleeping in the tent. 'The children need to look up to their teachers, he said. If I were sixteen and my teacher was sleeping in a tent and cooking over a fire, I'd be looking up to him, you can bet on that. I don't think I'll be able to hold him off for long though. Gotta pick your battles. Do you know of any places in town?"

I told him I had only just arrived myself, but I would ask my landlady.

"Maybe I'll move from the tent to Indiantown. What would they say to that I wonder?"

"I was warned to stay away from the Indian side of town."

"Were you now? Just arrived and already they're making you take sides."

"What do mean, 'take sides'? At home, I've been warned about the bad sections of Toronto. Brother Christopher warned me about the lumberjacks too. Nobody's taking sides."

He stared at me. "I find it hard to believe that you're that naïve. But you don't come across as a liar, so I'll choose to believe you. So here's a piece of advice from me: don't pay any attention to that crap. People have always been afraid of the 'other'. Maybe one day we'll figure out that the things that make us different are less substantial than the things that make us the same. Until then, make up your own mind about who you can trust."

He paused and looked me up and down. I had been proud of my reflection when I left Mrs. Norton's that morning. Now, under Jonathan's gaze, the red polka-dot skirt with its tightly cinched belt, freshly ironed white blouse, stockings and white pumps made me feel like an advertisement for Ivory Soap. "You don't look like a rebel, and I'm willing to bet adventure isn't your middle name. So what brought you to this place?"

He sounded vaguely insulting, but I decided not to take the bait. "I saw an ad and thought it sounded interesting. Something completely different."

"It'll be that," he said. "Now, I'm off to meet the head man, Father James. Any advice before I darken his door?"

"Father James? No, I haven't had a chance to meet him yet. Just a quick hello at the staff meeting. You'll have to advise me."

"Sounds like you elementary teachers don't have the status we high school teachers have. Although I'm not sure status is something I really want in this place. Brother Peter has already tried to get me to toe the line; Headmaster James is sure to be even worse! Especially if I'm late. Shall we leave this gentle sunshine and move indoors?"

He gave me his arm and a charming smile, and escorted me back into the building, where he made an exaggerated genuflection in front of the giant crucifix. His smile became a mischievous grin as he turned to stride down the hall to Father James's office.

In spite of myself, I found I was grinning too.

Jonathan's flippant attitude got me wondering. Before returning to my classroom I stopped in to see Sister Bea. When I asked her whether she thought the students were pagans, she laughed. "Wherever did you get that old-fashioned idea, Mary? No, I don't think they're pagans. Pagans run around without clothes on and poke holes in dolls. Their grandparents may have had some outlandish customs, but they come here too young to know about those things, and they're all Christians when they leave. These schools have been around long enough that some students are even second or third generation. This school's been here in one form or another since the late 1800s."

"Then let me ask you another question, Sister Bea. Do you think it's more important that they get an education, or that they're Christians when they leave?"

"Well, aren't we in a serious mood! That's an interesting question. I don't know quite how to answer it since I don't see it as an either/or proposition. Our job here is to do both. Well, our job from the government is to give them an education, but our role as Christians is to help them see the true path as well. I've never thought about it the way you're presenting it."

"How do you think Mother Magdalene would answer that question?"

"Oh heavens, Mary! I'd be in trouble if I tried answering for Mother Magdalene! If you ever get up the courage to ask her though, I'd be curious to hear her answer."

"All right then, if you had to choose, would you rather they left here with Christianity or an education?"

"I'll only answer that if you can promise me that this discussion goes no further than this room. I feel I'm on dangerous ground here, although I'm not sure why. Especially since I would hope that most of the staff would give the same answer. Though I'm thinking it's not the one you'd give."

I waited, not sure I wanted to hear her answer.

"I'd prefer they were Christians."

She slipped her hands into her sleeves and sat back in her chair, her wide blue eyes looking at me, unblinking, waiting for my disapproval.

"But this is a school, not a seminary."

"True, but we are a special school. We are here to give the students tools they can use for the rest of their lives, not just a knowledge of the periodic table. The English language will always serve them, whether or not they can spell; Christianity will always serve them, whether they become doctors or farmers, bakers or businessmen. You might disagree, but I believe that when one knows that God is there, come good times or bad, then the bad times are much easier to cope with, and heaven knows these children will grow up and face many hardships. I'd rather give them a resource to help weather their storms, than the ability to factor a number."

She paused again, warming to her argument, while I wondered what else Jonathan might be right about. My politics had always been simple. There were good guys and bad guys, right and wrong, and usually there was no problem distinguishing between the two.

"Thankfully we don't have to choose between Christianity and an academic education. So I can teach my charges how to factor a number and they'll also benefit from the comfort of the church. They're luckier than some."

I disagreed with her, but I could see her point. I also felt some measure of comfort in the knowledge that, despite her priorities, the children were getting a formal education at the school. Maybe it wasn't such a big deal. They could get the best of both worlds.

I didn't see Jonathan again until the next day. He walked right into my classroom without even so much as a polite knock, then closed the door behind him.

"I don't know if I'm going to last here Mary."

"Already?" I said.

"Brother Peter, and now Mother Magdalene, are after me about living in the tent, the clothes I wear and my 'casual' form of language. That was after I called Brother Thomas Brother Tom, I kind of like Brother Tom, don't you? Sounds kind of like the song."

He hummed a few bars of 'Frère Jacques' before continuing.

"And our paternal top dog, Papa Jim, excuse me—Father James— was no better. Did you know that the high school only convenes in the morning for the first few months? 'They have valuable non-academic skills to learn,' he told me. And what might those non-academic skills be, you ask? Well, let me tell you a few, and of course this is not the whole list: farming, milking, wood splitting, vegetable harvesting. Certainly, cleaning toilets is something they could never figure out how to do without the school's help. Oh, and of course there's the discipline of mind that a clean toilet promotes. Now, if someone was teaching them how to skin a moose, then I might see the point. But milking a cow? Come on, when are they going to use those skills after this place?"

He didn't wait for an answer; there was no stopping him anyway.

"I don't know Mary, I really don't know. It's not like I avoid doing my bit, or taking part in something I don't fully approve of. Hell,

I joined up, even though I hate the military. There's something about that top-down, do-what-you're-told-and-don't-question-anything mentality that grates against my soul. Fortunately for me, the war ended a few weeks after I got my uniform. I am eternally grateful I never had to shoot anybody. So you see, my point is, I'm able to put up with things I don't like if I see the need. And I understand that this is not Toronto and some 'non-academic' training would be useful, but if they don't get enough of the academic stuff then options like college and university are nothing but pipe dreams. And that's not what I came here for."

He was interrupted when the door opened and Brother Peter, the high school principal, whom I had met only at the dining room table, walked in.

"We do not condone closed doors when men and women are alone together," he said.

He waited for us to respond.

"Right. Understood. Sir," said Jonathan.

"Of course," I replied quickly.

"Jonathan, we need to go over a few things. Are you free now?"

"I'll be right with you," Jonathan said.

"I'll wait in the hall," said Brother Peter. "We can walk back to your classroom together."

Jonathan blew a silent kiss in my direction then stood to turn and face Brother Peter, "Why wait in the hall? Let's get this show on the road."

The army would have killed him.

SEPTEMBER
1947

FIRST DAYS

The rest of that week I rarely saw Jonathan except when all the staff was gathered. Everyone was busy as new students arrived daily and we prepared for the year ahead. The night before the first day of classes, I spent an hour going through the possible outfits I could wear. I envied the nuns their easy choice. Trying to find a balance between modesty, professionalism and staying cool in the sticky heat was not easy. I didn't want to stand out as the city dandy, and with everyone else covered from head to toe, bare skin was beginning to look a bit licentious, even to me.

At seven the next morning, in a plain grey skirt, a white blouse with long sleeves, stockings and my useful black pumps, I opened the door to my classroom. Everyone was still at breakfast, so I had the place to myself.

I organized pencils and paper and went over the first week's lesson plans one last time. By the time I heard the bell summoning every-one to the chapel for morning mass, I had nothing left to do but fret. In deference to the fact that I was an Anglican, Mother Magdalene had told me it wasn't necessary that I attend church services. But I wanted to know all about my charges, and daily rituals are influential in shaping our outlooks. So I made my way over to the chapel.

I arrived just in time to watch two rows of students with freshly cut hair and freshly pressed uniforms move silently along the covered walkway that joined the chapel with the main building. A few curious heads turned in my direction, but most walked with eyes front and arms at their sides.

I followed the last of them into the chapel. Once again, I was greeted by a large crucifix. This one hung over the altar, which had been draped in a green and white cloth. Christ, morose and helpless, stared at the congregation with a mute, guilt-inducing look. Inside, the students' silent uniformity continued. Except for the irrepressible little ones, everyone stood in the pews, tight-lipped and still: boys on one side, girls on the other, the youngest up front, the eldest at the back.

Before the mass began, Father James delivered a welcome-back message, and his words were translated by one of the altar boys. After my night in the dormitory, where I had been warned that they were not allowed to speak their language, I was pleased to think that this rule was now being relaxed.

As if he had heard my thoughts, Father James spoke again. "This is the last time you will hear your native language spoken. From now on, English will be your language. It will not be easy at first, but gradually you will come to understand it as easily as you understand Cree or Ojibwa. If you speak anything other than English you will be punished. Is that clear?"

When this had been translated he said, "Repeat after me: I will speak only in English."

All eyes turned to the translator, who said something in his native tongue, then finished with, "I will speak only in English."

It was impossible to understand what was said next as the new children tried the unfamiliar language for the first time.

After this brief introduction, the students were invited to sit down, and morning mass began. I caught a few glances across the aisle between the older students, but otherwise they were like automatons, repeating the phrases without having to look at the books, kneeling and standing with military precision.

As they filed out after the mass, the little ones chattered to each other, presumably about the new developments revealed to them in the chapel. As calmly as if she were straightening a slouching posture, a nun gave each of the children a sharp slap across the face.

"You will speak only in English," she intoned, after each quick snap of her wrist.

"And you," she said to my shocked expression, "will see that they do."

The rest of the walk was undertaken in silence. Few faces showed any expression at all. On one or two a silent tear could be seen drying up halfway down a chubby cheek.

Sept 2, 1947
The new girl went to mass this morning. She's not Catholic, or at least that's what I've heard, so I wonder what drew her there. Jonathan, of course, was nowhere in sight. He stopped by yesterday and we had a good chat. He's an intelligent lad but a bit too impetuous for his own good. One of those boys who thinks he's smarter than everyone else. I thought he'd do well here, but now I'm not so sure. The rules are going to strangle him and I don't see much willingness for compromise on either side.

I had a terrible sleep last night. It's been horribly hot and muggy and it finally broke with a big thunderstorm. You would think I was two years old, sitting in bed in my little room, trembling with fear as each bolt of lightning sent its stroke of energy to earth. It finally calmed down enough for me to get a couple of hours of sleep before prayers. I sometimes wish I knew what it was that makes me so afraid. Mostly I'm glad I don't know.

Sister Beatrice and I began our first day with everyone from both of our classes in her classroom. I waited nervously as the children filed in. Most of them didn't look at Sister Bea or me when they arrived, but some couldn't suppress a smile when they saw me. I was pleased at those reactions. I worried that Sister Bea was not.

Sister Bea gave her own welcome-back talk: how much we looked forward to this year with them, and although we were two classes we were one group and behaviour was important. Then she read off my student's names and I led my group across the hall.

I had assigned them seats in alphabetical order, the boys on one side, girls on the other, the way I was told they were supposed to sit. I told them to find their desks, which they did, without a sound. They stood until I asked them to sit, and then it began.

From my platform at the front, I looked down at a sea of brown faces staring back at me. They all looked the same, and I felt a momentary pang of despair at ever knowing one from another. The girls wore blue tunics with white blouses, their hair cut in two straight lines, one across their forehead and the other above their shoulders. No bright red ribbons or saucy pony tails, upset the uniformity. The boys all wore pale blue shirts and navy blue trousers, their crew cuts freshly trimmed. Two beautiful almond eyes looked out from each face, all directed expectantly towards me.

In that instant, when the enormity of what I had taken on sat staring me in the face, I wondered where I got the gall to think I was up to this. The excitement and confidence that had been building since my arrival deserted me like a bat in the light.

I moved around to the front of my desk and looked at them with what I hoped was a stern, but warm, expression. Thirty pairs of dark orbs looked back. Our mutual examination complete, I took a deep breath, strode to the blackboard behind my desk and picked up a piece of chalk.

Miss Brock, I wrote, in large cursive letters.

"My name is Miss Brock," I said, "and I will be your teacher this year." I was saying it for real this time, and I felt like a bride must on her wedding day, having practised her meaningful "I do" so often.

And, like a marriage promise, it was over in an instant, and the real work began.

"I'm looking forward to getting to know each and every one of you. I'm sure that you're all ready to work hard and learn lots this year.

"Since I don't know any of you, I would like you to say your name before you speak, whether to answer a question or to ask one. That way I can get to know each of you as quickly as possible.

"Before I get started, do you have any questions?"

One hand went up. I nodded at a little girl and she stood up.

"My name is Ruth York, Miss Brock. My question is: Why did you come here?"

Of all the questions I had prepared answers for, this was not one.

"Thank you, Ruth. That's an interesting question. I came here because I want to teach. I could have taught in Toronto, which is where I am from," and—I thought to myself, the answer to one of the questions I had prepared for— "but I decided to come here, because for me, this place is an adventure. I haven't spent much time out of the city. I'm hoping that you'll be able to teach me some things about living in the North."

This answer elicited some giggles, and some looks of incredulity. Ruth sat down, apparently satisfied, and I waited for another question. After a few uncomfortable moments of silence, I asked again.

"Does anyone else have something they'd like to ask me?"

What would I have asked my grade five teacher? Are you a nice person? Are you fair? Do you like to play outside? I could only imagine the questions they didn't have the courage to ask. I hoped that as the year progressed, they would come to trust me and ask whatever was on their minds.

But there was no trust today, so I went on with my basic introduction.

"I come from Toronto, which is a big city on Lake Ontario. Later we'll get a map and I'll show you. I have two brothers who were both in the air force in Europe and they both made it home safely. My father is a businessman who works in insurance and my mother works with the blind as a volunteer."

They stared up at me with polite, expressionless faces. I ploughed on.

"I'm very excited about being here with all of you. I think a good education is the key to future success in our world and I'm sure that each of you will do well in your lives if you work hard in school.

"Are you all ready to work hard this year?"

I waited. Silence reigned. I waited some more. One or two quiet yeses could be heard, and a few hands went up.

Clearly, they had no idea what was expected in answer to this question.

This was a good time to show I could take charge. "I'll ask again, and if you're ready to work hard then just say, yes, as loudly as you can."

"Are you ready to work hard this year?"

A few weak yeses answered me, one loud one (was that Ruth?), but most of the students looked quizzically at each other, still unsure.

"That was only a few of you, and certainly not loud. Let's try it again.

"Are you ready to work hard this year?" This time I raised my voice too.

"Yes."

"Better," I said, "but not good enough. I don't know how to believe you're going to work hard if you can't even say yes!"

Various yeses came at all levels from all corners of the classroom. I raised my hand for quiet.

"I'm going to try one last time. I want Mother Magdalene to hear you all the way in her office. Are you ready to work hard this year?"

"Yes!"

"That felt so good!" And indeed, it did. "Let's do it again.

"Are you ready to work hard?"

"YES!"

It was at this moment that Mother Magdalene popped her head in my door. "Is everything all right, Miss Brock?"

"Come in, Mother Magdalene. Everything is just fine. My class was telling me that they are going to work very hard this year. Isn't that right class?"

After our exemplary practise, I expected another loud yes. I was disappointed.

Ruth bellowed her's out and a few others managed to say something, but most just nodded their heads.

"I asked them to say yes loudly enough to be heard in your office. If you were disturbed by that it was entirely my fault, Mother Magdalene, and I apologize."

"I was not disturbed," she said, her eyes scanning my students, most of whom had their heads down. "I make it my habit to wander around the school from time to time so that I can keep in touch with what's going on. Especially in the first few days."

This sounded more like a warning than an opening for conversation. I nodded. "Thank you, Mother Magdalene. We'd love to have you drop by any time."

She nodded in reply.

"Goodbye, grade five, I know you will work hard—and politely—for Miss Brock."

"Goodbye, Mother Magdalene," the class chimed.

Not a good start.

By lunchtime I was exhausted. Trying to get more than "Yes, Miss Brock," or "No, Miss Brock" was the hardest thing I had ever tried to do. My student teacher days of mysterious projectiles and pulled pigtails were heaven compared with a class of woodenly polite children who were afraid to make the slightest mistake.

Fortunately, I could rest in the afternoon. It wasn't just the high school students who did non-academic work in the afternoons. Twice a week the grade five class worked outside, which meant that I could use that time for planning and marking. It was a teacher's dream, but I worried that the students wouldn't be able to finish the curriculum with so much time out of the classroom.

"They rarely meet the curriculum standards anyway," Mother Magdalene had said when I asked her about it. "You'll find a wide range of abilities in your classroom. The few that do well won't need the whole day to do it, and for the others, the afternoon chores are good training for what lies ahead. In fact, they're good for everybody. They learn useful skills, take responsibility and the school stays clean. In the winter, they'll have more classroom time, but in the fall, with all the harvesting on top of everything else, we need all hands on deck or our food will rot in the fields."

I wanted to prove her wrong on one score. I couldn't see how a curriculum built around the needs of the average child could overwhelm the average Indian child. But it wasn't going to be easy with half days.

The second day, I had the students make name cards for their desks. I told them to draw a picture of something that made them happy, something that made them sad, and something that made them different from anyone else. They responded with blank looks, so I did an example on the board. My artistic skills are minimal and I hoped that seeing my pitiful drawings might encourage them.

I drew a big square on the blackboard to represent their piece of paper.

"The thing that makes me happy, is teaching," I said, and drew a stick figure of a teacher in front of a blackboard in the middle of my square.

"The thing that makes me sad, is people fighting." I drew stick figures again, very small, in a corner of my square.

"What makes me different, is that I'm from a big city." That one was easy. Lots of tall buildings along the bottom of my square.

"Do your happy thing first, make it really big, as big as you can, then do your sad one, but make it as small as you can, in a corner like mine, and then put your different one in any blank space. It doesn't matter how well you draw because when you finish we'll be writing your names over everything."

I wrote, MISS BROCK, in big letters across my clumsy sketches.

As they worked, I wandered around the classroom. Most of the children were hesitant to commit to anything. One girl said she couldn't think of anything that made her happy. I found this unbelievable at first, a ploy to avoid the work. But her worried expression made me re-think my hasty judgement. I told her to draw something that didn't make her sad and left her struggling to draw a butterfly. Over and over I was told, "I can't draw." Over and over I directed them to look at my example, and gradually, encouraged by each other as much as by me, pictures began to emerge.

As each finished they sat with their hands in their laps, waiting. It didn't seem to matter if they had nothing to do: they weren't going to misbehave. Did I just get the "good" kids, I wondered? I thought that was unlikely. Maybe it was early days, and things would change as they got used to me. I didn't want problems, but there was barely any life in the classroom.

Despite my artistic examples, the exercise took up the better part of an hour as they tried to get it "right." I couldn't convince them that there wasn't a right or a wrong way to do it. Some of the children added some colour with the crayons, but most left it in pencil. Before recess I went around with a big black crayon and wrote their name over what they had drawn. Then tape was passed around and they all attached their newly minted name tags to their desks.

While they were outside, I checked their pictures to see what the children saw as their happy things. Many had drawn trees and water, one had a big fire, and another had what looked like a small tent. A few were crude drawings of dogs and houses. In their sad place, almost all of them had drawn a large building. At first, I took it to be my picture of the city. But it appeared over and over and I soon realized that it bore a remarkable resemblance to the school. A few had drawn a barn, and another had put a smaller building that I didn't recognize as anything in particular. On one, I recognized a copy of my teacher-in-front-of-the-blackboard picture.

After recess, when they were all back in their seats, I spoke to them about their drawings, hoping to create a connection.

"While you were outside I had a closer look at your pictures. I noticed that for many of you this school is your sad place. I'm sorry to hear that. I can understand how hard it must be to leave your family for such a long time and be so far away. I hope that this year I can help make your time here a little better. I'll do my best. But in return I expect all of you do your best for me. I expect you to work hard and to ask questions when you don't understand something. I'm more concerned that all of you leave here understanding what you've been taught than I am in having all of you leave here with As in your report cards. Do you understand that?"

Solemn faces made solemn nods. I knew I would have to repeat that speech a few more times before they really heard it, and I would have to prove it even more often before they actually believed it.

My first priority for the term was to find out what they did and didn't know. But given their reticence, I didn't think either a test or oral work would be the best way, even though I had prepared both. So I asked them to write the typical summer vacation story. I felt like a failure, resorting to such an unimaginative gambit, but I needed something from them.

They took out the notebooks they had been given and opened them to the first blank page. When I was in school I loved that first page. I used to run my hand over it. The page was like a new paintbox, so clean, so full of possibilities. I didn't see any little brown hands run over their first page. Instead they looked like they were being asked to write out their worst sins and post them on the bulletin board.

So once again, I did a small example on the blackboard to help them get started, and most did. But getting started is one thing, and getting finished is another. I finally said they had to fill the entire first page of their notebook and I spent the rest of the morning responding to questions about how to spell everything from "mum" to "disgusting."

During those first days, I despaired of ever being able to have a real class. A class that, despite the diverse personalities and skills of its students, has a life of its own. With no personality or personal style to tell my students apart, I was grateful that we had made the name tags and that they were in alphabetical order. There were a few exceptions, and as the first week drew to a close, those exceptions started to distinguish themselves.

There was Ruth, of course. She was always the first to answer a question, and the only one unafraid to ask one. In those days, children were required to stand up when they spoke in class. Even today I can picture Ruth, one hand on her hip, her head tilted to one side, asking me unique questions. She always started politely with, "If you please Miss Brock."

"If you please Miss Brock, why don't the rivers run out of water?" or "If you please Miss Brock, where do worms have their eyes?"

The next one I got to know was Billy, the one Sister Bea had warned me about. Billy was the boy who, had he grown up in my neighbourhood, would have been dipping pigtails into ink bottles. He delighted in getting into trouble himself, or getting someone else into trouble. He would drop his books loudly onto the floor while everyone was reading quietly, trip someone coming down the aisle, or write so hard on his paper that it would tear.

Donald was one of my most fearful students. If I came too near he would cringe. I stopped asking him questions after the first two tries, when it seemed that the effort of standing and saying something out loud was about to bring him to tears.

Then there was Shirley, a teacher's dream. She was the brave little girl from my night in the dormitory. She raised her hand for almost anything, wanted to stay after school and help clean the chalkboard erasers, put up pictures, or do any job that needed doing. Her work was always neat and tidy and she loved to help the others.

My failure to get any questions on the first day led me to create a "Question and Suggestion" box. The children could slip a piece of paper into the box, with a question or a suggestion, with or without their name. I warned them that I would post them on the bulletin board, but I also promised to answer every question and respond to every suggestion. The first month or so, the response was tepid at best. But as the year wore on I sometimes felt I was devoting more time to questions and suggestions than I was to lesson planning.

As Mother Magdalene had promised, their academic skills were as varied as their personalities. Some found it difficult to read simple texts, while others could read as well as I could. During our daily math minute—a minute of simple mental math—some could answer all twenty questions with time to spare, and some struggled to get five questions answered correctly.

In addition to the work I gave them, they also had chores outside the classroom, their non-academic lessons. The students played an important role in school maintenance: cleaning the inside and working in the gardens and fields outside. Early fall was harvesting time for much of the garden, although I use the word garden in a very general sense. Fields of potatoes, carrots, turnips and cabbages, required many hands to clear. It was back-breaking and time-consuming work. But residential schools were chronically underfunded, and any food they could generate themselves went a long way to ease their financial burdens.

Sept 9, 1947
The harvest is progressing by leaps and bounds. The heat is not so bad now, as the storm swept most of it away, and the nights are turning cool. I love to see the cellars fill up with carrots and potatoes and onions, it makes all that hard work in the summer worthwhile. The good Lord has provided well this year, despite our crazy weather.

Simon came by today. He's getting that look about him that I hate to see, that sullen, the world-hates-me look. I was hoping he would be able to avoid it. He's such a good student and he wants to please. I don't know if something happened over the summer or if he's just a teenager. I think we might do a better job with our charges if we were allowed to marry and have families. I try to remember how I felt when I was fourteen, but it was so long ago. And too, I was probably a lot different than the boy

I remember. Still, I'm glad Simon comes around to play horseshoes. They have so little free time these days.

Father James wants a list of the boys who come to visit, other than the milking boys. He says it's so that he knows where to look if they need someone. I'm not so sure, I feel like I'm giving names to the enemy, but when I try to reason out why, I can't. No one's telling me they can't come, but I worry that edict is coming down soon.

FATHER JAMES

It wasn't until the second week of school that I got the summons to visit Father James.

Mother Magdalene was the principal of the elementary school and in charge of the nuns and the girls' side of the residence. Brother Peter was head of the high school and the brothers. Father James was the head of the school as a whole. His imprint was on everything from the number of pounds of potatoes the garden was expected to produce, to the number of hours staff was expected to spend in prayer. He was probably in his fifties when I met him—ancient by my standards. He stood well over six feet, slim, and athletic, with limbs that seemed too long for his torso, like a gangly teenager with a wrinkled face. His thick grey hair, combed and oiled in a suspiciously vain manner, was a slightly darker shade than his piercing grey eyes. He was a formidable man, in every sense of the word.

Father James had spent the First World War as a chaplain in the army and it was rumoured that he was sometimes heard screaming at night. If that were true, he gave no hint of it during the day. I never heard him mention anything of a personal nature, and I couldn't imagine him entertaining the notion that something might disturb him in any profound or irreparable way. His back was ramrod straight whether he was inspecting a horse or deep in prayer. Father James always carried a stick in his right hand, and every so often I would see him in the school's halls, his stick, like a rider's crop, slapping against his thigh as he walked. He was stern, but fair, with high standards and swift punishments for anyone not living up to what he expected of them; students or staff. Sister Bea told me of a time one January when he made her kneel for an hour on the cold stone floor of the chapel because she had forgotten to lock the doors to the girls' dormitory the night before.

Father James was the disciplinarian when students fought among themselves. While I wasn't aware of it until well into my time there, the school was rife with rivalries, and gangs took a swipe at each other whenever they could. Usually I only saw the black eyes or bruises, they were good at keeping it underground, as punishments could be severe. Fights between individuals were more common, and it was not unusual to see Father James outside supervising a couple of boys who were going at each other with boxing gloves.

The other underlying violence at the school was bullying. It was not an easy place to be different, or weak, and some children were easy prey. Most of the time the bullies managed to terrify their victims unobserved, but heaven help the bully if Father James caught him in the act. The one time I saw him mete out punishment to a bully was the only time I saw him lose his measured, solemn poise. His stick was quick and merciless. Whether or not this helped the victim I never knew, but the bully was left bruised and humiliated by the time Father James was done.

Perhaps it was an extension of this fierce protection for the under-dog that prompted his actions during recess one sunny afternoon in early October. The normal bustle of activity quieted as he strode across the playground on the boys' side towards a young boy who was sitting alone against the fence. Father James sat beside him in the dirt and started talking, both of them staring at the ground between their feet where Father James drew haphazardly with his stick. He and the boy conversed quietly for about five minutes, until the bell rang. Then they got up, dusted themselves off and went back to their day.

I hadn't seen either the fierce protector or the gentle conversationalist before my first interview with Father James, but his reputation was enough to make me nervous. I was due at his office at exactly 3:40 p.m., so when the bell rang at half past three, I rushed the children out the door and ran to do a quick once over in the mirror of the staff bathroom. I tried to maintain a sedate pace from there as I walked to his office door, where I knocked with what I hoped sounded like confidence.

When I opened the door in response to his booming invitation to come in, he stood with a smile and the offer of a comfortable chair beside a coffee table. His office was much like Mother Magdalene's, large and sparsely furnished. A crucifix and two paintings of saintly looking men decorated his walls and a plain wooden cross hung in one window with a prie-dieu below it. The only other items in the room were his bookshelf, two comfortable chairs which sat close to a wooden coffee table, and his wide desk. On the coffee table, two empty cups sat on china saucers beside a steaming pot of tea. I was pleased I had been prompt. I doubt he would have found cold tea palatable.

"Thank you for coming Mary. I'm sorry I haven't been able to meet you properly before today. But perhaps this is better, since you've now had a chance to get to know us and your students a little bit."

"It's been busy, but everyone has been very helpful," I said, taking the cup of tea he had poured.

"You've come into a very different world than the one you're used to, Mary. I'm curious; what made you want to join us here?"

He said this while helping himself to a sugar cube, then gave me a straightforward stare while he stirred his tea with a tiny teaspoon.

I took a sip of my own tea and put it down on its saucer before answering, trying to decide on the best response. "I felt a need to do something for the greater good. The patriotism of the war created a feeling that we should all help Canada in any way we could, and I didn't feel that I had done much during the war."

"I'm sure there were other things you could have done."

"Well, I had my teaching degree. I wanted to teach, and this seemed more interesting than living at home and teaching in Toronto."

He nodded. An uninspiring, but honest answer. I wasn't sure whether it stood in my favour or not. I took another sip of tea.

"And how have you found it so far? Is it interesting?"

"Oh yes," I said, too eagerly. "Bear Lake is like nothing I've ever experienced, and I've never been to a boarding school either, so there's a lot to learn. Mrs. Norton, my landlady, is very nice, and she's introduced me to some people in town so I'm getting to feel more at home there. Sister Bea has been particularly helpful here, getting me settled in and answering many, many questions."

"Well," he said, "please keep asking them. We want you to feel at home here too."

I tried desperately to think of an intelligent question to ask him and came out with, "What brought you to Bear Lake?" A perfectly acceptable question at my parent's dining-room table, but it felt far too personal in this context.

Father James took it in stride though, and like me, paused for a sip of tea before answering. "Your question is interesting, Mary. While it shows some ignorance of how our system works, it's a gracious question in that it implies that I might have had some voice in my posting here. Normally, Mary, we go where we're sent. Of course, we can say no, and our wishes are taken into account. Depending on our relationships with our superiors, we can also ask for a posting we would especially like to have. But generally, those kinds of personal preferences are frowned upon, and more than once I've seen it backfire. So, I had little influence in obtaining this position. That said, I've been here five years now, and I hope to stay for many more. I find the students challenging. It's a unique opportunity we've been offered here, to take small children and try to mould them into responsible, capable, Christian adults. It is not a responsibility I take lightly and we're a long way from doing it well."

He paused to take another sip of tea, then placed the teacup gently back on its saucer.

"What do you think, Mary? Each generation brings something new and innovative to the table, even though we older ones like to think we've got things figured out. You may not have been here long enough to answer this question, but I'm sure you've given it some thought. What do you think we could do to improve our school?"

My mind raced, I wasn't sure if I was being given carte blanche, or a test. "Well sir," I stalled, "it's hard for me to know at this point. The Christian part, I think I'll leave to everyone else, but I do have some ideas about the way we teach." I paused. I wanted to take advantage of this golden opportunity, but after Mother Magdalene's visit to my classroom on the first day, I knew I had to be diplomatic if I was going to get anywhere.

"Go ahead, Mary. I'm always ready to hear what the latest ideas are. We don't get much opportunity to explore emerging educational philosophies here."

"Well, educational philosophies are changing. There's a move towards a stronger development of analytical skills and less dependency on rote learning, even at the elementary school level."

I kept going, but later, in trying to reconstruct this meeting, I couldn't remember much of the rest of the conversation. Despite his courteous manner, I was on pins and needles the entire time, trying to appear relaxed and confident, but certain that I was appearing young and naive. He was pleasant, and even entertaining at times, but when I left his office I heaved a sigh of relief. And went straight to Jonathan.

"Had your interview with the old man did ya?" he said. "I had mine a few days ago. He's one scary guy. I saw a very different person than the man I met when I first arrived. He couldn't have been more charming then, 'So nice to meet you, Jonathan. Welcome to Bear Lake Indian Residential School.' When I had my interview he asked me the same question you got, although he was a bit more direct. 'What would you do differently if you were in my shoes?' he asked. 'Send 'em all home,' I said. 'And let their parents teach them.' I felt pretty smug being able to just say it out loud, I ain't afraid of you Mr. Hotshot, I thought. He just looked at me, 'I'm disappointed in you Jonathan,' he said. Just like that, cool as a cucumber, don't waste my time kid. He was pretty even-handed, just said, 'Since that's not possible, Jonathan, do you have any other ideas?' Made me feel like I'd just told him my favourite subject was recess. So I gave him a few options: let the kids outside more, let them have a chance to be rough and make mistakes, offer them less preaching and more experimenting, blah, blah, blah. He said thank you and showed me the door. I don't know, maybe he really is interested in what we think, but personally, I think it's more of a way to find out the kind of person we are. He's a smart guy, and he watches everything. I'd keep my eye on him."

Two weeks later, Father James walked unexpectedly into my classroom.

The children, who had been working on math problems in small groups, stopped in their tracks and stared. I felt my heart lurch at the sight of him, despite his smile and deferential attitude, as he stood in the hall, waiting to be invited in.

"I thought I would drop by for a visit," he said. "I do this on occasion, it helps me keep in touch. I don't like ivory towers."

"We're delighted to have you, Father James," I said. "Please, come in."

"Say hello to Father James, children."

They stood as one, hands at their sides, "Hello, Father James."

"Hello, children. Please go back to your work. I don't want to disturb you."

He smiled pleasantly and made his way to the back of the classroom. There were no extra seats, and the children, confused about what was expected, went back to their desks. I found a chair for Father James and the children sat still and silent, looking up at me expectantly when I returned to the front of the class.

I tried to teach an arithmetic lesson that was better learned with group work, as Father James watched from his perch beside the coat hooks. I was glad I was no mind reader.

When the children finally stood to chime, "Goodbye, Father James," my relief was equal to their's as we listened to his footsteps recede down the hallway.

I went straight to Jonathan after school to see what he had to say.

"Don't you worry, my friend. He'll find what he wants no matter what you do."

"What's that supposed to mean?" I said. "What do you think he's looking for? Do you think he's just going to ignore my terrible lesson?"

"Were the kids quiet?"

"Yes."

"Did they do their work? Pay attention?"

"Yes."

"Then what're you worried about? You think he cares about your teaching strategies? All he cares about is whether or not the kids behave themselves and you stick to the curriculum. It makes no difference to him if it's a boring class or an exciting one. They want obedient Catholics more than they want eccentric Einsteins. You'll be fine."

It was reassuring, but Jonathan hadn't been in my class and he was as green as I was, regardless of how knowledgeable he appeared to be about the school's objectives.

I spoke to Sister Bea who said that, yes, Father James does visit classrooms on occasion and it wasn't any reflection on me. I didn't quite believe her, and certainly, after the miserable job I had done while he was there, I was sure he'd be back to check on me again.

Sept 9, 1947

The new school year has started off well. The students have lots of fresh energy for the harvesting, which is much easier now we have so many hands. The new teachers, Jonathan Jessop and Mary Brock, are both settling in. Jonathan moved out of his tent and into a room in Denis Dubois's house last week, much to the relief of Father James and B. Peter. I assume he'll be glad of it too, once he recovers from the ignominy of being forced to live under a solid roof. It makes doing everything so much easier. Denis has obviously been convinced to let Jonathan use his taxi to get back and forth, although Mary seems to prefer her bicycle. Either way, it's taken a load off us here. At first B. Samuel and B. Christopher took turns driving the new teachers between school and town. One of them will probably need to buy a car before long.

I enjoy the long summer with nothing but the farm to occupy me, but every September I'm reminded of how much I also enjoy the children and the life they bring to this place.

MUSIC

My classroom was next to the gymnasium, which was also used by
the school for assemblies and performances. It had a large stage with
curtains, a donation I was told, from a wealthy patron of the arts, a
friend of Father James.

Included in the donation was a piano. It was an upright, nothing
special, but it was the pride of Bear Lake Indian Residential School.
Piano lessons were given to students who showed an aptitude and
often as a reward for good behaviour. In my class, there were two
students who took piano and they loved the opportunity. Sister
Ursula gave lessons to the younger children, and Brother Peter took
over when they were more advanced. The students practised their
pieces on a strip of cardboard with the piano keys drawn in black
and white. Not being able to practise on the real thing didn't seem
to dull their enthusiasm. Like Beethoven, I suppose, they could hear
the music being beautifully played as they tapped each note on their
cardboard pianos.

Being the classroom closest to the gym meant that I often heard the after-school classes and the students' struggles as they went from cardboard to ivory. It wasn't Beethovenesque, but Sister Ursula was an enthusiastic teacher, and along with attempts to find all the notes to "Twinkle Twinkle Little Star" I would hear giggles and laughter. Despite the hesitant plinking and dissonant notes, it made a pleasant backdrop to marking and lesson planning.

Things were different on Thursdays. On Thursday, Sister Ursula's classes were cut short by Brother Peter, who taught the advanced students. Brother Peter had a reputation as a strict disciplinarian with a short fuse. In staff meetings he was impatient with anything that didn't directly concern him, and he had had nothing but a cursory, if polite, welcome for me. After he interrupted Jonathan's visit to my classroom, he was even more distant and cold on the rare occasions that I ran into him. He was a handsome man, tall and dark-haired with startling green eyes that could penetrate with a glance. He carried the air of someone who was used to getting what he wanted, when he wanted it. Whether he had to use charm or coercion, he didn't seem to care; he was competent at both. He did not fit my image of an artist, especially a musical one. So the first time I saw him stride past my door for the gym, I was unprepared for what followed

He began with scales and nursery rhyme tunes, played well. But once his warm-up was done, the rundown upright strained to do him justice, and I had to put my marking aside to listen. As unexpected as an avalanche, dramatic, emotional music stormed down the narrow hallway. At some point I must have closed my eyes, because I didn't notice anyone else pass my door and enter the gymnasium. But someone obviously did. First, the music changed, no longer loud and aggressive, it drifted out the gym door and floated softly by my open one. Then, between the waves of piano, a female voice lifted, strong and gentle, assured and vulnerable. And last of all, a male voice entered the mix, providing a beautiful counterpoint.

Music was one of the few joys in the school that was not considered a sin. Wonderful harmonies were often heard escaping from the laundry room or the kitchen as nuns sang through their work. But this was different.

I crept down the hall to see who was singing. Sister Abigail, the wrinkled nun with the drooping wimple who sat behind the counter in the school office, now stood with one hand resting gently on the dark wood of the piano. Her eyes were closed. The face she lifted to the heavens held only a passing resemblance to the one of my first impression. It was as though she had shed twenty years. Brother Peter, too, had changed. The rigid line of his shoulders had softened, his head rolled with the music and his hands danced gracefully across the keys. They were both wrapped in another world, far from misbehaving students, Spartan classrooms and proscribed days.

As I stood there watching, I heard someone come up behind me. I was surprised to see Mother Magdalene. I started to retreat but she laid a hand on my arm and we stood together.

Finally, an error made them stop to practise a few difficult bars and they noticed us in the doorway.

"I'm sorry, we'll close the door. We didn't mean to disturb you," said Brother Peter. His deference surprised me.

"On the contrary, you drew us here with your voices! I hope it doesn't disturb you if we stay and listen for a while," Mother Magdalene said.

"I didn't know anyone was here. This next part will be boring anyway, we're just going over this section here to get it right."

We could take a hint. Mother Magdalene left with me.

"They're wonderful singers," I said, as we walked back down the hall.

"Ah, yes," she said. "They're one of the great blessings we have here. Once a month they sing us an aria or anthem. It's always a highlight. God has given each of us special gifts. Do you remember Mathew's recounting of the parable of the talents?" She didn't wait for an answer, perhaps my blank face was all she needed.

"Three slaves were given money, called 'talents'. The two who invested their talents and made more were rewarded. The one who buried his money was punished. It's no accident that we use the word 'talent' the way we do. Our God-given talents are meant to be used and developed. The fact that these two use their talents to praise God is one of the joys of living a religious life."

"I've always wondered about that story," I said. "It always seemed to me like a tale to encourage capitalism."

Mother Magdalene chuckled. "Wait until winter comes. You haven't seen Brother David play hockey yet. He's an excellent player and our team has improved immeasurably under his coaching. We build the rink over the Christmas holidays, and there's hardly a boy at school who doesn't yearn to be on the hockey team. They practise day and night. Last year there was talk that they might even be good enough to play in the regional tournament. But it's not just the extra-curricular skills like hockey and music that we appreciate here. We couldn't do without Brother Thomas and his knowledge of animals, Brother Samuel with his handyman's skills and Sister Irene with her medical expertise, to name just a few of our irreplaceable talents."

She smiled at me. "It may seem that we lead boring lives, devoid of pleasure, but really we get a great deal of pleasure from a great many things. We're not a cloistered group. We've chosen to live in the world, as well as with each other. Though it might surprise you, we have both an interest in and a knowledge of worldly things. It's because of Brother David that I now know the names of some of the great hockey stars. I can't decide whether I'll cheer for the Toronto Maple Leafs or the Montreal Canadiens. Brother David likes Montreal, but since we're an Ontario school, cheering for a Quebec team feels disloyal somehow."

Leaving me at my classroom door, she gave a small smile before she walked away, her back straight, her hands, as always, tucked into her sleeves. I hoped she would choose my Toronto Maple Leafs.

BROTHER THOMAS

The school had six dairy cows, and every afternoon at four-thirty, as I sat in my empty classroom correcting papers or preparing for the next day, I could hear them bellowing and complaining. After three weeks of listening, my curiosity had to be satisfied. At the familiar sound of their plaintive bawls I put down my pen, and walked outside to the cowshed. Stepping gingerly to avoid cow pies and mud, I followed the last of the herd as they clomped into the barn. Each cow went to her stall without direction from the boys who stood waiting, shiny buckets at their feet. As the cows bent their heads into the mangers, the boys, after securing their cow's head, pulled up small stools, sat down and placed their buckets under the full udders.

That was when Brother Thomas noticed me. He managed the farm side of the school and I had met him briefly when I first toured the school, but we had not crossed paths since.

Brother Thomas was a short stocky man. Whenever I saw him he was tramping around in his uniform of overalls and rubber boots. He had a weathered face of indeterminate age and carried himself with an air of authority. He was not a man to suffer fools lightly, and that day, I was the fool.

He walked the length of the cowshed to where I was standing, keeping a wide berth between himself and the boys, who were bent over their tasks.

"What are you doing here?" His voice was quiet, but his anger was unmistakable.

"I've never seen milking before, I hear them every day, so I thought I'd come and see."

"You are not to come into the barn while milking is going on. Is that clear?"

"Yes. Sorry."

I turned to leave but he grabbed my arm.

"Stay right where you are until they're done."

Then he walked away.

I wasn't going to be spoken to like a student! I left, quietly, and I hoped, unobtrusively. Unfortunately, as I sidled out the door, the cow nearest me managed to knock over the half-filled bucket at her feet. I kept going before Brother Thomas had a chance to chastise me again.

I stayed away from the barn and Brother Thomas after that humiliation. I wanted no part of this grumpy, bitter old man. Asking around, I was surprised to find that others did not share my view of him. They claimed the boys loved him, and work in the barn was a coveted position. He kept to himself, but he was always warm when approached, ready to help build the skating rink, fix a broken bed frame or repair a leaky faucet. Trying to see both sides of the man, I decided that perhaps they were right, but only when you didn't step on his toes. Brother Thomas must be one of those rough-hewn men, scratchy inside and out, a benign but insecure tyrant, master of his menial cow-barn kingdom. Thankfully, the farm part of the school was quite separate, physically and socially, from the academic part. Brother Thomas was not someone likely to darken my door and not someone I was likely to need.

September 12, 1947
I suppose if I'm honest, a few things went right today, but when I look
back on my day I see only a string of disasters.
It started in the early hours of the morning when I knocked over my
water glass. It landed on the floor and shattered. It wasn't easy to clean it
up in the dark, but that wasn't the worst part. When dawn finally broke
and I knelt to say my prayers, my knee landed right on a shard of glass.
It bled badly enough that I had to go and get Sister Irene to patch me up,
which made me late for the barn, which meant that when I got here every
animal was making some sort of noise. When I got around to feeding the
horses Godfrey was banging his stall with his hoof like a spoilt little boy.
Thank goodness my milking boys can handle the job on their own now.
The one bright spot in my morning was seeing everyone in their place with
the cows quietly eating and offering up their bounty. Thank you Lord!
Later in the day, when we had the senior school students out in the
potato fields we found one corner all dug up by something. Could be
anything, squirrels, rabbits, skunks, who knows. I guess we should count
ourselves lucky that it doesn't happen more often. But I wasn't in a count-
ing mood.
The final straw was the end of the day milking. That new teacher,
the one from Toronto, came into the barn because "I hear them every
day, I just thought I'd see what it's all about." I don't walk into her
classroom uninvited just to "see what it's all about." Something about
a barn, people seem to feel that it's a public space and they can come
and go as they choose. I told her to stay put, but she took off anyway
and Jerry's pail got knocked over. He felt badly, which was completely
uncalled for, and it was a waste of good food. I suppose one advan-
tage is that she'll never want to cross paths with me again. I usually
try to make a better first impression though.

After telling my story to some of the other teachers I learned
that I'd been presumptive in going into the barn without talking to
Brother Thomas first. Learning this helped me to understand his
reaction and softened my harsh judgement of him. I felt I should
apologize, or at the very least, make amends for my inconsiderate
cowshed invasion. A golden opportunity presented itself one day in
mid-September.

Fall comes early in Northern Ontario. After the first week of school, I needed a sweater both indoors and out. Then, just past mid-September, we were blessed with an Indian summer. The afternoon sun shone through my big windows and the classroom warmed up. Too much in fact, so I tried to open my windows. They wouldn't budge.

My mother had taught me that an easy way to get on a man's good side was to play the helpless female. So after school, I walked over to the barn to see if Brother Thomas could help me get the windows open. I found him in the midst of a group of teenaged boys lounging behind the hay barn throwing horseshoes. The boys stood up politely when I arrived, but the casual looks they gave me were a bit disconcerting. I turned to Brother Thomas for support.

"Hello, Miss Brock. Is there something I can do for you?"

I felt like he and the boys were some sort of clique, and I was interrupting their male bonding with my, once again, unannounced arrival.

"I need someone to help me open a window," I said. "I was hoping you might be available."

The boys stared at me blankly but I pressed on. "It's stuck. I'm not sure when it was opened last, but I don't think it's been open for a while."

"What window are you trying to open?" asked Brother Thomas.

"My classroom window."

The boys all gave each other wide-eyed looks.

"The windows aren't meant to be opened," Brother Thomas said. "They've all been nailed shut from the outside."

The boys turned their faces to look at me, politely neutral, waiting like a cackle of hyenas for my next foolhardy remark.

I obliged. "Really? Well, can we un-nail them?" I asked.

Before answering, Brother Thomas's face seemed to tighten, which I interpreted as a subtle, or involuntary, message to give it up.

"No, we can't 'un-nail' them. Most of the year we don't want them open anyway."

The ball was back in my court. There was a moment's quiet while he waited for something more, but I wasn't going to give him, or them, the pleasure. I thanked him and left, with my back straight and my pace even, my dignity hanging by a slender thread.

Turning my back on the barn, I walked along a path that led past the playground and into the woods. Jonathan had told me that there was a pretty little waterfall not too far off. I had no desire to return to my stuffy classroom and sit in humiliation, so I decided to take advantage of the unexpected warmth and go exploring. The path wound through the trees alongside a small stream. Within a few minutes the school was out of sight and I could hear the distinctive sound of rushing water. A few minutes more and a small clearing opened up and the falls were in front of me. The water cascaded down over numerous rocky ledges into a clear pool, decorated by the ragged remains of lily pads. Beneath the surface, a small school of minnows swam lazily among the reeds. Along the shoreline, I spotted a garter snake curled up on a warm rock. A few feet behind it, the sun poured through the leafy canopy onto a rough log bench.

I was tempted to sit there and enjoy the last warm rays of fall, but I saw paths leading off from this sanctuary and I didn't know when I would next have the opportunity to explore them, so I kept going. My practical black pumps were good for the classroom, but not very practical for scrambling over fallen logs or up steep inclines. So as each trail grew faint, I returned to try another. My third attempt faded to another disappointing end, making the sunny bench look like my best option, when I spotted an unusual shape almost hidden by the underbrush.

On closer inspection, I saw that it was it was a short, round structure made of sticks tied together with leather, sort of like an emergency shelter. It was about seven feet in diameter and sat about four feet high, comfortable enough to sit up in, too low to stand, but good enough if someone wanted to spend the night. I wondered if anyone had. I got down on my knees and crawled inside for a look, but there was nothing there, just a big hole in the middle, probably used for a fire.

By then, afternoon was turning to dusk. The cool of autumn returned with the sun's departure, but the chill I felt when I crawled back out of that derelict shelter had nothing to do with the temperature. In the semi-darkness it felt like some unseen person was watching from the among the trees. I took a couple of deep breaths to calm myself, and headed straight back for the security of the school.

September 17, 1947
Mary Brock came by today. She wanted someone to open her classroom windows. I had a group of the older boys playing horseshoes with me behind the barn. Although they weren't rude, there was something in their demeanour that didn't sit well with me. Mary looked uncomfortable too. After she left they made some choice comments. I put a stop to it, but it would appear that they need more respect for me as well. I'm not their peer. Given the circumstances, she handled them pretty well, I must say. I think I might be able to get along with her, although I'm not sure that she'll give me another chance. But she did well with the boys and didn't let my coolness put her off her mission. I like that.

It doesn't seem possible that these boys will all be set loose on the world in less than a year. They have a harder time taking responsibility than last year's crop and they tend to follow the one who will get them into the most trouble. I've got some work to do.

My second meeting with Brother Thomas only reinforced my initial opinion of him, and I had no interest in pursuing a relationship. But on a gloomy Wednesday one week later, I ran into him again and met a different man.

On Wednesday afternoons we had our weekly staff meetings. Normally, I kept my mouth shut and listened, as Jonathan did enough agitating for the two of us. But I was starting to feel more confident and decided to mention some strategies I wanted to implement in my classroom— more group work and less testing, some of which I was already doing. Mother Magdalene sighed, and the others kept silent, as she explained to me with a clear voice and simple words the intrinsic value of their teaching methods, letting me know that it was not for me to question their wisdom. Even Jonathan stayed quiet as she preached at me.

When the meeting finally finished, I felt as gloomy as the weather, which had turned to a cold rain. But after my dressing down I needed to get outside, the school building and all it represented felt like a prison. So, despite the weather, I turned towards the forest, thinking

I might go to the waterfalls. I had heard that there were bets over whether Jonathan or I would make it past Christmas. I was beginning to wonder if I wanted to.

What I wanted to do at that moment was to punch a tree or shout my frustrations to the heavens. But by the time I got as far as the barn, the wind and rain had dampened my clothes along with my enthusiasm for an angry walk. The milking shed was out of bounds, so I slipped into the attached hay barn. My Uncle Floyd owned a farm, and I had many happy memories of summers spent playing with my cousins in his barn. Crossing the threshold to stand under the big open ceiling, the quiet cathedral atmosphere was the perfect antidote to my frustrations.

Just like Uncle Floyd's barn, this one had a loft on each side of the central open space. Bales of hay were piled high in both, as well as underneath. The earthy smells that lifted on the damp air and the staccato fall of heavy rain on the metal roof reminded me of one of my most cherished summer traditions. The fort. It was built in the hayloft in whatever space was available. Some years we had lots of room, other years we had to make do. The fort was our rainy-day playroom. I knew that the barn, like the cowshed, might be out of bounds, but with some residual self-righteous anger to bolster my curiosity, I mustered the courage to climb the slats nailed across two supporting posts and up into the loft. I hoped that some intrepid students might have built a fort here too.

Sure enough, at the back, a few out-of-place hay bales gave it away. Ten feet by four feet, the fort's walls were a respectable three bales high. It was minimally decorated. An empty milk bottle and two filthy pillows lay on an old horse blanket that covered the bale floor. I smiled as I imagined the fun the children must have in this place and I adjusted my view of Brother Thomas just a bit. Surely he must know of this secret haven in his barn.

My courage thus rewarded, I climbed back down to explore the rest of the barn. I found the oat bins and ran my fingers through the kernels, remembering how much fun it was to sit in these bins and let the oats form around me. Farther on were horse stalls. In two of them, huge Clydesdales watched me quietly as I neared. A little afraid that Brother Thomas was going to come around a corner to reprimand me, I couldn't resist reaching in to rub their soft noses. They bent their big heads to my hands, hoping for some treat. I was sorry to disappoint them and vowed I would bring apples the next time. Now that the tractor ruled, the rest of the stalls were being used for storage. I saw old saddles, hay rakes, long tractor attachments and—Brother Thomas. He was sitting behind a desk in a room made up of what had once been two stalls.

"Hello there," he said as I passed by the open door. "I wasn't expecting a visit."

"I'm sorry," I said, startled. "I didn't know you were here. I... I was just looking around."

"Perfectly all right," he said. "Did you find anything of interest?"

"The horses are sweet, and the smells reminded me of a barn I used to play in as a child."

"Won't you come into my humble abode?" he said. "We didn't get off to a very good start. Let's give it another try."

His voice was deep and rich, and his unexpected openness disarming. The next thing I knew I was sitting in an ancient well-stuffed chair that took up a large part of his 'humble abode'.

Brother Thomas was only in his forties when I met him, but he looked much older. His jowly cheeks were covered in a grey stubble, which gave me the impression he only shaved to meet society's expectations. His deep-set eyes were topped with feathery eyebrows that made his face appealing in a clownish sort of way. His thinning salt and pepper hair was as unkempt as the room. Under his overalls, his red flannel shirt was rolled up to his elbows revealing a long scar along the top of one hairy forearm. His hands, now clasped in front of him, were large and as well-worn as his shirt. This was a man comfortable in his own skin.

"As you can see, I took two stalls and made them into an office. That way I have space for a bed in case I need to spend the night, as well as room for my desk and papers."

His narrow bed stood along one wall and was topped by a few cushions so that it could do double duty as a sofa. Other than the bed and my chair, a teacher's desk and a bookshelf were all that the room could hold.

The desk was cluttered with papers of all sorts, ledgers filled with numbers, farming magazines, something that looked like a tractor manual, and lots of notes. Behind him three shelves were overflowing with books. Tractors for the Modern Age and Veterinary Basics for Bovines sat next to a brand-new, History of Western Civilization, by Bertrand Russell, and another by C. S. Lewis, The Screwtape Letters, one of my father's favourite books. On the top shelf I saw a row of journals, bound with red leather, the year stamped in gold on the spines. His collection started in 1936. He hadn't missed a year.

"Yes," he said, following my eye. "I have an eclectic taste in books. And I write in my journal every day. I'm not sure why. I think it's a good discipline as much as anything. I'm sure most of what I've written will never see the light of day, and even less would probably be worth reading. Still, I keep it up. A bit of a vanity I suppose."

"I kept a diary during the war," I said. "But I haven't written anything since it ended. I should probably keep one this year. I have a feeling this place is going to be important in my life."

"First jobs are always important. And this one will be unlike anything you ever expected to be doing. For example, I'll bet Normal School never prepared you for the cowshed. By the way, I must apologize for the way I treated you, but cows, while they may not appear to be, are very sensitive animals. If you treat them nicely, they'll return the favour. They're fond of routine and they get to know the people they come into contact with. At milking time it's especially important that things are as calm as possible. I could've handled it much more pleasantly though. I hope you'll accept my apology."

"Of course! I didn't mean any harm; I don't know anything about cows. Could I come by sometime and learn?"

"Maybe. I have two new boys this year, so let's wait a while. I'll let you know."

An idea had started to form during my walk through the barn. I was still burning from my dismissal at the staff meeting, and it seemed that Brother Thomas was feeling the need to make amends. "I have another idea," I said. "It would involve you."

Brother Thomas looked at me. His face bore what I can only call an impish grin, and his eyes, buried deep in folds of skin, were bright. "I'm feeling that, like your innocent invasion of my cowshed, this may be something not in line with what normally goes on here. But you've piqued my curiosity. What exactly might this idea involve?"

"The girls never get a chance to see the farm side of things. What if I arranged for a class visit to the barn? We could see what you do here. Maybe the boys who milk could explain how that works. They could play a bit in the barn. It would be fun!" The more I said it out loud, the more I warmed to the idea.

"Fun doesn't sound like education to me. I don't see how Mother Magdalene would approve." But his eyes were twinkling.

"Oh, I could make it very educational. I could work some math into it, English would be easy: they could write about their experience. We could probably even work some science into it if I needed to!"

"Is that what they teach at Normal School nowadays? How to make everything educational?"

"But everything is educational! What do you think?"

"I think you'd have a very hard time getting it approved. But if you can manage that, I'll support you."

I don't know why, perhaps Mother Magdalene also felt the need to make amends, but one week later I walked from my classroom to the barn, followed by two neat rows of students.

Each carried a notebook, a pencil and a grin. It was the first time I had seen genuine excitement.

We started in the hay barn, where Brother Thomas gave them a tour and explained about the workings of this part of the farm. Then we went into the milking shed, where Bessie stood quietly, chewing her cud in a stall. Anyone who wanted could try to milk her. Ruth was the first to volunteer and she did surprisingly well. A few of the girls ran screaming as soon as their hands touched Bessie's teats and Brother Thomas got a face full of milk when he bent to help one of the boys. Soon everyone wanted a turn—even I tried my hand at it. Bessie was one very patient cow!

Mother Magdalene had allowed me an hour-and-a-half for the trip. When we finished with Bessie, we still had fifteen minutes, and Brother Thomas said it would be all right if the children played in the hay barn. They were thrilled!

The only grey bit was when Brother Peter showed up and saw us all playing. The look on his face was thunderous, but he turned and left without saying a word. Most of the children didn't even see him. Then, just before we were about to leave, one of the high school students poked her head in the door.

"Cathy!" Ruth shouted. She and a few other girls ran over to give her a hug, but Cathy barely responded and seemed uncomfortable with the show of affection. They talked for a moment and then she, too, left quickly. I hoped she wouldn't get into trouble because of us.

September 26, 1947
I underestimated that lovely Mary Brock. I wonder if she's wormed her way into Mother Magdalene's affections the way she has into mine. She has an innocence that is disarming, combined with a confidence that one mustn't, as I did, sell short.

Today she brought her class into the barn for what she calls a 'field trip.' Bessie was most compliant, allowing inexperienced hands to milk her, with nary a complaint. Would that we were all so accommodating! The children were quiet and polite, taking copious notes as I dropped my pearls of wisdom. I don't get much time with the younger ones, it was refreshing. They played in the hay when we were finished with the tour and I loved hearing their delight as they jumped from bales and ran obstacle courses through the barn.

I was just heading up to the milk shed when I remembered that this was the day Brother Peter usually comes. I enjoyed the milking much more today, imagining his horror at seeing a barn full of happy children. Maybe there is some truth to the Buddhist notion of Karma.

BEAR LAKE

Bear Lake was a small community, especially by my big city standards. It lay like a roughly drawn rectangle with the lake in the south, and the railway to the north. The eastern and western borders were formed by the forest, a more flexible barrier. Church Street, so named because all three churches were on it, ran east to west, through the centre of town. King Street, the main artery for downtown Bear Lake, ran north-south, ending at the lake where there was a small park and a public wharf. East of King Street and south of Church was the "bad" corner of town. On the eastern edge of this section was the sawmill, with a bunkhouse for the men. I had passed through this section on my trip to the school from the train station. There were a couple of bars in the area too, and a hotel for those who didn't want to stay in the bunkhouse. The hotel was also reputed to be home to the "ladies of the night." Better-off families lived in the southwest corner, with the lake lapping up against their backyard lawns. Mrs. Norton's house was in the residential area to the north, known as Spruce Hill. This neighbourhood spread east and west of King Street.

North of it was the poor section of town which extended up to the train tracks. North of the tracks was Indiantown, and beyond; the ever-present forest.

The commercial district of Bear Lake was made up of a few stores, a bank, two restaurants, one hotel, a bar and the police station. The town also had a medical clinic run by two doctors who shared a building with the town's only lawyer. Their offices were on Church Street and their building boasted the grand title of "The Professional Building". At the corner of Church and King was Johnson's General Store. It had once been the focal point of downtown, but by the time I arrived its glory days were fading. It still had a bit of everything, but as the town grew, specialized stores were becoming more popular, and a few were already doing well. A green grocer had opened right next door to the General Store, and closer to the lake, a ladies clothing store sold ready-made clothes and hats. The Eaton's catalogue was also a popular shopping option.

The school was about five miles out of town. Mrs. Norton found a bicycle for me to use and pedalling got me to school and back. It also became my favourite way to tour the neighbourhoods and beyond. I loved to take my bike outside the city limits and explore the side roads Brother Christopher had pointed out when I first arrived.

Bear Lake was the biggest lake in the area, but hundreds of other lakes, large and small, dotted the region. It seemed that every man in town had his well-guarded secret about the best lake for fish, and every man liked to get to his favourite lake with his truck. This meant that small laneways had been cut into the bush all along the main road. Some roads led nowhere, some I never got to the end of, but most, after a short ride, ended at a body of water. After that, animal and human trails were plentiful and I would leave my bike by the shore and wander aimlessly, until hunger or dark sent me home.

Like the trails I tried to follow by the waterfall at school, many paths faded away to nothing. But with the advantages of sensible shoes and a packed lunch, I was more adventurous on these rambles and every once in a while I would get lost. Usually, it was a simple exercise to find my way to the water and follow the shoreline back to the laneway I had come in by. On one occasion, I got to the lake and instead of turning towards the laneway, I turned away from it.

By the time I realized my mistake, the sun was down. As I struggled along the rocky shoreline in the dark, I met a rescue party out looking for me.

After that incident, Mrs. Norton, who had given up on trying to convince me not to walk in the woods, made arrangements with a friend of hers to teach me some basic navigational skills.

I will be forever grateful to Mr. MacIntyre, an old hunter and trapper who spent hours teaching me how to see in the woods—to pay attention to sun, shadow, wind, and every kind of landmark. I learned to look behind me to see how things might look on the way back, to break twigs or leave little ribbons on branches to guide me on my return trip. And, I never left home without my "survival" kit, matches, a fishhook, first aid and a flashlight.

On my excursions outside of town I often saw evidence of human activity. Trappers' shacks and hunting cabins or clearings with an old fire pit in the centre, were not uncommon. But with summer over and hunting season yet to begin, I rarely came across any people. So I was surprised one day when I met a man at one of the trappers' cabins.

It was a Saturday and I had brought a picnic lunch so I could be out all day. The trail leading up to the cabin was wide and well used, which was unusual, but the cabin itself was no different from any other I had seen. It was built from unstripped logs, and chinked with moss. Windowless, it was topped by a simple tarpaper roof. I never saw a lock on any of these shelters, and I could never resist the urge to take a peek inside, despite a twinge of guilt for trespassing, and this cabin did not escape my scrutiny. From the light of the open door I saw a narrow bed along one wall, a table and in the centre of the room, a wood stove made from an old oil drum. Hoops for stretching skins hung on the walls along with a yellowing newspaper photo of Pope Pius XII. I was surprised to see a few plates and cups piled on the table and tins of food on a shelf above it. A pair of boots was tucked beneath the bed, and some neatly folded clothes had found a home in wooden crates that were nailed to the wall. It was simple, but clean and cozy. I wondered who might live there.

It was fun to have the day and be able to go deeper into the woods. Jonathan would love this, I thought. I came across a freshly killed deer that looked as if it had been ripped apart by wolves. I had my lunch beside a beautiful little pond created by a beaver dam, where I watched a heron fish for his meal. On my return trip, I came face to face with a skunk, who, after seeing that I was too petrified to move, ducked into a hole under a rock, leaving me with nothing but my own scent to carry home.

It was shortly after this, close to the trapper's shack, that I smelled smoke. I was excited to meet the person who lived in the little cabin and I picked up my pace. But once I had broken through to the clearing, I hesitated. Bush people are a strange lot, and I wasn't at all sure he would want a visitor. I started for the door, stopped, started again—then it opened.

He was a short man, with a full beard and a red, bulbous nose. He stood in his stocking feet, his legs spread, his thumbs hooked into dirty yellow suspenders, a green toque on his head.

He didn't say a word, just stared at me.

His stare felt like an accusation of some sort, which I thought was unfair.

I tried to be nonchalant, to defuse the tension. "Hello. I didn't mean to invade your privacy, I was just out walking."

He didn't respond to this overture, so I tried again. "My name is Mary Brock, I'm teaching at the Indian school. I'm new, I just started this year."

This seemed to interest him not at all, so I kept on walking. "Well, goodbye. I hope I didn't disturb you."

He continued to watch me as I continued to walk across the clearing. After a few, tortuously long minutes, I finally reached the path at the other side that would get me back to the laneway and my bicycle. As soon as I felt he couldn't see me anymore, I ran.

Mrs. Norton had no idea who he was, but she warned me to stay away from "his type."

"There are a lot of odd men out there in the woods. Some Indians too. They're still trapping and hunting and they act like they own the land. I know you like your adventuring, but I'd do it a little closer to home if I were you."

When I talked to Jonathan about it, he laughed at Mrs. Norton's concerns. "There's very little danger for you out there, unless you count tripping on a rock. Those guys just want to be left alone. If you respect their need to be unsociable, you have nothing to fear."

By this time Jonathan had left his tent and was living in town with Mr. Dubois. Mr. Dubois drove a big old school bus and the town's only taxi, neither of which got much business. I never saw the taxi on the street, and the bus was used mainly to shuttle the loggers between the bush and town or to transport sports teams to competitions. On rare occasions, if we were invited to a special event in town, our school also used the bus.

Despite his admonitions that I had nothing to fear, after my meeting with the bush man, Jonathan started to make himself available to come along with me on my explorations. Whether it was because my stories had whetted his appetite or because he felt the need to act as protector I never learned, but I enjoyed his company. He knew a lot about the forest, and was able to spot animal tracks and dens I would have passed by without seeing. He always brought his wild food guidebook with him too, and we would look for, and usually find, something edible.

One sunny Sunday afternoon we harvested arrowhead tubers. The arrowhead plant grows in shallow warm water with the edible tubers deep in the muck. On the day Jonathan suggested we try, the air was warm but the water had already turned cold. As a girl, I had often fantasized about living the bush life. I would be well provisioned with meat by my handsome, skillful husband, and I would augment our diet by collecting food in season from the woods outside our door. Most of the edible plants Jonathan and I collected were easy enough to find and harvest, even if they weren't the tastiest. But harvesting arrowhead tubers was another story. After three hours in the cold muddy water we were completely soaked and freezing cold. All we had to show for our patience and icy fingers were twenty small, hard, and very unappetizing tubers. My romantic vision of pioneer life was quickly revised.

As the days got darker and colder, I spent less time exploring the bush and more time in town, and at home. Mrs. Norton was a wonderful, but basic, cook and liked nothing better than sharing her table with as many children and grandchildren as possible. When her friends dropped by, the kitchen table was where they sat, coffee and fresh baking within arm's reach.

She said she would be happy for me to do some cooking too. But with my busy schedule and her efficiency I don't think I cooked more than a dozen meals the whole time I was there. The only thing I made was tea.

Mrs. Norton was a coffee drinker. When someone wanted tea, she would put a tea bag into a mug of hot water and add some milk and sugar. Not my style. I had grown up with strict rituals around tea and by the time I got to Bear Lake they were immutable. Tea had to come out of a teapot, one that had been warmed beforehand, and poured into a teacup with a bit of milk already sitting at the bottom.

My first purchase in Bear Lake, and one of my only non-perishable purchases, was a big yellow teapot I found at Johnson's General Store. The store had opened in 1925, and the big yellow teapot looked as though it had been waiting on the shelves since that time. It sat on an upper, hard-to-reach shelf, above a row of electric coffee percolators and toasters. When I spotted it, I knew it was mine. It looked exactly like my grandmother's teapot, and I needed something familiar in this foreign land.

I brought it home, stopping on the way at the grocery store for some Red Rose tea. I cleaned it up, and after dinner that night, introduced Mrs. Norton to the joys of a properly made cup of tea. She was unimpressed, and after a few sips apologized and hurriedly made herself a cup of coffee. But for me, it was heaven.

I never did buy myself a teacup, but that big yellow teapot found a spot for itself on the cookbook shelf in Mrs. Norton's kitchen. It never failed to make me feel warm and cozy whenever I reached up for it. It was like tasting home.

OCTOBER
1947

LOSING GROUND

My bicycle ride back and forth to school was one of the things I loved most about Bear Lake. It took about five minutes to traverse the residential area, then for the next half-hour or so I pedalled through the woods. The road had a few ups and downs, nothing too onerous, except at the halfway point, where one long hill either delighted or dismayed. On my way to school, I got off my bike and walked up it, but on my way home I'd bounce my way down and let my hair fly.

Jonathan had also found a bike, and sometimes we would meet and go to school together. But I loved it best when I rode on my own. When the sun shone down through the yellow leaves of autumn it was like a caress. Even a rainy-day ride invigorated me. I loved the smell of wet earth and the feeling of accomplishment as I pulled into the long school driveway.

The crunch of my wheels usually kept the wildlife at bay, but the exceptions never failed to delight. Most of the route was deep in the forest, but there was one stretch beside a large marshy meadow and it was here I was most likely to spot an animal. Startled rabbits would leap above the grass in a rush for the safety of their burrows. Sometimes I would see the proud tip of a fox's tail as he pranced unconcerned through the vegetation. Occasionally, I would get a glimpse of bright eyes and alert ears as he sat up on his haunches to check me out as I passed by. One time I saw an enormous moose lumbering along the edge of the road, not a care in the world. He didn't even bother to look at me as I rode past, giving him a wide berth. Partridges were a problem: they would dash out unexpectedly when they heard me coming, and I almost ran over a few.

As autumn wore on, the days got shorter. Soon, dawn was breaking as I headed out from Mrs. Norton's, and darkness was falling as I returned. But, like the rain, this made the experience different, not miserable. I loved watching the sun rise or set through the trees, sending long shadows across the road and painting the clouds with crimson, gold, and mauve.

By the time September came to a close, my life in the classroom had settled into a comfortable routine. Most of my students were still cautious, reluctant to answer questions unless they were confident they had the right answer. But as the name tags we made on the first day deteriorated and fell off, they were not replaced. And then one day, I realized that the habit they had gotten into of saying their names before answering or asking a question was more annoying than helpful.

Father James never returned after his initial visit, and I no longer listened for his distinctive footfalls. Although, at times I wished he would show up, just so he could see how well I was doing. I felt at home in the classroom. I looked forward to meeting my students every day, and already I was seeing some improvement in reading and arithmetic.

Then, the honeymoon ended.

First, the weather changed. The gentle rain of September changed to cold downpours in October, which made the road a sloppy mess. It got worse when cold nights froze the mess, and I had to ride to school through ice and slush. I felt no pride of accomplishment on those mornings. Warm and damp was one thing, cold and wet quite another. My part-time solution was Jonathan, who, with the slow taxi business, had the temporary use of his landlord's car. However,

I was well aware of the gossip circulating about the two of us, and I had no intention of encouraging it. Jonathan insisted that the best way to quell gossip was to ignore it, but I wasn't so sure. He hadn't let me down yet, but there was something indefinable about him that made me reluctant to be dependent on him. I wanted to get my own car, the sooner the better.

I noticed a change in the classroom too. The students, knowing that I was more lenient than the nuns, started pushing boundaries. And there were other considerations. As the dark days settled in, I'm sure that the students, like me, looked ahead. Christmas was a long way off. We were in this for the long haul. This was the period when I was most homesick, and perhaps they were feeling the same way. Whatever the reasons, a cranky teacher and unhappy children are not a good combination.

One day Bobby threw an eraser at Susan. Ordinarily, I would silently celebrate such an expression of normalcy, but not this time. I scolded him in front of the class and made him stand with his nose to the blackboard. This made the whole class shut down. I could hardly get a word out of anyone, which made me even more frustrated. The next few days were no better, and then I heard myself say, "If you children can't answer simple questions, I don't know how you're going to manage the difficult ones." It sounds like a minor chastisement, but getting these children to open up was a delicate balancing act. I knew that any trust I had banked was quickly being eroded with my impatience; but I couldn't help myself.

My annoyance with everything peaked one morning when one of the boys fell asleep on his desk. I woke him up with a cuff on the cheek. It's a powerful feeling being able to do that sort of thing with impunity. It shocked me how good it felt. The same day at recess, I grabbed one of the girls who was hanging around the fence that divides them from the boys and pulled her away. You're learning how to be a proper teacher, I told myself, growing up, not being so soft. But it didn't feel right.

Brother Thomas said it was a part of the process. He said I would find a middle ground soon enough and not to worry. Sister Bea said that the children needed a kind but firm hand, and I was doing the right thing. She seemed pleased with me. I was not pleased with me at all, and a middle ground was nowhere in sight.

Behind the scenes, in our staff meetings, things were no better. Whenever I brought up any changes in classroom conduct and discipline that I wanted to try, Mother Magdalene would sigh and ask me to please wait. "As a new teacher it's best that you start by sticking to the tried and true. Once you have been here a while, you will see that some of the things we do are not as old-fashioned or as unreasonable as you may think. Get to know your students and us a bit before experimenting." The others would nod in solemn agreement. Jonathan would try to stand up for me every now and then, but he had his own battles to fight. We had meetings once a week and by the time October rolled around I had given up trying to say much of anything at all.

As October dragged on, the days growing shorter and colder, I felt more and more alone. In the morning, when my alarm went off, instead of leaping out of bed ready to start a new day, I would look through the crack in my pink curtains to the dark outside and wonder why I was still here. Leaving the cocoon of my blankets took every ounce of energy I had. When my feet hit the floor, any warmth they had was stolen by the tendrils of cold that rose through the floorboards and hung in the pre-dawn air. It was depressing to realize that my father was right after all. I hated it here. I hated the school, I hated the town, I hated my pink bedroom. I couldn't think of one good reason to stay.

Then, Jonathan left.

With his departure it felt like the rug had been pulled out from under me. His irreverence for everything had balanced the seriousness with which everyone else took everything. His crazy lifestyle had made me feel better about mine. His independent assertiveness at meetings had given voice to some of my own concerns. Now, I was really alone.

I didn't even know he was leaving until he dropped by my house on a Sunday afternoon, the day he took the train south. It was the first and only time Mrs. Norton met him. He had spent the weekend with some friends in Indiantown and with his woodsmoke smell, unshaven face and well-worn pack, she wouldn't let him past the front door until I came downstairs and assured her that he was indeed who he said he was.

Jonathan told me that Brother Peter had booted him out. He had called Jonathan into his office on Friday and told him that he had been given plenty of warnings and plenty of time to both clean up his act and change his attitude. Jonathan had done neither. They wished him well, but he was not suited for life at Bear Lake Indian Residential School. He was not to come back on Monday.

"So, I'm off on the evening train," he said, and shrugged his shoulders.

"Give me a minute," I said, "I'll get my coat and walk you to the station."

When I went into the kitchen to retrieve my jacket, Mrs. Norton had her back to me, busying herself with something on the stove. But the telltale sign of a chair, pulled up close to the hall gave her away.

"We can talk when I get back," I said. "And please, no gossip. At least until you hear what I have to say."

She turned with a "who me?" look on her face, but she smiled and nodded. Only slightly reassured, I went out the door with Jonathan.

As we started walking the familiar route to the railroad station, I buttoned my coat and stuffed my bare hands into my pockets. I don't know if it was the winter wind blowing through my fall jacket, or the realization that Jonathan was leaving, but the chill went straight to my bones.

"I don't know how I'll manage without you," I said.

"You'll probably do better without me. No one to get you riled up or pull you into some scheme or other. I'm just not suited for compromise."

"What's that supposed to mean? Are you saying I'm compromising by staying?"

"Yeah, I suppose so. But don't take it so hard. I don't mean it in the terrible way you make it sound." He looked down at me. My face always gave away whatever I was feeling. "I know that without compromise nothing gets done. But whenever I do it, I feel like I'm surrendering, and it kills me. Maybe that's why I'm out of here and you're not."

We walked a few blocks in silence, Jonathan kicking at the autumn leaves that littered the sidewalks.

"What are you going to do now?" I asked.

"I don't know." Jonathan stopped walking for a moment. "You know, what surprises me most about this whole thing?"

I looked at him, wondering where this was leading. "I feel disappointed," he said. "It's partly because I can hear my dad saying, 'I told you so'. I've always had a hard time keeping jobs I don't like. But, it's more than that. It wasn't all bad, and I was starting to get to know some of the students, the boys especially. They're good kids. But they get treated as though they'd burn the place down if they weren't supervised every second. I feel like I'm letting them down by not being able to handle the rough stuff. Compared to what they have to deal with, it isn't rough at all. How can I hope to make a difference in their lives if I can't even say, 'Yes Sir' to Brother Peter without an argument? Is it vanity to think that I might have made a difference? Ha! Look at me! Talking like a Catholic already!"

I laughed. "Yes, it probably is a vanity, but it's probably true too. I'll bet the boys loved you. I'm just not sure it was for the right reasons. You probably appealed to their sense of rebellion."

I smiled at him, but his face was serious.

"Did I fail Mary?"

"Fail? That's a weighty question Jonathan. I guess you have to ask yourself what it was you set out to do."

"Since you're not giving me a straight answer, I'll take that as a yes."

"Well," I told him, "you failed at keeping your job, but it didn't sound like you were asking me about that."

"How do you manage it, Mary?"

"Manage what?"

"I don't know. All of it. How do you manage to smile at Mother Maggie when she shuts you down every time you try to do something different? How do you chat with Sister Bea like she's your best buddy? How do you teach your students to read with stories centred on lives they've never seen? How do you supervise a recess where brothers and sisters aren't even allowed to talk to each other? How do you keep your sanity when you're participating in a system that's insufferable at best and downright cruel the rest of the time?"

Jonathan had never let me into his thoughts like this before. I was taken aback by his vehemence. "Jonathan, you're sounding almost hysterical. You said yourself that it's not so bad. There are good people here doing good things. No child likes rules and regulations, but we all have to learn to live with them. I'll grant you that I don't like a lot of their ways, but really, I think 'cruel' is an exaggeration."

"Really, Mary? Really? Don't you think it's cruel to keep brothers and sisters apart? Don't you think it's cruel to tell a child that if he doesn't brush his teeth within five seconds of being told, that he's going to hell? Isn't it cruel to prevent children from speaking the only language they know? I could go on and on, you know I could! How is that not cruel?"

"I guess I never thought of it that way. The people are so nice."

"*Some* of the people are nice, but even if they all were, they're supporting a system that's rotten to the core. The more I think about it the angrier I get. Brother Peter probably did me a favour by booting my ass out. I couldn't have stood it much longer anyway. You're right, maybe I would have inspired the boys to revolt. I'd love to be there for that day!"

"'That day' would be terrible. Can you imagine the punishment that would be meted out for a revolt? I don't even want to think about it."

"My point exactly, Mary! They get beaten into submission from the time they first walk through the door. Maybe I'll be more help to them from the outside. I can tell the world what a horror show we have right in our own backyard. The people running the schools aren't going to change. But everybody has somebody telling him what to do. I'll just go on up the chain of command until I find someone with the authority and the will to make some changes."

His pace quickened. Now that he had a purpose he was eager to get on the train and get started. I wasn't so sure that his resolve would last the trip home.

"I see that look on your face, Mary! Don't you think I don't." He laughed. "You think I'll go home and find a boat to sail around the world on, or get a job working the lifts on the ski slopes of France.

Well, I can't blame you for thinking it. A month ago that's exactly what I would've done. But this boy has grown up some these last few weeks. I thought this job would be an amusing way to learn how people live in the North. But it turns out that I actually came to care about my students, and I will fail if I don't try to make their lot better than it is."

We reached the station, and the distinctive sound of steel wheels turning on steel tracks came to us from across the water as the train made its way along the shore towards the rickety wooden platform. The Bear Lake sign squeaked on its chain in the cool autumn wind.

"I'm going to miss you," I said.

He looked surprised, then his face softened. "I'll miss you too, Mary. I'm counting on you to keep Brother Peter on his toes!"

As the train's whistle pierced the dark, I realized what was being taken away. I was losing the one person who understood me. Jonathan and I shared a common background and a common goal at the school. He was the one person who could be counted on to listen sympathetically to my frustrations and complaints. He could make me laugh with his sacrilegious irreverence for everything everyone else held dear. Jonathan never accepted the status quo without examining it first. He could be frustrating, opinionated and egotistical, but he was always honest. Our last conversation would haunt me over the coming months, but all I could hear right then was the train's whistle, telling me that he was going away.

October 16, 1947
It's been a while since I've written. Bessie took a turn when the cold hit, and she died a few days ago. I didn't think a cow's death would make me sad, but it has. She was a good girl who lived a hard life. She kept on giving no matter what, stoically, uncomplaining, milk and calves year after year. We could all learn a lot from her. We were able to use some of her meat, so even in death she gave us what she could. I'll miss you Bessie. I hope there's a cow heaven for you with lots of green grass and sunshine.

The other big news is Jonathan's departure. No one knew about it, or if they did they didn't tell me. He just didn't show up on Monday. Brother Jerome had to take over his classes, which he wasn't too happy about, but the boys are even more unhappy. They all loved Mr.

Jessop and I do believe he loved them back. I enjoyed our raucous conversations on the value of the school, whether or not Mackenzie King has overstayed his welcome in parliament, or if the war was the only way out of the Depression. He was engaging and lighthearted company. I'll miss him too.

MELTDOWN

A week after Jonathan left, while sitting in my bedroom after school pondering my options, I heard a determined knock on my door. I usually sat with Mrs. Norton after school, she with her coffee and me with my tea. But her chatter and constant questions were becoming more than I could handle after a day with students. So lately, instead of heading for the kitchen when I got home, I headed upstairs to my room. It had been at least a week since I last heard the whistle of the kettle, and I took this to mean that she had accepted the change in our routine.

Apparently not. I opened the door and there she stood, filling the space with her wide form. Uninvited, she stepped in and looked around the room. I followed her gaze and was surprised at what I saw. Clothes lay everywhere—on the floor, the chair, the dresser. My shoes were scattered wherever I had dropped them, and books and papers topped the mess. I was grateful that I had brought my half-filled cups of tea down to the kitchen that morning.

"I'm sorry," I muttered, "I'll clean it up right away."

"What's wrong Mary?"

I looked at her, standing there just inside my door. Her floral housedress hung shapelessly on wide hips. Tight blue-grey curls, which she maintained by sleeping in pin curls held tight with bobby pins, framed her plump face. She wore her husband's old leather slippers "so as not to pinch my bunions," and one of her stockings had fallen down around her ankles. She represented everything my own mother was determined never to become: a dumpy housewife whose skill set included a great macaroni and cheese recipe and a low-cost way to bleach the sheets.

But if there was one thing I was learning in my time at Bear Lake, it was that social class is a poor indicator of character. Mrs. Norton's simple question of concern touched a lonely place inside me that had grown beyond my ability to contain it.

"Nothing's wrong," I said, before tears made me incoherent.

She sat me down on the bed, and held me as I wept. By the time I was finished, a pile of tissues had been added to the mess on the floor.

"Now my dear, let's go down for a cuppa, then we'll come back and clean this place up."

Down in Mrs. Norton's simple kitchen, I spilled my heart out while she sat and listened. Normally, it was hard to get a word in edgewise, but this time it was me who talked nonstop. I told her of the friends I missed, the activities, the boys, and my family. I told her about my misery at school where anything I wanted to do was against the rules, and children got hit for speaking their own language. When our cups were empty and I had run out of reasons to be miserable all she said was, "Now, let's go back upstairs and get that room in order!"

As we folded shirts and hung up dresses she took her turn to talk.

"Did you know that I was born in England?"

I had never even thought about where she was born, or anything about her life before Bear Lake.

"I started life in the grand city of London. I came here as an orphan."

She laughed at my expression. "Oh not like those children who came during this war. This was after the first war. In fact, it was the influenza that made me an orphan. Took both my parents within a week of each other, it did. I have two younger brothers who were taken in by my mother's brother and his wife, but they couldn't take all three of us. My father's sister was in Canada, so I was sent here while my brothers stayed in England. My aunt and uncle lived in Saskatoon. So I understand about landing somewhere new and finding it not to your liking.

"Believe me, I hated it when I first arrived. I didn't think I'd ever seen a more provincial place than Saskatoon. My uncle drank away any inheritance I arrived with, and my aunt didn't know what to do with this almost-teenager with a funny accent. I learned to keep my head down at school and my door closed at home. Finally, at seventeen, six years after I'd arrived, I had enough money for a bus to Toronto. I found a place to live and a job behind the counter at Eaton's: Ladies' Gloves and Hats. I felt I had arrived! Finally, I was back in touch with women who cared about the latest fashions and making a good impression on the world!"

She caught her image in my dresser mirror and stopping folding the blouse in her hands. "Look at me now." She chuckled. "You'd never know I cared a whit about fashion, now would you? I did though. When I was a little girl I had a scrapbook of debutante pictures cut from the social pages of the newspaper. My father was a physician and we lived well. So you see, I understand a bit about your change in lifestyle too.

"As wonderful as Toronto was, my dream was to go back to England. In my mind it was the perfect world. I assumed that when I returned I would step right back into the life I had expected to grow into when I was a child. I couldn't afford the trip, but I didn't see that as a problem. All I needed was the right man, and then money would be no object. We would move to England and life would be perfect again."

At this she raised her arms and face to the ceiling, a broad smile crossing her face, and I could almost see the young Mrs. Norton, full of dreams for the perfect future that the '20's promised.

"In Toronto, I spent every penny I could on clothes and make-up and being seen in the right places. I started to meet people and get invitations to private parties in the Annex and Parkdale. Every

Saturday afternoon a crowd of us would go to the Sunnyside Amusement Park, down by Lake Ontario—I believe it's still there."

"Yes," I said. "In the summers when we were young we'd take the bus down to swim in their huge pool. When I was eighteen, I was allowed to stay on for the dances at the Palais Royale."

"So you danced at the Palais too!" Mrs. Norton said. "What a wonderful coincidence. My memories of it are full of light. Big chandeliers, moonlight and starlight streaming through the windows, and my Charlie. That was where I met him, you know, at the Palais Royale. The stars couldn't have shone any brighter than my eyes the night I met my Charlie. It was love at first sight it was. Things were turning out just as I'd planned."

"Was he handsome?" I asked, imagining this romantic meeting.

"As handsome as a prince! With good prospects too. He was studying mechanical engineering at the University of Toronto and wanted to go into business for himself. He had a great mind, my Charlie. We were married in '26, and in '27, two months after he graduated, our first, Janice, was born. Life was grand. He got a good job at a manufacturing company and we started saving for a house. Well, you know what happened soon after that. The crash left us penniless and Charlie without work. To top it off, I was pregnant with James. We moved in with his parents while he searched for work."

Mrs. Norton sat down on my freshly made bed. Her shoulders slumped and the springs creaked beneath her.

"He finally found work up here. At the lumber mill." She turned to look at me. "It wasn't even anything mechanical. He was just a labourer on the planing saws. I was horrified. Not what I had planned at all. He came up first, to see what it was like. But jobs were scarce, and I was expected to follow. James was born a few months after he left. A few months after that, I joined him. It was the end of winter and the logs were coming in after break-up. There was plenty of work for him, and not much time for me. I'm surprised our marriage survived that first year here. We were not a happy pair, each of us feeling misunderstood and hard done by."

She paused, "Well, look at me would you! Telling you my whole life story when all I really wanted to say was that you can get used to anything, and that if you take some time to look, you can find friends, find things to do, maybe even a find a boyfriend, although we'll have to talk about a few rules if that happens! There are wonderful, interesting, intelligent people everywhere, even if they don't come from the same background as you. Believe me, even though I barely graduated high school, I was the biggest snob there ever was. This place taught me a few things I can tell you, good things. I hope you find it does the same for you."

"Trust me," I said, sitting down beside her on the bed. "It already has. I can't imagine coming up here in the '30s. But you stayed. Did you like it better after a while?"

"Well, thank you for your question, my sweet! I'm glad my story didn't bore you to tears, I do go on sometimes. So, let's see: did I like it better? Not for a long while. It wasn't so bad for Charlie. He worked in the mill, and eventually made his way up to foreman. When the second war came, business got better, and he finally got to use his engineering skills. He knew the plant inside out by then and had lots of ideas about ways to improve things."

She took my hands in hers and gave them a squeeze, warming to her story.

"The turning point for me though, was a chance to go back to England. That was before the war, '34 it was, a time when travel was not as easy as it is today, and certainly not a time when people did much travelling. But after our first year, he agreed that we would save up money so that I could go 'home.' I kept having babies and of course money got tighter, but we finally had enough and in 1934 I went home for a month."

Mrs. Norton stopped here, her eyes glazing over.

"Was it wonderful?" I asked, imagining the joy a family reunion would bring in the midst of the Depression.

She looked at me with a start. "It was horrible, absolutely horrible. We laughed about it afterwards, Charlie and me. That $500 probably saved our marriage. When I got back here, I was more than content to call it home, and happy to be in a place where I belonged."

"Horrible? What was so horrible about it?"

"My brothers were strangers to me. They'd both grown up in the comfortable upper class that we had all started in, and the crash brought them down hard. They didn't know how to cope. No servants, no grand parties, no nannies. They were lost. Full of complaints and excuses and reasons why it was everyone else's fault. Their wives and children were no different. The whole lot of them were whiny and unhappy. And the weather! Oh my dear Mary, the weather in England is terrible! Rain and grey, then more rain and grey. I'll take white snow and blue skies any day! I could hardly wait to get home. Oh! And you remember how my accent made me stand out in Saskatoon? Well, it appears I had lost my posh British accent too. I was miserable. I felt as if I didn't fit in anywhere. Until I got back home and realized that I fit in perfectly right here. It wasn't what I imagined my life to be. It wasn't even what I wanted. But it turned out to be just what I needed.

"So that's my story, my dear. I'm a British rose who's found roots in northern Ontario. It can happen to you too. You've no idea where you'll end up. Maybe here, maybe Timbuktu. But wherever you are, you can make a mess of it, or you can make it work. It's up to you. Hopefully, it won't take a few years and an expensive trip to make things right!"

She gave me a hug and went downstairs to start dinner. She was right. I needed to smarten up and make the best of things here. It wasn't forever, unless I wanted it to be, and I wasn't going to waste any more time moaning about what I didn't have. I would start appreciating all that I did have instead. Problem solved.

MY SECOND
PURCHASE

I knew that not all my problems could be solved with a change in attitude, but it was a good start. The second order of business was a car. With Jonathan gone, all I had was the bicycle, which was already untenable. Mrs. Norton said that there would probably be a few cars available as the summer workers left, so I put up an advertisement in the post office, and Mrs. Norton asked around.

Sure enough, the day after our chat, I came home early to find a note saying that a man named Martin Shroud had a car for sale. He was a friend of Peter Proctor, the green grocer. When I called Peter, he told me that Martin was at Birling's Bar and he would let him know I was interested.

Birling's Bar was on the "bad" side of town. But, I reasoned, how bad could the bad side be at four-thirty in the afternoon? My curiosity got the better of me, and against all the rules, I decided to go and find him myself. In those days, bars usually had two sections: one for men, and one for women with an escort, the only way a woman could get into a bar. The Birling didn't have a men-only side, so I was just breaking one rule when I marched bravely through the front door—all alone.

The bartender, after his shock at seeing an unescorted woman in his bar in the middle of the afternoon, answered my query about Martin Shroud by pointing over to a group of men playing pool. One of them was an Indian. I had never seen an Indian in a bar, or even in a restaurant, not here, or in Toronto. While there were no laws against the races mixing, for the most part people tended to stay with their own. One's "own" wasn't just defined by race. The Chinese had Chinatown, but the Ukrainians had their neighbourhood, the Italians theirs, the Greeks too. I had accepted this unwritten rule of racial and cultural segregation without question. It took seeing an Indian man in a bar to make me aware of it.

I introduced myself and met Dennis, Stephen, and Sam. Martin, the one with the car for sale, was the Indian. Martin was from Owen Sound, not too far north of Toronto, and he was headed back. He had been working as an assistant cook in the summer logging camp but had no interest in staying on for the winter.

"I'll need the car for a couple more days," he said. "A friend of mine is going to use it, but he's a responsible guy. I'm sure there won't be any problems. Let me show it to you."

We went out to have a look. It was a bright blue 1938 Ford sedan with a wide running board and big grille. We both got in so I could take it for a quick test drive. It felt strange to have an Indian sitting beside me as though it were the most natural thing in the world. It made me realize how, with the exception of my students, I'd thought of Indians as belonging to a group with no connection to mine. Maybe Mother Magdalene was right. Maybe I did need to spend more time figuring things out before trying to change them.

In my short time at the school, I had seen how anything considered "Indian" was disparaged and discouraged. At the time, I knew nothing about Indian culture myself. The problem was, I thought I did. And, like most of the people I was working with, I saw it as pagan, as Jonathan had so concisely stated, or at best, old-fashioned. My understanding of Indian culture was limited to stories of potlatches and sun dances, both of which were incomprehensible to me. I thought Indians believed in little spirits in trees and leaving their old to die all alone when food was scarce. I also felt perfectly comfortable in lumping all First Nations people across the Americas into the same basket. Mohawk, Ojibwa, Cree, Haida—they were all just Indians to me, their differences limited to longhouses or teepees. In my formal education, Indians were barely mentioned, except in the context of how they were "dealt with" so that European settlement could continue. Martin didn't fit my stereotype of an Indian. Martin was just a normal person, and it surprised, bewildered and relieved me.

I took the car over to Sid at the garage first, so that he could have a look at it. Sid said he thought it was a great car; he didn't even have to look under the hood. He'd done a few repairs on it just a month ago he said, and it was in good running order. He thought Martin should drive it back to Owen Sound, but Martin just smiled at this suggestion. I agreed to buy it.

We went back to the bar so I could make arrangements with Dennis, who was the one who needed the car first. He and the rest of his friends were eating and I was invited to join them. Feeling braver than I had when I marched in unescorted that afternoon, I accepted their invitation. I called Mrs. Norton on the bar's phone to let her know that I wouldn't be home for dinner and tried to keep my whereabouts as vague as possible. I assured her that I was with friends of Peter and she was satisfied.

They say that life keeps giving you the same lesson until you learn it. My year in Bear Lake was a lesson in seeing past the book cover. Mrs. Norton, with her empathy and her story of coming to Canada was one of my first lessons. Martin was another, and his friends proved to be a third. I guess I was a hard study. These men were the first lumberjacks I'd met and I was surprised to find they weren't coarse simpletons. Just as Martin surprised me by who he wasn't, as much as by who he was, these men were not what I expected. They spoke of books they had read, and philosophized about the war. They were curious about the school, and I didn't hear a swear word from anyone.

After dinner though, a few of their buddies arrived. More than a few actually—Mr. Dubois must have brought in a busload. In minutes the bar filled with loud, obnoxious men. The gentlemen I had eaten with became the lumberjacks I had expected, and no one seemed to notice when I left. When I got outside Martin was there, smoking a cigarette.

"I'll drive you home," he said.

"That's okay Martin, thanks. I'd like to walk anyway. Nothing's too far around here." I wanted some time to prepare for Mrs. Norton's interrogation.

"Its dark; I'll walk you."

"Honestly, Martin, I appreciate the offer, but I'll be fine."

"If you don't want me walking beside you, I'll walk behind you. But I'd like to see you safely home."

This startled me, and then embarrassed me. Not only was he normal, he was a gentleman.

So I found myself walking with an Indian on the white side of town. I wasn't sure what the busybodies behind the curtains we passed would see, but Martin seemed not to care. I tried not to as well.

"I don't like it when they get together like that," he said, gesturing back towards the bar. "It's as though they're two different people. I'm never sure which is the real one. It can be dangerous for me when they're in a crowd."

"I think we all want to do the right thing," I said. "I guess sometimes we do the right thing for the people that we're with, even if it's the wrong thing."

"You're a wise woman," Martin said, smiling.

I laughed, "I think that's the first time anyone's referred to me as a woman."

It was Martin's turn to laugh. "But wise," he said. "You've been called wise many times I should think."

His flattery and his open, easy manner charmed me. It took only a few moments for me to forget about the ladies behind their curtains, and focus my attention on the person beside me. He asked about my teaching, and I found it easy to confide in him. I told him how it felt like the students were treated like delinquents at a reform school instead of little children, taken from their families. I spoke of my frustrations at trying to change this attitude and my fear that if I pushed too hard, I too, would follow Jonathan and be told to take the train home. As I talked, it dawned on me that he had probably been in a residential school himself. I was embarrassed by my own lack of sensitivity. I couldn't think of any way to find out, except to just ask.

"Did you attend a residential school?"

"No," he said. "They had a school on the reserve I lived on, so I was able to live at home. I didn't finish high school though. I went as far as grade eleven, then I couldn't take it anymore."

I looked at him, surprised. His intelligent questions and thoughtful observations had led me to think of him as a peer, and my peers were mostly university educated. My idea of a high school dropout was nothing close to the polite and perceptive person Martin was.

We got to the house much too quickly.

"I live here, but why don't we walk a bit and talk some more?" I said.

He agreed. We walked over to the small neighbourhood playground, sat on the swings side by side and talked. It was easy and comfortable, like talking to a good friend.

Finally, a full two hours later, he walked me to the door, we shook hands and he left.

When I walked in the door, Mrs. Norton was waiting for me. I had never seen Mrs. Norton angry before, and the woman waiting for me was furious.

"What has gotten into you?" she said. "To spend the evening wandering around town with a redman? I've gotten at least three phone calls and Mrs. Virtanen actually came over to let me know! I am completely humiliated in this town!"

Mrs Norton's reaction stunned me.

One of the advantages of growing up in a monoculture is that you rarely have to face bigotry or prejudice. Everyone was white in my neighbourhood, in my classrooms, my clubs and my camps. I rarely even ran into anyone whose heritage was south of the English Channel. People's cultural differences were marked by being English or Irish. In my world, if anyone was seen as "different" in any substantial way it was usually due to income.

I knew people would notice Martin and me, and that many of them would disapprove and read more into our walk than was there. But I was not prepared for the vehemence or self-righteousness of Mrs. Norton's response.

I had no idea how to answer her accusation.

"That was Martin Shroud," I said. "He's the one who has the car for sale."

"So buy his car, shake hands and drive away," she said. "Do you have dinner and walk all night with every salesman you meet?"

"If he hadn't been an Indian, would this be a problem?" The words were out of my mouth before I could stop them.

Mrs. Norton paused a moment, then she let loose. "Don't you wave your snotty big-city flag at me. Of course it makes a difference that he's an Indian. Maybe you can wander the streets with whoever you want in Toronto. Maybe no one cares, or you can hide it from anyone who does, but things are different here, and if you want to live here you'll have to live by our rules."

That stopped me. In my world, there may have been prejudices and biases, but people in polite society hid them from each other and found other reasons to explain any unpleasant behaviour.

"Well, he's leaving, so I won't be spending any more time with him." It was a facile way to escape, but it deflated her anger somewhat.

"Mary, you have to understand. Everyone here knows everything that happens, and after you leave, I will stay. We live by unspoken rules that I've chosen to accept. You may not like them, and I know that the world is changing, but, well, that's just the way it is."

She looked at me, her eyes soft, willing me to understand.

I apologized for putting her in a difficult position, which mollified her enough that we were able to sit at the kitchen table and talk. When we retreated to our bedrooms, we were both feeling a little better. But neither one of us was willing to admit any wrongdoing, and it took a few days before we were almost back to our original conviviality. But things were never quite the same after that.

October 14, 1947

Thanksgiving is over. B. Richard got us some geese, a real Thanksgiving treat! We even had butter for the mashed potatoes. The pièce de resistance, though, was dessert—apple pie—enough for everyone! Sister Maria deserves an award. I hope that the kitchen students got a little something extra to tuck under their pillows; they all worked very hard.

Of course the rest of us have been working hard too. With winter almost here the last of the work to prepare the soil for next year is almost done, and the last of the vegetables are in. We used Godfrey and Justin a lot this year. Clydesdales can pull a big load, and they don't need even ground. I'm glad they were kept on. They like to be working too. Everyone needs to be needed, even animals.

It's nice to see things winding down, I must admit. I've had no time for a social life, and I miss my talks with the boys over horseshoes or games of Crazy Eights.

BARN DANCE

My social life in Bear Lake, to put it nicely, was quiet. I was an outsider wherever I went, in school and especially in town. Mrs. Norton had done her best to introduce me to people, especially to people my age. But most women my age were already married with children. Some of Mrs. Norton's friends tried to interest me in their sons, but for the most part, I was a novelty, and the people I met were more curious about me than interested in me.

One notable exception was Mrs. Norton's third daughter, Nancy. She was twenty-three, just a few years older than me, and already the mother of two girls, two and four years old. Her husband worked at the mill and she stayed home with the children, helping her mother out during busy seasons in the post office. Despite our different circumstances and upbringings, Nancy, with her easy laugh and enthusiasm for any adventure, was the person I dropped in on whenever I needed a friend. She never failed to offer me a cup of tea, a child to hold and an ear.

Society on the white side of Bear Lake was divided into two distinct groups: permanent residents and temporary ones. I didn't fit into either, but was nominally a member of the former. These were the people who had lived in Bear Lake for ages, or were committed to living there for the foreseeable future.

The transient group was primarily made up of the lumberjacks. A few of them had lived in Bear Lake for as long as any of the townspeople, but they were often eccentric and more likely to live in the poor section of town. Most of the lumberjacks though, came for a year or two, some just for a season. If they worked at the mill, they usually stayed at the bunkhouse or the hotel. The rest of the men lived in the bush camps and came into town to go wild for a night or two, sleep it off, and then go back to the bush. The only respectable townspeople who had anything to do with the lumberjacks were those who took their money in the bars and hotels.

This rule was broken three times a year: Harvest Festival, which happened near the end of October, Winter Festival, a mid-February extravaganza of bonspiels and dog sled races, and Dominion Day in July. Each celebration involved the whole town, at least the white side, including the men in the lumber trade. The churches held rummage and bake sales, there were wrestling matches in the high school gym, and hayrides ran from Cuvier's Feed Store to the Foster's farm. At every public venue, from churches to baseball diamonds something was going on.

My first introduction to these celebrations was the Harvest Festival. I went on the hayride, and then competed in a dart game set up against the side of the Foster's barn. I bought a beautiful home-made sweater at a rummage sale, and enjoyed hot dogs cooked over an outside grill while watching the men play football. It was dark by late afternoon, and by five the outside activities had shut down and everyone was gathered at the elementary school for the talent show. This was followed by a potluck dinner and the grande finale, a barn dance at the Foster's farm.

The barn dance was the highlight of the season and I wanted to do it right. Nancy started preparing me in September.

"A band and caller are coming all the way from Winnipeg!" she told me. "I've found a pattern for a dress. Can you go with me to buy material? You know what everyone is wearing these days! It's only a month away, so I don't have much time. Tom's even promised to wear a tie! I don't think he's had one on since the day we got married. I'm so excited! The last time we had a dance here Tom was in the band and I never got even one round with him." On and on she went.

I listened with fascination. At home, we had dances every weekend. There were dance halls all over the city and bands were a dime a dozen. I tried to enthuse along with her, but I felt a bit like an anthropologist, about to participate in a cultural experience unknown to modern man.

As the date for the barn dance got closer, my awkward status in the community made me increasingly apprehensive. I wanted to belong, but I was scared I'd wind up feeling like the new kid in the cafeteria, tray in hand, wondering where to sit. Thank goodness for Nancy. She helped me with everything from my dress, (the one I thought was perfect would have looked like a ball gown at a birthday party), to square dance lessons. She also took me around to meet all her friends. By the time the big day arrived, I had met with just about every female between the ages of eighteen and twenty-five.

The dance started at seven, and when we got there, a few minutes after seven, it was already bustling. A true community affair, there were people of all ages. Nancy and Tom had brought their young children and Mrs. Norton, her bright flowered dress topped by her Sunday hat with its lacy black veil, was there with her bridge group. The ministers of all three churches, easy to identify in their starched white collars, were deep in conversation by the punch bowl.

When I first arrived at Bear Lake, despite Mrs. Norton's best intentions, I had had no choice but to accept many invitations to tea with the ladies of town. At many of these teas, the subject of conversation would turn to the mention of a handsome son. Sometimes an awkward young man was forced to join us. I'm sure they were all as delighted as I was when their mothers finally tired of me. I wasn't too optimistic about the offerings at the dance, but it was exciting to think that there was a possibility.

One of the men at our table during the potluck dinner had appealed to me. His name was Frank and he was a lumberman, which was one strike against him. But, like the men I met at the bar when I bought the car, he and his friends impressed me with their good manners and intelligent conversation. They were the hit of the talent show, much to the disappointment of ten-year-old Sandra Mayfair, who had been practicing her violin for weeks. Frank and his friends won top prize with a short musical skit parodying their life in the bush. At dinner, they were loud and boisterous, but in a funny, inclusive way. I loved their sense of adventure and brash confidence.

Upon arriving at the dance I scanned the barn and saw a few of the lumbermen lounging around the drinks table. We had passed a crowd of them outside, laughing and sharing a brown paper bag. Frank was nowhere in sight. I hoped he wasn't in another tightly knit group sharing some other paper-wrapped bottle.

Inside the barn, both the lumbermen and the local boys looked as uncomfortable as I felt. Dressed in their Sunday best, they were like fish out of water, their rough hands and weather-stressed faces in stark contrast to their freshly pressed shirts and neatly knotted ties.

Each lady was given a dance card when she arrived. Nancy stuffed hers into Tom's pocket but I was acutely aware of all the blank spaces in mine. Would anyone write his name?

When the music finally started there was a surge of excitement as everyone took to the floor en masse. Reluctant farmers were dragged by wives, and the lumbermen rushed for the women they had been eyeing. I stood on the sidelines, my dance card empty, and considered running back home.

At the start of the second song, Frank walked in and I got my first invitation to the floor. When he had to pass me on, he made a point of writing his name a few more times on my dance card; by the fourth tune, every dance was taken. From anxious newcomer to Cinderella, the barn dance lifted spirits that were sorely in need of lifting. My plain frock swung provocatively and my feet never seemed to miss a step. With each successive dance, I became more energized and my missteps during the square dances were nothing more than a silly girl's mistakes, easily forgiven. It was wonderful.

Before the last notes rang out, I had given Mrs. Norton's phone number to three different men: Frank, another logger named Paul and a pilot who just happened to be in town. I floated home on a cloud. Bear Lake wasn't going to be so bad after all.

Frank was the first to call, and it wasn't by phone.

The next day was Sunday, and as usual, I went to church. When I came out, he was waiting on the curb, leaning against a fancy yellow Chevy. He said he wanted to take me out for lunch, but since he knew that the restaurant didn't open on Sunday until dinner, he had some food in his hotel room.

"Oh no!" I said. "I'm not headed to your hotel room."

He laughed. "I thought you might say that. So," he gave the car an affectionate pat, "I borrowed a friend's car. Are you willing to come in a car with me?"

I was torn. I wanted to spend time with Frank, but I knew Mrs. Norton would not approve, and I wasn't anxious to upset her again.

I told him it might be better if we waited awhile and he told me that he was going back to the bush camp that night. I weakened, he saw it, and pushed his advantage.

"I'm a good guy, really. I know we loggers have a reputation, but I can assure you there are plenty of gentlemen among us. We can sit on the park bench if you want to make sure I don't try anything unseemly."

His charm, and the lingering glow of the previous night, gave me courage. "All right," I said, "but I want to get out of my church clothes. Let me go home first, then I'll meet you back here."

"I can pick you up," he said. "In fact," he grinned, "I can even drive you home."

"No, that would be a terrible idea. I'm sure my landlady wouldn't approve."

"That lovely lady who was sitting with you at dinner?" I nodded. I'd never heard Mrs. Norton referred to as "that lovely lady."

"I'm sure I can win her over. It's probably best that I meet her first and disarm her with my charisma, so that she knows you're not in any mortal or moral danger."

I wasn't sure how effective his charisma would be with Mrs. Norton, but I agreed it would be better if she met him before hearing about the two of us from somebody else. So Frank drove me home, then sat and chatted with Mrs. Norton at her kitchen table while I went upstairs to change. When I opened my door to go back downstairs I could hear her laughter—not an unusual sound, but one

I hadn't heard much lately. He had done his job well. As we walked out the door, she saw us off with a cheery wave and an admonition to get home before the rain.

We drove to the landing at nearby Mitchell Lake and walked along the shore until we came to a small beach tucked between two rocky outcroppings. With a grand flourish, he spread out a blanket and set down some cheese and bread.

"I hope you're not too hungry," he laughed. "This was all I could find on short notice."

We ate a few pieces of bread and cheese, then, with another dramatic flourish, he produced a white ceramic mug, took off his shoes and socks and waded into the freezing lake to get us some water. Very romantic!

And it was romantic. We talked and shared a few kisses on our tiny beach, wrapped in the blanket and huddled together against a cold wind that brought the rain Mrs. Norton had predicted. With the first big drops we ran back to the car, laughing. For one afternoon, I forgot all about school.

We parted chastely on Mrs. Norton's front porch. He said he would come calling when he got out next, in two weeks time. In the meantime, we could write to one another. Overseers and supervisors from the camp came into town during the week and they could leave letters for me at the post office and pick up my letters to bring back. No stamps necessary! As Mrs. Norton was the postmistress I was wary of this arrangement, but he promised to write soon—and politely enough for a snoopy postmistress!

SILAS

One morning, near the end of October, I opened my eyes to find my world completely changed. A blanket of snow had covered trees and cars, sidewalks and front lawns. I could hardly wait to get outside.

The storm had started its silent work while I slept, and by the time I left for school at least three inches had fallen. I drove my familiar route through a fairyland of snowflakes. Stark, bare trees had blossomed overnight with frosty winter blooms. The tall cattails in the marsh were dusted with a flimsy coating but the trees, many still holding on to their autumn leaves, were bent low over the road, stoically accepting piles of snow. Inside the car I ducked instinctively as I passed under them. At school, the children could hardly be contained until recess liberated them. The excitement that burst through those doors, was wonderful to see. Even the most retiring child revelled in snow forts and sliding games. It gave us all a badly needed surge of joy.

By day two, the wonderfulness was wearing off. Instead, I was beginning to wonder if the snow would ever stop.

The road to school was ploughed, but the big hill was slippery, and my tires were not made for snow. It appeared that my coat and boots were not made for snow either. At least not a Northern snow. My beautiful high-heeled leather boots, the ones that had cost me a week's wages and made my calves look so shapely, were as slippery as my tires—and as warm as a pair of galoshes. My long camel hair coat, the one I could wear with pride to the opera, kept the worst of the cold out, unless the wind blew, and then it flapped like a flag and I froze.

The discouraging part was that, when I looked around Bear Lake, the winter outerwear of choice was a big heavy parka with an equally large, attached hood, balanced below by big, heavy boots, the liners popping out the boot top. To complete the ensemble, a woollen hat and scarf, and thick leather mitts were worn. It looked as appealing as the coveralls which had greeted me at the train station. But until I could find the time to get to the store to see if there was some sort of in-between, I went back and forth to school in my impractical, but gorgeous, winter wear.

Then, disaster struck.

Despite my best efforts, the long hill got the better of me and I slid off the road into a big pile of snow left by the snowplough. I managed to get out of the car, sinking almost to the tops of my fancy boots. There was no need to think about my options. I could sit there and freeze, or walk the rest of the way. Gathering my school supplies, I faced the hill.

It looked as formidable on foot as it did in the car, and I despaired of getting to school at all, let alone on time. When my coat flapped open and the wind blew in, I hoped I wouldn't be found frozen to death on the side of the road later in the day. If I survived, I wasn't going to wait for the weekend to buy proper winter wear, or chains for the car's tires.

Clutching my books to my chest, I was almost half way up the hill, trying to keep my footing on the slippery road, when I heard the reassuring crunch of tire chains coming up behind me. Through the haze of falling snow, I watched as a dark shape slowly materialized into a beat-up truck that looked like it had once been a cheerful red. It came to a stop beside my disabled vehicle.

A large man in a wool jacket, wool trousers, a fur cap and a pair of those ugly boots emerged from the cab, gave my car a once over and then strode confidently up the hill to where I was standing.

"Bit of trouble I see," he said.

I was getting used to the habit some people had of getting right to the point, without bothering with superfluous niceties like, "Hello. How are you?" And as there didn't seem to be much to say to this comment, I kept silent as I watched him look from me back to the car.

"Won't be able to get you out without a bit more help," he said. "I'll give you a ride."

With that, he headed back to his truck.

Walking downhill was as bad as walking up. I finally discovered that putting my feet sideways to the hill resulted in an awkward but more sure-footed way to get to the truck. When I reached it, he was waiting inside and the passenger door was open. Once I was seated, he leaned over and grabbed a piece of rope that hung from my door handle and pulled the door closed. He wrapped the rope around one of the hooks on the empty gun rack hanging in the rear window, and put the truck into gear. As we began to crunch up the hill, I turned to get a better look at my rescuer. In a small town, where everyone knows everyone else, I was not familiar with his truck, but with a start, I realized I was familiar with him.

It was the "Chief." The last time I had seen him was in August, when he stood outside the school gates in the small tent encampment that had been there before school started.

Sitting beside him in the rusty red pick-up was disconcerting. In my mind he belonged to another era, one of dog sleds and canoes. It was an anachronism to see him steering the big truck, handling the gears and foot pedals with ease.

The truck had obviously seen better days and the cold air coming through cracks in the body did nothing to diminish the odour that hung like a fog in the truck's cab. Impregnated into the worn vinyl of the seats and torn plastic of the dashboard was the strong smell of cigarettes, wood smoke and sweat. It filled the small space in a surprisingly agreeable way and humanized the wooden image I had of my rescuer. At the same time, something about his character reached out like a physical force. Sitting in such close proximity, it wasn't just his smell that filled the draughty cab. The Chief had a presence.

Maybe because of that he didn't feel the need to talk, but I felt the silence like a straightjacket, cinching tighter with every crunch of the wheel.

"Thank you," I said. "I wasn't sure I would make it to school."

He glanced over at me. "Mighta been tough."

"Do you live in town?" I asked.

"Yup."

"Do you work with the lumber company?"

"Nope."

Despite the fact that I was beginning to feel like an interrogator, I kept going.

"What's your name?"

"Silas."

"Hello, Silas. I'm Mary Brock. Where are you headed today?"

I could see a small smirk form on his lips. This road only went to one place.

"Oh, of course." Feeling foolish, I offered this up before he had a chance to answer.

"Do you have children there?"

Silas sighed. "I'm going to see my nephew. I hear he's been sick."

"What's his name?"

He looked at me, his eyes narrowing with annoyance.

"It's just that I might know him. Maybe I even teach him!" I said brightly. His mood was unsettling.

"You do."

I thought desperately of the rows in my classroom. Who had been absent lately?

"Mark Hurrit," I said, relieved to have remembered. "He wasn't in class yesterday, but the nurse says he's getting better."

He nodded, staring through the swirling snow at the road ahead. For some reason, his reticence was making me feel I needed to take some responsibility for Mark's poor health.

Our conversation patently closed. I took surreptitious stock of my rescuer.

Close up, he was older than I'd thought. His face was leathery, marked with deep creases and a webbing of fine lines. His hair was long, hanging in a thin braid down his back. He was going grey and a streak of white played hide and seek throughout his braid, showing up in startling contrast to the black. His hands were hidden inside those ubiquitous leather mitts, the kind with an extra finger and a wool patch on the back to wipe your dripping winter nose.

His hat sat on the seat between us, a sleek, dark fur, mink maybe, or beaver. My mother would have loved a coat of whatever it was. But this, too, was built for business, not beauty, with large earflaps and a visor.

I tried to get up the courage to ask more questions, without success. Instead, I sat quietly in my thin city boots and leather driving gloves, which were no match for the cold blowing through the cracks and crevices that were everywhere in the old truck. Eventually, I had to stamp my feet as the cold crept from my toes and fingers towards my core. He glanced over at me and then turned a knob on the dash sending a blast of welcome heat into my face.

I was so surprised that I laughed.

My laugh made him smile, which turned into laughter, which changed everything.

I don't know why, but I knew I had found a friend.

When we got to the big double doors of the main building, I thanked him for the lift, and said I was sure Mark would be happy to see him.

He looked at me, and in the direct way I was already coming to know, said, "You watch out for my Mark. He's a special boy."

I wasn't sure if this was a request or an order, but I assured him that I would, and made a mental note that, friend or not, I must never underestimate Silas.

October 21, 1947
Mary stopped by again today. I'm pleased that perhaps she has changed her mind, and doesn't think me the dour old man she met in the milking shed. I never thought she'd outlast Jonathan. She's got her ways, but she's willing to follow the rules too.

She stayed late today so Brother Samuel could drive her back into town. She drove her car into a ditch on her way to school this morning. This unseasonal snowstorm is wreaking havoc on our unprepared resources, including Mary's. She doesn't have chains on her car yet, and she couldn't keep any traction on the big hill. She was lucky that Silas Hart came by with his truck and gave her a ride. Surprisingly, she likes him. She must have a soft spot for surly old men. I haven't spent much time with Silas, but I've heard enough about him to know that he can be a force to be reckoned with. I hope he has a soft spot for her too. I don't trust him myself, he's an angry man who keeps it contained. One day, it's inevitable, he'll blow.

And Mary has a boyfriend! I thought she'd meet somebody and she hasn't wasted any time. A lumberman, she says, and once again, I find myself questioning her judgement in companions. I can see how he'd attract a city girl like her. He's probably the big bear type, rough on the outside, warm and cuddly inside. It's charming to see good manners in a plaid shirt, but it's usually the plaid shirt that wins out. I'm feeling a little paternal I suppose. I'd love to be able to give him the once over, shotgun in hand. I'll just have to encourage her stories!

We managed one last cut of hay from that warm September growth. There's still some buried under this mountain of snow, so I hope we get some bright sun to burn it all off fast. I don't hold much hope though. We can use it for bedding at least.

Brother Samuel dropped me off at Sid's Garage where there would be someone with a winch who could pull my car out of the ditch. Although the storm appeared to have passed, one more dump of snow and my car would be buried. And so, still in my city coat and boots, I walked into the chilly front room of Sid's Garage.

There was no one about, so I went through the swinging door marked "Employees Only" to see if anyone was in the garage itself. I saw a large pick-up and a car, but no mechanic. Disappointed, I was about to leave when I heard the sound of metal wheels rolling on the concrete floor. I went around the pick-up and saw feet, then legs, and finally Silas, rolling out from under the car.

I was surprised to see him, but he didn't look in the least surprised to see me.

"Come to get your car out I see," he said.

"Yes, I am. I didn't know you worked here."

"Well, now you do. You ready to get out there?"

"Sure, but am I supposed to do anything?"

"Just keep me company," he said. "Let's go."

He grabbed his big woollen coat off a hook on the wall and headed out the back door.

We passed by his once-red truck and got into a tow truck with "Sid's Garage" painted on the side.

A slight grin softened his features as he turned the key and then pulled the knob that sent hot air into the cab. On this drive, I rode with a different person. He wasn't one to chat, but he filled me in on Mark, who was doing well, and would be back in class tomorrow. And although I didn't learn a lot about his life in Bear Lake he gave me more than one-word answers. By the time we got back to the garage, my car trailing behind us, I knew that Silas lived in Indiantown, had worked with Sid for five years, and had grown up near Sault Ste. Marie. It was enough for starters.

Before I left the garage he took a look at the car and told me that I would probably be without it for at least a week: I had done some damage in my slide off the road, and they had to order parts from Winnipeg. He told me he'd keep me posted. I was without a car once again.

HOUSE HUNTING

If getting to school without a car was not easy in the early fall, it was going to be doubly hard now. The snow was already starting to melt, but the road was a sloppy mess, and would be for a while. Bicycling was out of the question. There was always Mr. Dubois's taxi, but money was precious and it would be an expensive trip. Mrs. Norton didn't own a car, although she had a friend she was sure would be happy to drive me. But I decided to try a fourth option—I was going to walk.

Mrs. Norton had a pair of sensible boots that would fit me until I got my own. I thought the walk would take about an hour and it might actually prove to be a nice way to start the day. I would soon know.

I got up early to find that Mrs. Norton had gotten up early too.

"No toast and tea for you this morning, my sweet," she said. "I wish you'd let me talk to Mr. Chandler. I'm sure he'd be happy to drive you."

"I'll try this first. It may not work, but for a week it might be good exercise. Besides, it's already started to melt. If I'm lucky it may melt enough for my bicycle. And the road's ploughed, so walking shouldn't be too hard."

Mrs. Norton sighed and passed me a plate of greasy fried eggs and toast.

Halfway to school, the sun still below the horizon and long before I'd reached the big hill, I was already reconsidering my decision. As I plodded along the road, my nose dripping, I envied Silas his big mitts with the soft woollen pad for just such a situation. Despite the "warm" weather prediction it was cold enough at this hour that I couldn't feel my fingertips; and my legs, with the unaccustomed weight of Mrs. Norton's boots, were feeling the strain. This was not going to work. I would call Mr. Chandler as soon as I got home.

Then, for the second time in two days, I heard the welcome sound of chains and turned to see headlights round a corner. A now-familiar truck pulled to a stop beside me.

"Hop in, Mary," Silas said. "I'm going up to do some work on that old pick-up of theirs. It costs them more to fix it than it's worth, but they don't seem to care."

By the time we got to school he had volunteered to come and get me at the end of the day. And by the end of that ride, he had volunteered to chauffeur me back and forth until the car was fixed, "I've heard they do this in the cities sometimes," he said. "Think of it as good customer service."

"It's more than good," I said. "It's exemplary! I'll pay you back somehow."

He drove to the garage and I walked home from there. I explained to Mrs. Norton that someone from the garage was going to take me back and forth to school. I didn't say who, and she didn't ask.

Until a few days later.

I returned home from work and Mrs. Norton met me at the door.

"Did you get into Silas Hart's truck today?"

"Yes. Is that a problem?"

"You are not to ride in a truck with him."

"Why? Is he dangerous?"

"Mary, we've been through this before."

"But this is different. He's a mechanic; he's fixing my car. It's part of the service."

"It's not part of the service that anyone else gets. Besides, whatever your sympathies may be, in this town we know about Indians. They're unpredictable. Nice and friendly one day, drunk and belligerent the next. You never know what he might do."

"So far, I've seen nothing but nice and friendly."

"So far! You mean you've done this before?"

"Yes," I said. And I'll probably do it again, I thought

"Mary, we went over this when you bought the car. This is not the city where you can do whatever you want and keep it secret. Here, everyone knows everyone else's business. It can be a blessing and it can be a curse, but there's no getting around it. The Indians and the rest of us live separately, and we're both happier that way. He's as likely to get into trouble from someone in Indiantown for driving you around as you are to get into trouble here."

"What kind of trouble would I get into?"

Mrs. Norton eyed me, as though wondering if I were old enough to hear the truth. "I hate to say it, it sounds like some old religious punishment, but people will shun you. It's real, and every small town uses it. It works. No one likes to be alone."

But I wouldn't be alone, I thought. I'd have Silas. Or would I?

Mrs. Norton and I stared at each other.

"Mary, if you can't keep away from Silas Hart, you won't be able to stay in this house."

I stared hard at Mrs. Norton to see if she meant it. There was nothing in her look to suggest that she didn't. The stakes were getting high. I couldn't believe it had come to this.

"I'll need some time to think about it."

Mrs. Norton's face relaxed a little and she reached out for my arm. "Mary dear, I know you like him, and I'm sure he's a very nice man. But there are unwritten rules in this town, and I have to live here. I'm sorry it has to be this way. If I could make things different I would."

"Maybe you can," I said. "Would you like to meet Silas yourself, and then decide if he's appropriate company for me? It will only be for a few more days. My parts will be here soon and then I won't need him."

Mrs. Norton dropped my arm and stood a little taller. "Mary, you haven't been listening if you think I'll change my mind. I can't make your decision for you, but I will expect you to have made one yourself by tomorrow. Let me know."

I walked heavily up the stairs to my pink bedroom. I had hated the room when I first arrived, but already it wore the memories of my time here. The crack in the ceiling above my bed that, when the light hit it the right way, looked like a sketch of my dog, Sparky, who waited for me in Toronto. The frilly curtains that made the shadows on the wall dance when the sun and wind played together. The soft pink carpet, always warm and gentle in the cold of early morning. Where else could I live?

The next day was Friday and I was allowed to ride to school with Silas, but I was also expected to tell him my decision. I couldn't. All I said was that I had a ride home, so he didn't need to pick me up. If Silas was aware of my forced brightness, he said nothing about it.

I needed someone to talk to who knew the community. I decided to try Brother Thomas. My relationship with him had improved, but having seen as much of the brusque and unfriendly man as the warm one, I was still wary of him. However, he was plain speaking and I needed some plain advice. At lunchtime, I made my way over to the barn where I found him at his desk, bent over his leather-bound journal. At my tentative knock he looked up and I watched a trace of annoyance cross his features. But he put his pen down and invited me in.

"Hello, Mary. What can I do for you?"

"I have a personal problem that I need some advice on. I hope you don't mind."

"Mary, I'm a middle-aged man who's never been married; I don't know what help I could be to you."

"Oh, it's not that kind of a problem," I said.

"If it's about the school, then I'm not the best person to come to either. I'm not at liberty to discuss or to debate school policies or politics, nor would I want to."

"No, it's nothing to do with the school either."

"Well then," he leaned back in his chair, "you have my attention and my curiosity."

I explained the situation with Silas. Brother Thomas listened carefully. I found that just saying it out loud to someone gave me some relief.

"You have a difficult dilemma, Mary. The question I always ask myself in these sorts of situations is this: What will I have to live with afterwards? Finding another place to live will not be easy. Leaving your friendship with Silas will not be easy either. It's up to you to decide which will be harder for you to live with afterwards. When we're comfortable, it's easy to take the high road, to say that Silas is your friend and you won't betray him. But what Mrs. Norton says is true. If you do take that decision, then not only will you be searching for a place to live in a town with few options, but you will be searching in a town that will not appreciate your decision to continue your liaison with Silas."

"Liaison! It's not a liaison! There's nothing romantic about our relationship."

"People may or may not believe that. Nevertheless, they won't like it. Especially in a teacher who's working with the Indians. They don't like to see sympathy for them. And Silas is well known in town and here at school. He has a reputation for keeping the old ways; people don't like that. Some even think he has powers as a medicine man and children are warned to keep away from him."

This seemed ridiculous, but it made me wonder if perhaps that was part of the problem with Mrs. Norton. Maybe that was what she meant by "unpredictable." Maybe she thought he was using his medicine-man powers to seduce me into thinking he was just an ordinary guy, and then he'd pounce when the moment was ripe.

October 23, 1947

I have to interrupt this interesting tome on cows to write about a visitor who just dropped in. Mary Brock, that innocent young thing from Toronto popped her head in my door today at lunchtime. I can usually count on this time of day for a little peace and quiet, but she had a serious dilemma to discuss. Mary Brock has come face to face with small-town politics and prejudice. I get the impression that her life so far has been fairly straightforward, with few opportunities to challenge her own moral compass. She has a problem with her landlady, the postmistress Mrs. Norton. Mrs.

Norton wants her to stop seeing Silas Hart. What Mary sees in Silas I'll never know, but they have formed an unlikely friendship. Mrs. Norton wants it stopped, and Mary thinks this unreasonable viewpoint should not be honoured by acquiescing. I remember when I saw things clearly too. It's refreshing, on the one hand, to see someone who is ready to fight against the tyranny of the small mind; depressing on the other to know what little impact she'll have. Although, I have to admit it's usually the young people who change things. It's that clear-headed determination that one is right, combined with the naive belief we teach our children that right always wins. I had nothing much to offer her beyond what I hope was a dash of realistic expectations. Personally, I would be happier if she no longer spent time with Silas. She is woefully unprepared for life here. But I like the girl, she's not a whiner.

I wanted to take the high road. I wanted to shove Mrs. Norton's platitudes back in her face and move forward with a clean conscience and a strong will. I wanted to. But I didn't know if I could. The only other place I knew of to live was Jonathan's old room, and I had no desire to live with odd Mr. Dubois. And who knew if he'd even take me?

Brother Samuel was making a run into town, so he drove me home after school. By the time I got home, Mrs. Norton had already left for Friday night potluck and bingo at the church. I was grateful for the respite and made myself a sandwich before heading back out the door. There was one more person I had to talk to.

In all my exploring, I had never ventured into Indiantown. It wasn't until I reached the railroad line that I stopped to wonder about the hold this invisible social wall had on me. I thought I was above Mrs. Norton's racism, but it was part of me too. Before crossing the tracks I took an almost instinctive look over my shoulder. Did I really care if anyone was watching me from their window? I suppose I did, because my heart beat a little faster as I stepped over the steel lines that formed Bear Lake's unofficial boundary between the white and Indian sides of town.

To a casual observer, the homes on either side of the tracks would be indistinguishable. The houses on the white side, belonged to the poorest people of Bear Lake. Most were squat wooden structures, many with broken or boarded-up windows. Bare yards were muddy from the melting snow, and littered with the detritus of everyday life: broken toys, fishing rods, empty beer bottles, lost mittens. Some homes had their winter supply of firewood neatly stacked, while others had left it in a heap, wherever it had been dumped. It was dinner time, and smoke drifted skyward from a few chimneys. But many houses looked vacant, their inhabitants elsewhere, working in the bush, on a trapline or still sleeping off the previous night's indulgences.

On the Indian side, the houses were also squat wooden structures, some with a porch or an extension added on. Smoke came from almost every chimney, but the homes were not unlike the houses on the white side. The front yards were littered with rusting animal traps, tangled fishing nets, sleds and wood piles. Outside many homes I saw animal skins stretched out in hooped frames, and drying fish hung like still life paintings underneath roof overhangs. And everywhere, there were dogs. Dogs in backyards, dogs in front yards, dogs chained to little doghouses and dogs just hanging around. There was nowhere that I could go without a cacophony of noise announcing my arrival.

The streets had wooden sidewalks in some places and trails through the weeds in others. I had no idea where Silas lived, but I assumed that I would meet someone who knew him and ask the way. Despite this, I hesitated to ask the first people I passed. Mrs. Norton's warning about the trouble he might face made me nervous. I decided to look for his truck before I talked to anyone. Sure enough, after I had gone down a few streets, I saw it parked in front of a white house. Silas's wood was stacked and his chimney was blowing smoke. He was home.

Still, before I turned to go down his walkway, I stopped. Did he live with anyone? Surely neighbours would see me go in, which would make my attempts to avoid people on the street a wasted effort. I wondered if I should just go back to Mrs. Norton. I wasn't going to be staying in Bear Lake forever anyway. Would I rather have Silas as my only friend or enjoy the company of Nancy and all her friends? What would Frank make of this? It was a terrible choice.

I was about to walk away when I heard his familiar voice. "Mary! What brings you here? Come on in."

Silas was standing at the top of the steps to his house, an unreadable expression on his face. He held the door open with one hand, the other held a wooden spoon. I crossed in front of him to go inside and was assaulted by a smell. A primal odour permeated the small house, like his truck writ large. It was muted somewhat by a stew bubbling away on the wood stove. I hesitated a moment, causing Silas to bump into me from behind.

"Keep going Mary; you're letting all the heat out!"

I kept going, at least enough to allow Silas to shut the door. In contrast to his cold truck, the room was hot enough for shorts.

"Come in, Mary, come in. Take your boots off. Have a seat."

He gestured to his left where hooks lined the wall and a pair of boots sat below a single woollen coat. I took off my boots and coat and sank into one of the two overstuffed chairs that were pulled close to the wood stove.

Silas sat in the other chair and looked at me expectantly.

I started to cry.

Silas's response was to get up and lift a heavy black kettle off the stove. Soon he was handing me a thick, cracked mug filled to the brim with sweet, milky tea. He sat back down with his own mug and waited.

"It seems," I began, "that you and I are not supposed to be friends."

"Ahh," he said.

"Mrs. Norton told me that if I continue to ride with you then I am no longer welcome in her house. She told me that the whole town would shun me if I keep it up."

Silas nodded.

"Is she right?"

"I don't know. Maybe she is."

"She also said that you might be in trouble with your friends for giving me rides."

Silas smiled. "Did she now?"

"Will you?"

"Let me worry about my friends and you worry about yours."

"I don't know what to do."

The simple truth shamed me. But Silas's expression of concern stayed the same at my admission.

"You'll have to do what you have to do. Friendships around here don't usually cross the tracks. And since we're a man and a woman, people will talk."

"You don't think of it as romantic do you?" I couldn't believe I had asked that, but I needed an answer.

This time Silas laughed. "I'm as good as married, Mary, and I don't need any problems."

This surprised me. I didn't know him well, but in my mind he was only slightly more socialized than the hermits who lived in the trappers' shacks. He had never mentioned a woman, and I didn't see him as someone who would want any kind of an obligation.

"Are you engaged?"

"No, and she lives in Winnipeg so we don't see too much of one another."

"Why don't you live in Winnipeg with her?"

"So many questions, Mary."

It was true; once again I was the interrogator.

"I'm sorry. I'm just surprised. Wouldn't Winnipeg be a nicer place to live?"

"My children are here."

Children? First he had a girlfriend, and now he has children?

"Yes, Mary," Silas smiled again. "I have six children."

Six children? I was incredulous. Six children!

I looked around, as though expecting them to suddenly appear from under the table or behind one of the doors that led off from this main room.

"But where are they?"

"The first four are grown and on their own; the last two are still at school."

"But school was out hours ago," I stopped. "They're at... at my school."

Silas nodded.

I stared down at my feet on the rough wooden floor and noticed absently that one of my socks needed mending. For the first time,

I wondered what it was like to send your children away to school when you'd rather they be at home.

"It's all right, Mary. I'm here; they know it, I can keep an eye on things, and they get home more than most of the other children."

"Did you go to Bear Lake?" I asked.

"No, I went to another school, near Winnipeg."

"Are you a medicine man?"

I don't know what it was about Silas that allowed me to ask these outrageous questions, but he took them in stride.

"Whoever told you that? Oh, never mind, let me guess—Mrs. Norton, the source of endless information."

Silas looked grim and I couldn't tell him it was Brother Thomas, not Mrs. Norton, who had let that one out.

"'Medicine man' is a strange word Mary, even coming from you. In my culture, you don't ask questions like that."

He still hadn't answered the question, but I wasn't going to ask it again.

"In your culture?" I asked instead. "What do you mean, in your culture?"

Silas looked at me and laughed. I laughed too, although I wasn't sure why, I was just glad that the atmosphere had gotten lighter.

"It's time for you to go home, Mary. You have a decision to make and whatever you decide, I'll understand. I know how hard it is to be an outsider. It's not something I'd wish on anybody."

The next morning, at her cozy kitchen table, Mrs. Norton handed me my plate: crisp bacon, two eggs sunny side up, and a piece of buttered toast. She was going all out. Maybe, I thought, Mrs. Norton would miss me if I left.

She retrieved her equally full plate from the counter and sat at her usual place at the table. We said grace together and ate in silence. When our plates were empty, she got straight to the point. "Well Mary, have you made a decision?"

"No, Mrs. Norton," I said. "I haven't. I'm sure you understand that this is a major moral decision for me. Should I give up a friend for the sake of a place to stay, or give up a wonderful place to stay for the sake of a new acquaintance? I need more time to think about it and I won't need a ride before Monday."

"I assure you, Mary, I'm asking this of you for your own good. I've never seen you with him myself. I learned it all from common gossip. You can be sure that what I heard was just the tip of the iceberg. There'll be a lot of trouble for you if people believe that you're getting cozy with the Indians. It suits both races for us to live separately. It's hard for people who don't live here to understand, but it helps everything to run more smoothly."

"I don't understand how it makes anything run more smoothly. What is there to run that can't happen with people being friends with each other?"

"Well, for starters, it prevents romantic relationships and keeps people with their own kind."

"So you mean I can't be friends with a man because no one will believe it's not romantic? If he were white would people be as concerned about a romantic situation? Anyway, he's married for heaven's sake!"

"Don't make me out to be the evil witch here, Mary. This is not my doing. This is what society has always done. People stay with their own kind. Perhaps if the whole town could agree that you and Silas were some unusual exception, it would work. But you know how impossible that would be. It's the principle of the thing. Once things get lax then other things start to happen. And believe me Mary, not everyone thinks your relationship is so platonic."

"I don't know what to do, Mrs. Norton. Surely you see my dilemma."

"I do Mary, and I sympathize, but on this I must hold firm. I'll give you a week to decide about your friendship, but only if you promise not see Silas during the week."

This would not be easy, but it was already Saturday, and with any luck my car would be fixed by Tuesday, so I agreed.

"You'll see Mary. It won't be so hard."

In spite of myself, my eyes filled at Mrs. Norton's small show of sympathy. I got up to take my plate to the sink and go upstairs.

Mrs. Norton was smiling as I left the kitchen.

I spent the weekend checking out my options for alternative places to live. I couldn't find anything. Except for the hotel, this was not a town accustomed to having to accommodate outsiders. My choice was getting clearer, but something in me refused to accept that I was going to have to give up a friend because of his race. Was I really being naive? I wondered if Silas was getting any of the same harassment.

On Monday, I accepted a ride from Mrs. Norton's friend, and by Tuesday my car was fixed. The issue of spending time with Silas was not as pressing, and Mrs. Norton, true to her word, found other things to talk about until the following Saturday. But once Saturday arrived, she jumped right in.

"How was your week without Silas?" she asked.

"I could probably spend a month without Silas and be just fine. But you don't just drop your friends because someone has an unreasonable reaction to seeing the two of you together. As you yourself said, it's the principle of the thing."

"You're free to go if you want to, Mary. No one's stopping you."

"There is nowhere else for me to go. I've looked."

She could hardly keep the smile off her face, although, to do her justice, she did try.

"So, you're staying here."

"It appears that I can stay here or pitch a tent. I'm not about to pitch a tent. But neither can I, in all honesty, say that I will never be in touch with Silas again. I think he's a wonderful man, and he's the one who came to my rescue when my car broke down. Everyone in town knows him, talks to him. It's not as though he's some hooligan with tattoos out to take advantage of vulnerable women. There must be some compromise we can both agree on."

Having the upper hand must have softened her a bit. By the time breakfast was over she had agreed that I could see him in town, for a cup of tea in the restaurant, as long as everything was always out in the open where everyone could see us. I was getting a reputation as an Indian lover and that would not be good for me, she warned.

It was exhausting trying to figure it all out.

CRIMES &
PUNISHMENTS

Looking back, I can see that October was a settling-in time for me in the classroom. It was, as Brother Thomas had promised, the time when I found my middle ground. The sip of state-sanctioned power I tasted had been a bit like getting drunk. It offered a sense of authority and omnipotence that felt empowering at the time and deeply regretful later.

In the weeks before I started testing the waters of absolute authority, I was beginning to feel that my students and I were finally getting to know one another. We had developed some routines and they had a better idea of what they could and couldn't get away with. Some of them were volunteering to answer questions and others were even asking them. These fragile threads between us were weakened with each breach of trust I engaged in. Fortunately, my students were a forgiving lot, and as I moved past my power days they returned the favour with a gradual return to our previous rapport.

As they slowly allowed their personalities to emerge from behind the masks of decorum, my sea of brown faces started to differentiate themselves, and I got to know them as individuals. I learned who to make allowances for and who was just taking advantage. I learned their strengths and weaknesses, what made them laugh and what they could not handle. There were some I never reached, some who took until Easter. But they stopped being a race of people who needed my help and evolved into my students. I, in turn, evolved from the educational equivalent of a saint who wanted to save the heathens, into an educator who wanted to teach.

Although I hate to admit to it, one little boy became a favourite. It wasn't because he was sweet or charming; in fact, he was quite the opposite. By the end of September, I knew them well enough that the trouble spots were rising to the surface and Bobby was trouble. He wasn't trouble the way Billy was, making life miserable for anyone every chance he got, or like Kenny, who could barely hold a pencil, let alone write a complete sentence. Bobby followed the rules with sullen, plodding steps.

He read aloud in a monotone. His stories had the proscribed beginning, middle and end but were as interesting as a to-do list. He never raised his hand but always had the correct answer when I called on him. He seemed determined to let nothing touch him, which made me determined to find out how.

One day at recess I found a crack in his armour.

A fence divided the boys' yard from the girls' yard in the outside recreation area. Children with siblings often snuck up to the barrier for a few words with a brother or sister. Sometimes the nuns turned a blind eye, and sometimes they didn't. I could never figure out what would trigger a reaction, but the threat of punishment didn't seem to matter. There was always somebody there, or hovering close by.

Bobby was often along the fence, but it wasn't until a cold day in October that I saw him connect. She looked about seven, the age at which children often started at the school. He held her hand, then said something that made her smile. It lasted a moment and then he was gone, lost in a group of boys kicking a ball. The little girl stayed by the fence for a while longer until someone came and pulled her gently away.

But trying to use her to get to him proved more difficult than I thought. A typical Bobby conversation went something like this.

"Did you get a chance to see your sister today, Bobby?"

"No"

"Is she having fun in Sister Maureen's class?"

"I don't know."

"I'm sure she loves having you around."

Silence.

"My older brother is my best friend."

Silence.

"Maybe you could write her a story."

Silence.

When I suggested to Sister Bea that we get the different classes together so the children could have some time with their siblings, the answer was no. I tried Mother Magdalene too. Surely she would see the advantage of giving the children some time together. But although she was understanding and sympathetic, the answer was still no.

"Our goal," she said, "is to prepare our charges for a new world. They must leave their old ways behind in order to become capable and productive adults in a different world than their parents. Some of the things we do may seem cruel or unnecessary, but I have been in this business a long time and I've seen how the kind of thing you're suggesting slows down their progress. In the end, it's not a kindness at all. They get a chance to see their siblings during the weekend and at special occasions during the year. The weaker their family ties, the easier it will be for them to assimilate. Give it some time, it's different from what you know and how you grew up. You'll understand it better once you've been here a while."

She was wrong. I never did understand it. But I did get the message, and some understanding of Bobby.

Could anyone make his sister smile the way he could?

I continued to watch him but I stopped trying to engage him so directly. He, in turn, gave me a little more. He raised his hand every once in a while, collected papers, and one time he even stayed behind to clean the blackboard.

Physical contact was different here. The first time I put my hand out to a child she recoiled. I adapted, starting with small measures—a touch on the shoulder as I went past, a clap on the back in celebration, a hand held to help with penmanship. The children were starved for physical affection but wary of it at the same time.

Of course, not every hand raised towards a child at Bear Lake was lifted in affection. I was not against corporeal punishment. "Spare the rod, spoil the child," was an unquestioned adage in the forties. I had had a few spankings myself, and one of my brothers had gotten the strap at school. But at the residential school children were hit for any infraction, major or minor. I doubt that anyone escaped the school without receiving more than a few smacks or strappings. There were many times though, when the punishments meted out went far beyond what was acceptable, even for the times.

One Thursday morning the children arrived looking solemn. Every once in a while I would see someone looking over at Janice. Janice was one of my quieter students, she liked to blend into the background. But now, instead of sitting at her desk with her back straight, her eyes front, as she usually did, she was perched on the edge of her seat with her eyes fixed on the classroom floor. Everyone else also did their best to avoid eye contact with me. The morning was spent with most heads bent studiously over desks. If they looked up it was only for a quick glance at the blackboard or when I forced someone to answer a question.

Finally, I walked over to Janice's desk and asked her to step outside the classroom with me. Janice looked pleadingly at me but responded with a weak, "Yes, Miss Brock."

Once we were in the hall, I bent down to try and look at her but she continued to stare at the floor.

"What happened, Janice? What's wrong?"

"Nothing, Miss Brock. I wasn't doing anything wrong."

"Of course you weren't. I didn't mean it like that. But something is troubling you, and everyone knows about it but me. I'd like to know too. Has something happened to you?"

Janice's eyes filled and her chin quivered. "I didn't do anything," she insisted.

"Janice, I'm not blaming you for anything. Honestly. I'd like to make your life easier, but I can't if you won't tell me what's wrong."

Janice took a deep breath. "Nothing's wrong, Miss Brock."

I stood up. "All right, but if you change your mind, please, come and talk to me. I'd like to help you if I can."

I waited a minute to see if she would take this opportunity to talk, but she continued to stare morosely at the floor. I gave up.

"You can stay out here a while if you want to compose yourself," I said.

"No thank you, Miss Brock," Janice said hurriedly. "I'll come in now."

My responsibilities at the school were minimal compared with the rest of the staff. I left the school when my day was over, and I had the weekends to myself. For everyone else, time for themselves was a luxury. Unless they were in prayer or performing some useful chore, the nuns and brothers were on duty, so I tried to rely on them as seldom as possible. Still, Sister Bea and Brother Thomas were the ones I went to when there was something I didn't understand.

After school that day, I went to Sister Bea to find out if she knew what had happened to Janice.

"Oh yes," she said, "she was punished because she was caught stealing from the potato bin."

"Stealing from the potato bin? Why would a child want to steal potatoes?"

"You'll have to ask her why. Anyway, it doesn't really matter why. The point is that she took something that wasn't hers and she was reprimanded."

"And how was she reprimanded?"

"She got the strap."

I thought about Janice not wanting to sit on her chair. When I was in school the strap was given on the hand. I had seen the same thing here.

"Where was she strapped?"

"On her bottom. Stealing is a sin and must be dealt with severely. The potatoes are for the whole community, so she was stealing from everyone when she took some."

Sister Bea knew me by then. She delivered her explanation in a straightforward, no-nonsense way—these are the rules.

I imagined Janice in Mother Magdalene's office, bent over a chair, Mother Magdalene with her arm raised over the little girl.

"She could hardly sit down. She must have gotten a very hard strap."

"She got ten straps, Mary. Stealing is a serious offence in a community like this. There are no locks here. We have to be able to trust each other."

"Ten straps! She's a little girl! I'm sure she could have learned her lesson with one."

"Perhaps she could have, but the rest of the students need to understand the seriousness of her crime. They have to know that we will not tolerate that sort of behaviour."

"The rest of the students? And how do they know? Did you make an announcement?"

Sister Bea sighed. "They watched."

"You mean it was done in front of everyone? Everyone watched?"

"Now Mary, don't turn this into something bigger than it is. The girls watched. We don't let the boys in, but they were outside in the hall so they could hear, and know, what was going on. She'll be fine in a few days, lesson learned."

I had to sit down. "Does this happen often?"

"Well you see," she smiled, "that's the good thing about a severe punishment. I know this is harsh, but it prevents others from doing the same thing. In the long run it saves the other children from punishment, and it teaches the importance we place on the basic values of honesty and trust."

"Surely it could be taught without a beating."

"Oh Mary, don't be so dramatic. It was a punishment, not a beating. We can't watch the children constantly; there are too many of them and too few of us. We have to know that they'll do as they're told. A few embarrassing punishments like this one, and the rest will toe the line. It helps the whole community run more smoothly when everyone plays by the rules." She reached out to touch my arm. "I know this comes as a shock to you. This isn't the way things are done in the city. I know that. I was shocked too when I first arrived.

It seems like a platitude to say that things are different here, but they are. These children come from undisciplined backgrounds. And they're used to harsh physical conditions. Some of them lived in tents during the winter before they came. They're tough."

"They're children!"

"Don't be ridiculous, Mary. I know they're children. I just mean that they're used to a tough life; they can handle a tough punishment. If we don't show our strength, they'll see us as weak and take advantage of it. It's like the military: the rules must be followed and not questioned, otherwise there is chaos."

"Sister Bea, please, this is terrible. You must see that. She's a little girl."

"It may be terrible for Janice, but without discipline it would be terrible for all of us. You haven't seen where they come from. They need to understand that the principles we care about are adhered to. In the end it will serve them well."

"What about the principles of compassion and empathy? Aren't they important too?"

"In Proverbs 23, it says, 'Do not withhold punishment from a child. If you strike him with a rod you will save his soul.' I'm abbreviating it a bit Mary, but the point is, compassion and empathy are not synonymous with permissiveness and indulgence. One can be compassionate and empathetic without being lenient."

I stared at her, unable to believe she really felt that way. Not everyone expected the children to behave like little soldiers. I thought Sister Bea was one of those who liked to hear the children laugh, who saw the spark of life in disobedience and the intelligence in seeing things differently.

"Mary, we're all doing our best here. It's not an easy place, not for them, or for us. They will grow up and leave, and I hope that when they do, they will remember the Christian values that are taught here, and carry those values with them wherever they go. I hope that whenever the temptation arises they will not steal, they will not lie, they will choose the right path. That is what will bring them true happiness. Sometimes we have to suffer in the short term in order to gain in the long term."

Her pale face, framed by her starched wimple, was soft and sympathetic. There were dark circles under her bright blue eyes. I wondered what suffering she was enduring in this life she had chosen.

I nodded my reluctant acceptance of her explanation and stood up to leave. The walls of her classroom were squeezing the air out of me.

Stepping out of Sister Bea's room I heard Brother Peter playing the piano in the gym. The sound was muted by the closed gym doors, but the beauty of it drew me like a bear to honey. I needed something sweet and innocent.

I slipped inside the doors and sat on the floor with my back against the wall while he played on. He moved seamlessly from hymns to marches to what sounded suspiciously like jazz. I closed my eyes and lost myself in his world of endless play. That Janice's beating and Brother Peter's beautiful music were both available here was a paradox I could never unravel.

After the incident with Janice, I became more sensitive to the moods of the class. When there was some noise, I was happy. When the children were quiet and submissive, I knew something was amiss.

Then I found out about another line of punishment.

This time I didn't need a quiet class to tell me that something was wrong.

Johnny, a new arrival to the school who was just starting to come out of his shell, came in late one day smelling like a urinal. The children were quiet, and kept their distance from him. Johnny himself kept his head down and didn't say a word the whole morning. When it came to the boys, I found that the best person to talk to was Brother Thomas. At lunchtime I headed to the barn. He met me on the path, coming from the milking shed.

"Mary! A delight to see you I'm sure! One of the cows had a blocked teat. I could use some pleasant company for a while."

I smiled and quickened my pace to keep up with him.

"How do you fix a blocked teat?"

"Believe me Mary, you don't want to know. Suffice it to say that it is unblocked. I do like it that we're able to provide them with a little fresh milk every day. It sure beats that powdered stuff most other places use."

"Do you ever make cheese?"

"Oh we tried, but it took too long and the children have enough to do without that. What brings your sweet face this way Mary? You're looking like there's something on your mind."

I told Brother Thomas about Johnny and asked if he knew why a student would be allowed to come to class smelling like that.

"Well, Mary," he said, "you aren't going to like what I have to tell you. And I don't like it myself, but there you are. Some things are worth the battle, and others, well, they're simply lost causes."

He was right. I didn't like what he had to say, but I wasn't ready to concede that it was a lost cause.

If a child wet the bed, they had to stand at breakfast, in front of everyone, with the offending sheets wrapped around them. Their own breakfast was a piece of bread in the kitchen. After breakfast, they had to go to the basement laundry room and wash the sheet by hand, hoping it would be dry by bedtime. Their school uniform, which had taken on the smell from the sheet, wasn't washed until their regular wash day. This meant that sometimes a child had to come to class for a week in a uniform that smelled of urine.

October 20, 1947
Mary was by again today. One of her students wet his bed and she didn't like the punishment. She's run up against a few punishments she considers too harsh for the crime and I must admit that, while there isn't much I can do, it's refreshing to hear her complaints. It's made me aware that I've come to accept what we do here as the norm, when perhaps it isn't. Perhaps it never even was the norm outside these walls. Regardless, things change outside, and they don't change much in here. We're like an isolated tribe in the Amazon: the modern world rarely touching us. While we may not want much that the outside world has to offer, I think it's important that we spend some time listening, with an open mind, to what it has to say. We may find that some things are improvements.

When I asked Sister Bea about this method of punishment, she was unperturbed.

"It bothered me a bit when I first saw it happen," she said. "But with so many children we can't be changing sheets all the time. It really isn't so awful."

"Isn't so awful? To be shamed in front of everyone? To smell like urine all day long? How could that not be awful?"

"Well, you may be right. I've probably gotten used to it, so it doesn't register with me. It happens a few times a week. It's not as though he's the only one."

"Please, Sister Bea, when it happens to you, it's as though you're the only one. Johnny was mortified."

"Well, he's a little older. It would be more embarrassing for him. But it's the way we do things here, and the children know it. He'll be back to normal in no time."

She eyed me sympathetically. "Ah Mary, look at you. I know what you're thinking. 'How do we change this?' Some things are worth the fight, but this isn't one of them, I can assure you. You've been here a few months now. Surely you know that."

"Brother Thomas told me the same thing. But things do change. Does the sheet punishment really work? What do you think would happen if I spoke to Mother Magdalene?"

"I think you would put in a crack in the thin ice you're already skating on. As you well know, she doesn't appreciate you telling her how to discipline her charges. The sheet punishment has been around as long as I have, and that's at least seven years. It's not going to change, Mary. Just let it go."

I was skating on thin ice, so I did let it go. But it troubled me. My students all smelled of soap when they filed in for the rest of the year, but I couldn't help but feel that I had to do something.

A few days later, Johnny was still subdued. I took him aside as the children spilled out for recess.

"Johnny," I said, "I know it was embarrassing for you the other day, when you were punished for wetting the bed. I want you to know that if that ever happens again, I'm happy to have you in my class. I understand that there are some things we have no control over."

He nodded, looked at me briefly to see if I wanted anything more of him, then dashed off to join his friends. I didn't know what else I could do.

ANIMIKIIKAA

I was grateful to have the car for school but as the snow melted, and the streets dried, I went back to my bike to get around town. After the big snowfall, the weather warmed up but it wasn't exactly warm. So when the last Saturday in October arrived with a bright blue sky and enough heat to burn off the frost by mid-morning, I knew I had to take advantage of it. I decided to risk the wrath of Mrs. Norton and her cronies and ride my bike to Indiantown to see if Silas knew of any interesting places to explore close by. Besides, I wasn't going to visit him, just to ask a question. Still, I rode the long way around to get to his house, so no one would suspect where I was going.

I was disappointed when he wasn't home, but instead of heading back into town, I kept going through Indiantown. I had never been to the forest on this side of town.

The houses went on for some way, growing farther and farther apart, until eventually the trees took over. The path continued though. It was a wide, well-worn trail clear of the branches and leaves that usually find their way to these open spaces. It was relatively straight too, with only a few bends to get around large trees or rocks.

When the path finally got too narrow for my bike, I leaned it up against a tree and continued on foot. I went slowly, knowing this might be my last forest ramble. It was cooler in the forest, where the trees were dense. Here and there the afternoon sun managed to find it's way through, especially now that the deciduous trees were bare. After about fifteen minutes I came to a fork. The trail to the left, the direction of the lake, was well worn. The one to the right, going deeper into the forest, was narrower, and rougher. My choice was clear. I wasn't going to waste what remained of this perfect day by going back to the lake. I expected the rougher trail might fade to nothing, but surprisingly, after the first few minutes, it got more established. This made me even more curious, and so, one niggling part of me wondering if I was being foolish, I plunged into the mystery of the woods.

I had been walking for about ten minutes and was plodding mindlessly along when I came around a narrow bend and was startled by a flurry of feathers. A partridge took off with a squawk of irritation into the safety of the underbrush. At its unexpected eruption, I tripped over a root in the path and went flying myself, giving my own squawk as I landed flat on the ground. When I looked up, I saw the sun glinting off a window in a clearing where the path, presumably, ended.

If anyone was home, they would certainly know I was there. I picked myself up and marched, as bravely as I could, into the clearing. My experience with the old trapper had made me wary of encounters with these hermits of the woods. I thought the best strategy would be to walk past the cabin out in the open, letting any suspicious recluse see me without having to interact.

In the clearing, as I expected, sat a small log cabin. Along one wall I could see the familiar shape of hoops for stretching fur. But that was the only thing this cabin had in common with the many I had encountered so far. First of all, it had windows, clean windows, and a wide front porch. On the porch was a bench and a rocking chair, crafted out of saplings and decorated with bright red and yellow cushions. A shiny metal pail hung from a hook on the railing and a kerosene lantern hung on a hook by the door. This place looked like a home, not a way station. Smoke drifted from the chimney and the path that led to the door had been freshly swept. I paused for a moment to take it all in. I was curious enough to consider knocking on the door. Who would keep a place with such meticulous tidiness in the middle of the woods?

Before I could decide whether or not to brave the door, it opened. I took an instinctive step back towards the shelter of the trees and watched as a short woman wearing a grubby apron stepped onto the porch. She stared at me across the clearing, her feet firmly planted, her hands on her hips. Skinny legs supported a wide torso with two long, grey braids lying atop her ample bosom. Perched on her tiny nose, wire rimmed glasses framed small dark eyes that showed no hint of welcome.

"You visiting?" she said.

I waved my hand in the direction of the woods. "I was just following the path, and this is where it brought me." She had caught me off guard. I couldn't think of anything to say but the truth.

"Well, since you're here, you'd best come in."

I wasn't at all sure that I agreed with her. It seemed to me that the best thing to do would be to run. But when she turned her back and walked into the shadows of the cabin, I followed.

"Sit yourself down. That's a goodly walk for a city girl like yourself."

"I'm fine." I protested. "It's just that I fell."

"That partridge is my best friend. Never lets me down. No one arrives unannounced."

I looked for a place to sit while she busied herself with a kettle, filling it with water from a wooden barrel then placing it over one of the burners of the cookstove. There was one well-stuffed chair, which was occupied by a fat grey cat, and a bench alongside a narrow, rough-hewn table. I sat on the bench, moving aside some papers to do so. She opened a small tin that sat on the counter and measured tea into a brown ceramic pot while I watched. From hooks on the wall above a basin, she took down two thick mugs. Then, pulling on a leather strap attached to the floor, she opened a trap door and took out a glass jar with milk. A white bowl with the word SUGAR written in fancy script waited on the table. It's delicate china lid protected its contents from flies, and cats.

She worked in silence, taking some biscuits out of a tin and arranging them on a plate she set on the table, along with two empty plates and a canning jar filled with a crimson-red jam. The kettle boiled quickly and soon she was sitting in the easy chair, the cat on the floor and the tea on the table, steeping in its pot.

She took a long look at me. "You're a curious girl, coming through Indiantown, and the woods too."

"I... I like to explore."

Despite the tea and biscuits, I had yet to see her smile. What did she mean by "curious girl"? I wondered where my explorations had led me.

"And what have you discovered?"

"Nothing, so far. Just the forest, and you. Which isn't nothing," I hastened to add. "I just mean nothing that you wouldn't expect to find, except you of course—I didn't know you were here. Do you live here always?"

"Not sure what you're asking exactly. I live here year round, but I lived somewheres else before."

"How long have you lived here?"

She paused before answering. The cat jumped into her lap and she ran her fingers along its back. She looked at me with the eye of a horse trader. I waited, wondering if I would pass inspection.

"I been here now about ten years. Had a man with me for the first five. A white man, a good man too. He took a chill one winter and never recovered. I buried him out back. It comforts me to have him near." Her gaze shifted to somewhere behind me. I almost turned to see if there was someone else in the room. "Could be I'll show you some day." She nodded at this, as though she and her man had just communed and agreed to this possibility. I felt a shiver go through me. I doubted I would be back for another visit. "Haven't seen you around afore," she said.

"I've only been here a few months. I teach at the Indian school."

"Ah, the school. Me too. I came for the school," she said. "My granddaughter went to that place. I wasn't gonna to leave her with no family in sight like some of them other poor children. It's a shame the way they take those little ones from loving families. They don't learn a damn thing at that school except how to hate themselves."

She didn't seem to be blaming me, but I wasn't sure how else to interpret her. After her denunciation she stopped talking and in the silence that followed I felt some need to justify my role there. Although she appeared to be in no hurry for me speak.

"It's not perfect by any means," I said, "but I don't think it's so terrible. Most of the children seem happy, although I have to admit, sometimes it's hard to tell. And they're learning to read and write and how to do mathematics and science. Things they'll need when they go out into the world."

"Pshaw. What they need to know is how to feed themselves and their families. Reading and writing don't feed a person."

I felt my back go up. This was against everything I had lived with all my life.

"Sure it does," I said, "with reading and writing they can get jobs."

"You don't need no job to feed a family. Alls you need is a gun and a good eye. And knowledge about the bush. I can hunt and store up food for winter, where you my little store-bought child, would starve the first snow. Who's got the better knowledge?"

Something in me did not want to upset this woman. It wasn't that she was dangerous, although I was willing to bet she could be, or that she could, apparently, commune with ghosts. Looking back, I think it was because I liked her. I would grow to love her, but at that point in our relationship, what did I know? Nothing really, but she appealed to me in the same way that Jonathan had. She wasn't afraid of anyone or anything. The difference was that her bravery came from experience, while Jonathan's was youthful arrogance. Still, once again, I felt the need to defend my position.

"But I don't live in the bush. I need to survive in the city."

"Who wants to live in the city? Not you, my friend. Pinch me if I'm wrong, but here you are, living miles from the nearest movie house and spending your spare time tromping through the woods." She paused. "You runnin' from someone?"

"Running? No, I'm not running from anyone." If she expected anything deeper from me, she was disappointed. As far as I was concerned, I was here for a new experience and in the woods for a pretty view, or an interesting birdsong. After a short wait for anything more, she continued.

"I've lived in your cities and I've lived on the land. I've lived a long time and I can tell you this. Fresh air and hard work is the best life there is. No one sleeps better than a person who's been outside all day, doing whatever needs doing."

"You like being out here?"

"Like it? If I didn't have this place, I don't know what I'd do."

"What do you like about it?" I asked. "I know I'd miss running water and indoor toilets. Wouldn't you like to have a furnace to heat your house so you don't have to chop wood all day? Wouldn't you rather go a few blocks to the store for food rather than maybe getting something on a hunt? And how on earth do you bring those big animals back to your house? Where do you store them? How do you keep everything from rotting?" The list of complications seemed endless.

She looked at me, and her tiny eyes twinkled as a smile finally lit up her face.

"You have no idea how satisfying it is to be able to feed yourself."

"But I do feed myself," I said. "I may not kill the cow, but I can afford to buy my own meat."

She looked at me doubtfully, as though this were a brand-new concept. "I was hungry once. Winnipeg it was, the summer of '36." She grew quiet for a moment. "Rough times then. I was on social welfare. In them days you got sixteen dollars from the government for rent. There weren't no place to rent for sixteen dollars. It weren't just me neither. Lots of people in my shoes, lots of people was hungry in them days. I took to laying rabbit snares for food. Kept me healthy, those rabbits."

She gave me wide grin, then turned serious again. "But in '36, in that summer, the heat was so bad it was killing people. It killed my rabbits too." She shook her head at the memory. "Nowadays, my granddaughter couldn't find a rabbit's trail in the snow. She woulda gone hungry long before the heat. The old ways are dying. Soon they won't know nothing."

"But we're teaching the children new ways so they can prosper in a new world. I don't live as my ancestors did."

She stopped and stared at me, as though seeing me for the first time. "You been tromping these woods, looking to discover something. You want to learn some old ways?" she said.

I didn't know what to say. Wasn't I the teacher? And what was it she was wanting to teach me? I looked at her while these thoughts ran through my head. Her face was serious and thoughtful. It was as though she was saying, I'm only asking you this once, take your time and be sure that you answer in a way that is true to your heart. Yes or no, she didn't care. She only wanted to know if I wanted to learn. She wasn't going to tell me what it was I was going to learn and I doubt she had a curriculum in mind. Feeling like I did when I took the left-hand path—a little bit foolhardy, a little bit brave—I answered her.

"Yes," I said.

Second thoughts flooded in immediately. What had I said yes to? Was I going to be introduced to some Indian voodoo? Made to dig for arrowhead tubers all day? Taken into the woods to kill a deer?

She smiled and raised her mug in a toast. "To lessons," she said.

"To lessons," I replied, trying to match her whole-hearted smile.

"First things first. Introductions. My Indian name is Animikiikaa, but white people call me Annie. I'm Turtle clan. I was born north of here, near Sachigo Lake. I never went to your schools. My parents taught me. After we came out of the bush I ended up in Winnipeg." She shook her head. "Not a good place for me, at least until I met my Henry. But I got the English there. I'm glad of that. My man couldn't speak Anishinaabemowin so my English got real good when we moved in together." She laughed. "When I left Winnipeg all I got to show for it was English and my handsome Henry. Henry was worth it."

She smiled wistfully, then nodded at me.

I tried to follow her lead, "My first name's Mary. I don't have a clan, at least that I know of, but my last name is Brock, so maybe that's my clan." I looked to her for a response, but getting none I went on to say where I had grown up. "I teach grade five at the school. It's my first year teaching. I have a boyfriend, but I doubt we'll marry, so that part of my history is yet to be written." I paused, she waited. I shrugged my shoulders, "I guess that's it." I said.

She waited a little while longer before speaking again. I fidgeted, wondering if there was something I should have told her. But when she spoke up again it was as though there had been no silence at all.

"When I was a girl we moved around a lot," she said. "We followed the animals. In winter we had a cabin. It was like this one." She waved her hand around her tiny cabin, grinning widely enough that I could see her almost toothless bottom row. "This place is high class compared to when I was young. No one had a place like this all to themself. We slept together, parents, children, grandparents too. Kept us warm," she chuckled. "Less need of that wood gathering you were thinking was such a chore."

I tried to imagine the scene. Everyone in one cabin. Where did they go to the bathroom? Where did they cook? Where did they store all their things?

Annie's eyes had brightened as she talked. "Maybe that's why this cabin suits me," she said. "Everything I need is right here. It's not for everybody. But you can be happy in a cabin in the woods."

She lifted up the cat that had been sleeping in her lap. "His name's Bartholomew." She laughed. "Quite a mouthful ain't it? Henry named him. I just call him 'cat'." She chuckled again. "Do electricity and running water make a person happy?" she asked Bartholomew.

She turned her attention back to me. "I had both in Winnipeg." She shook her head, as though she could shake the memory of Winnipeg out of it. "I was not a happy person in Winnipeg. It's not what you have, but how well you use what you're given."

I didn't get it. I understood how flush toilets might make me happy and how a trout on her line might make her happy, but I didn't understand how the way you used them could make someone happy or not. I wanted to ask for clarification, but instead I looked around her little cabin. The time had flown and it was already late afternoon. The light was low, and despite the kerosene lamp she had lit, it was difficult to see the details. She had a double bed, pressed against the back wall. It was neatly made and covered with what look like a handmade quilt. Two wide drawers under the bed presumably held her clothes. Above the bed, shelves tacked to the wall held an assortment of things: everything from a crumpled towel to a well used Bible. The only other pieces of furniture were the table with its bench, the easy chair and the cookstove. She had a few photos on the wall, but it was too dark to see them. One window had curtains, made from the same fabric as the cushion on the sapling chair outside, and an old guitar sat tucked away in a corner.

"Something to sit on, something to sleep on, and something to cook on. A cat for company and the big world outside to feed me and keep me close to Creator. The things I want that ain't in the forest or streams," she swept her hand across the table where the teapot sat cooling, "I buy with money from furs. It's a good life."

I nodded politely, not sure if this was a lesson or not. But as it didn't invite comment, I didn't make any. By this time the sun had slipped below the horizon. It was time to go home.

The woods had been dark enough in the day, with sunlight peeping through, but when we stepped out onto the porch, even with the early evening light, the forest beyond the small clearing looked like a black wall.

"I could walk you back," she said. "But you can do it yourself too. Lesson two!"

She went back into the dark cabin and came out with a small tin whistle. "If you get scared, blow it softly. If you are truly lost, blow it hard. But I doubt you'll need to do that."

Her confidence was inspiring, if somewhat misplaced. But I had little choice, so I wrapped my shawl around me and headed off, her whistle in my pocket. When I got to the edge of the clearing she shouted at me, "Don't forget my partridge!" I laughed, which made the dark woods a little brighter.

She was right of course. I did make it home. Once my eyes adjusted to the dim light it was brighter than I expected and I found that my feet were also useful tools, and could easily tell me if I was on the path, or veering off it. Still, I did a lot of soft whistling.

When I got home, I thought about the tin whistle and how I had used it. It looked like a cheap popcorn-box treat, but it had eased my anxiety on the way home, and, yes, it had even made me happy.

I visited Annie as often as I could, and each time I learned something new. My first visit after our initial meeting we talked about the tin whistle and how it had helped me. She spoke of her little brown teapot and how it helped her. It was her first gift from the man who lay buried behind the cabin. She said that every time she poured hot water into it she felt him keeping her warm.

Sometimes her lessons were practical, like the time I arrived while she was skinning a beaver. But most of the time it was like there was no lesson at all. We would sit, and she would tell stories that seemed to have nothing to do with anything in particular. Usually though, a few days later, or even a few years later, something would happen and I would remember her tale of a winter hunt or her first encounter with a bear and think, ah, that's what she was trying to tell me.

NOVEMBER
1947

BELINDA

In early November, my teacher's aide finally arrived. I had seen her
on occasion because she was one of Brother Peter's piano students.
Her name was Belinda Whitestorm, and as Sister Bea had promised,
she was an angel in a blue tunic.

Belinda had started at Bear Lake when she was seven. When I met
her, she was sixteen and in grade eleven. Since the school only had
classes up to grade ten, this was a remarkable achievement. Twice
a week she made a trip into Bear Lake to attend the public high school
for science and mathematics classes, the rest of her schooling was
accomplished through correspondence courses. At sixteen, she was
free to leave the residential school, but her home community had
no school at all. There was talk of letting her take grade thirteen full
time in town, at Bear Lake High School. If that happened she would
be a pioneer.

She was one of those people who appears to glide through life
without missing a beat, who is always able to see the silver lining and
cheer up everyone else by doing so. In our classroom, her presence

151

had the effect of relaxing even my most fearful students. To top it off, she even looked like an angel, as hard as that can be in a shapeless blue tunic. She had the well-defined face of a model, and a figure to go with it. The boys had a hard time keeping their eyes on their work as she moved around the classroom. The girls adored her too. She had a way of making each person in her orbit feel special and valued.

Belinda came twice a week, on Monday and Thursday afternoons, and I looked forward to her arrival as much as my students did. On Thursdays, she would stay for an hour after the children left and help me mark papers or prepare a lesson before going down the hall for her weekly piano lesson with Brother Peter.

One day I heard her singing.

Sister Abigail led the choir, and she had worked with Belinda during her first years of high school, but now Belinda was taking both piano and singing with Brother Peter. I was delighted. The more music that drifted down the hall and into my classroom, the happier I was. That first time, even though I knew Brother Peter didn't appreciate an audience, I couldn't resist sneaking in to watch for a while. Belinda sat on the piano bench and Brother Peter stood behind her, every once in while reaching over to guide her hands or straighten her back as she practised a hymn for the Remembrance Day service.

Then things shifted. I heard Brother Peter say, "All right, try something by ear. What's one of your favourite songs?"

"You mean, other than a hymn?"

"There are plenty of beautiful hymns, but I'm sure they aren't what you hum when you're washing dishes."

Brother Peter stood back as she played the first few tentative notes. It didn't take long for her confidence to grow and her hands to find their rhythm as she sang, with a plaintive assurance, Doris Day's "Sentimental Journey."

I didn't like Brother Peter. In fairness, I had little to go on. Other than listening to him play the piano on Thursday afternoons, my few interactions with him had been cursory at best. But those times had given me the impression of a man without a heart. I once saw him stop a student in the hall and hit him so hard the student fell against the wall. I have no idea what the student had done. No one said a word; everyone, myself included, just walked on like it hadn't happened. Brother Peter walked on too. He strode the halls like he owned the place and wore his good looks like a medal he had earned. How he had ended up here, or even as a member of the church, confounded me.

But he was a different man on the piano bench. Music changed him, made him real. As Sentimental Journey came to a close, he sang the last few bars with Belinda in harmony.

DIFFERENT HABITS

I rarely saw or heard anything of a personal nature from the nuns and brothers I worked with. My dealings with them were limited, for the most part, to professional contact. As a result, I rarely thought about what their lives had been like before they appeared in mine, or what they might want, or miss, from the lives they had left behind. Whether or not she was a true representative, Sister Bea was my model whenever I did try to understand the motives or actions of the nuns and brothers who lived at the school. She appeared to have the best interests of her charges at heart, genuinely concerned about the students' well-being and their ability to grow academically, physically, spiritually and socially.

But her relationship with the children was secondary to her relationship with Jesus, and sometimes the two would clash.

Sister Bea often complained to me about one of her students, a little girl named Milly. Milly was small for her age and slow academically. She was usually sweet and friendly, but at times she would collapse in tears or explode into anger for no apparent reason.

Milly also had a hard time with her fine motor skills, and writing was difficult for her. Each piece of written work took her twice as long to complete as anyone else. In one instance, in late November, Sister Bea asked her class to write a story about Christmas. For Sister Bea, this meant Jesus and lambs, wise men and angels. For Milly, this meant a story about Christmastime. She wrote about one Christmas when she stayed out to play in the snow and got so cold she barely made it home. Sister Bea was furious and made her stay in for recess to write the "real" Christmas story. Milly refused to do it. It took the strap to change her mind. Winning that battle wasn't enough, however, and Sister Bea made her rewrite her story several times to get it right. Milly and Sister Bea had to stay in for recess for almost a week, which was hard on them both.

Incidents like that, with Sister Bea telling me with satisfaction how she finally got Milly to do the "right" thing, made me want to take all the students she didn't like and put them in my class. They were starved for love and understanding. Some of the nuns were always surrounded by children, but most just swished by in their long black habits, as though the need for human touch had left them along with the ability to marry.

But as the first months passed, an awareness grew, as it had with my students, that the uniform set of attitudes and appearances I initially encountered in the staff were just surface layers. Each nun or brother that I came to know as a person was as nuanced and multidimensional as I was, although their devotion to the discipline of a religious life sometimes made it difficult for them to express their individuality. But every once in a while I would get a sneak peek past the walls of decorum and long black habits.

Shortly after Milly's week of indoor recesses, I stopped in after school to see Sister Bea about a science class we were teaching together. I pushed open the door to her classroom without knocking, as I often did, to find her at her desk, her head down, crying. I backed out quietly, torn between offering sympathy and offering privacy. When I went back fifteen minutes later, she was staring blankly at the back wall. I asked about the science project and we had a short conversation but she kept her head down, pretending to be writing something in her attendance book. I lingered, waiting to see if she wanted to talk, but clearly she did not, so I left.

I never did find out what had upset her so. But the incident made me look at the staff with more compassion. I had always felt they were happy at the school. They had their community after all; they had chosen a life of abstinence and poverty and they believed they were doing God's work on earth. Loneliness or discontent seemed almost sacrilegious.

But Sister Bea was not just a lonely disciplinarian. One Saturday in early November I went to the school to help supervise the students during their afternoon recreation time. On Saturdays, the girls and boys were allowed to play together. I was excited about the opportunity to see brothers and sisters together and maybe even some romantic alliances. They had chores in the morning, and study hall later in the day, so they made the most of their time to play.

On this Saturday, the sun was out and a group had started a soccer game. One of the boys kicked the ball in the general direction of Sister Bea whose face lit up with a smile. She ran to the ball and kicked it back. Then she astounded us all and ran into the field of play herself. She hiked up her skirts and showed off her skills, which were considerable. She maneuvered the ball between a multitude of players, who, once they got over their shock, did their best to get it back from her. Brother David was watching, and before long he too got into the act. Soon the two of them were playing around each other, acting out a strange dance of joy and tension while the other players bobbed ineffectively nearby. The rest of us stared in wonder. That is, until Mother Magdalene arrived.

The silence descended slowly. Most of us were too intent on the performance to notice her approach, but as she moved through the crowd it got quieter and quieter. Still, by the time she got onto the field, most of us were only just aware that she had arrived.

It would be lovely to be able to say that Mother Magdalene amazed us all by taking control of the ball herself. What a storybook ending that would have been! But this place was no setting for a storybook. When Mother Magdalene stepped onto the field, Sister Bea stopped dead, a look of horror on her face. It took Brother David a little longer to realize why the play had stopped, but when he did, he slipped into the crowd and disappeared. He left Sister Bea standing stock still in the middle of the field, looking for all the world like she'd just been caught having sex in the school gym.

Once Mother Magdalene knew she had Sister Bea's undivided attention, she turned to her spellbound audience and said, "You will all go straight to your study hall classrooms. Now."

She looked at me and said, "Miss Brock, would you be so kind as to take charge of Sister Beatrice's class? Sister Beatrice will be coming with me. There will be no talking."

Then she stood there, waiting for us all to follow her orders.

Which of course, we all did.

Back in the classroom I was torn between discussing the incident and following orders. I went for following orders. It was the simplest, but I knew that it was also an evasion, no different than Brother David's abrupt departure.

November 2, 1947

I had an interesting visitor today after lunch. Mother Magdalene stopped by. Apparently, my growing friendship with Mary has not escaped notice. Usually I'm able to stay out of school politics, and I wanted no part of this conversation. By the look on her face when she saw the chair she was expected to sit down in, it was obvious that she was equally anxious to make the meeting as short as possible.

In all my time here, I don't think I've said more than ten unnecessary words to Mother Magdalene. Today, she stayed for over an hour.

We started by talking about Mary. What did I think of her and her suitability as a teacher here? I surprised myself by defending her. For all her naiveté and inexperience, she is a breath of fresh air, and also, we both agreed, the wave of the future. This school, and others like it, are not going to manage without outside help. It's something we're going to have to get used to.

But the interesting part of the conversation came after all that. She had come because of the episode with S. Beatrice playing soccer with the boys on Saturday. She felt that it might be Mary's "unsettling" influence that had allowed such a breach of decorum. What did I think? Ah! How I love those kinds of questions!

If I had had the opportunity to go to university I think I would have taken philosophy and become an academic. But in truth, I'm glad I didn't get the opportunity. There are plenty of soldiers among religious communities, those who take comfort in clear boundaries and a clear set of rules. I think we all must on some level, but there are also the thinkers. I had never taken Mother Magdalene to be a thinker, but I was wrong.

We spent a long time talking about our school and its failure to graduate the kind of person we are striving to create. I have my own ideas about that, but I'll try to recreate what she said, since it was so unlike the person I've seen presented in public.

"I took the name Magdalene because, while the biblical Magdalene appeared to have changed after she met Jesus, I saw her instead, as a person who was finally able to come into her own. Jesus saw the good that was already in her and allowed it to blossom. I'm not proud of my life before I met Jesus. Suffice it to say that I was in jail when I met Sister Cecilia. She was the first person in my life who treated me like a whole human being, and not just an incorrigible person who did bad things. She drew out of me the good that I had buried, along with any belief in my own redemption, and told me that Jesus loved me. She said she loved the story in Matthew where Jesus said that each time we clothed the naked or visited the prisoner, 'As you did it to one of the least of my brothers, you did it to me.' She said that for her, this meant that Jesus is in each of us, and if that's true, then there is pure goodness in each of us.

"I keep a portrait of Mary Magdalene in my office," she said, "to remind me that Jesus is in each of us, but sometimes I'm ashamed to look at her. When I came to my first residential school, I was as horrified as Mary about the strict conditions and harsh punishments. Harsh punishments had done nothing to me except make me push back even harder. But I was a new nun, and I wanted to belong to this community more than anything. So I followed the rules, and soon got used to them. Not only used to them, but a believer in them. It was at that first school where I saw the homes that some of these children come from. I took on the mantle of saviour and when I was moved here as principal I saw it as my chance to really make a difference—but I haven't made any difference at all."

I didn't know what to say to her. In my little corner here in the barn, I believe that I am making something of a difference. However, after our conversation, I realized that the difference I am making is not in adding to the good, but rather in trying to provide some respite from the conditions the students deal with every day.

I wonder what Jesus would think of what is going on here in His name. John 13, "Love one another as I have loved you," He told us. We can spout the rhetoric with ease, and claim we are doing all we do here out of love, but frankly, love is a word that rarely sees the light of day in this school.

I hope this wasn't my last talk with Mother Magdalene.

BIRLINGS

The snow didn't come again until late November, but the days were noticeably shorter and colder, and the sun rarely shone. The mood, at school and at home, felt as grey as the skies. Fortunately, I never surrendered the way I had after Jonathan left. Instead, I tried to find some antidotes, but it was an uphill battle. At school, my attempts to introduce some games and fun as an alternative to rote learning continued to be suspect, and at home, a meaningful social life was elusive. Most young women my age were mothers already and few had any idea of life in a city. We came from different worlds and our common ground was a narrow strip. The three people that I did enjoy spending time with were Annie, who was hard to reach, Silas, who was considered verboten, and Nancy, who had a family to look after.

Thank goodness for Frank. He wrote often, and took every chance he could to come to town to see me. His attention made me feel whole. I was no longer the inept junior teacher flailing helplessly at old-fashioned rules or the awkward outsider who didn't know how to bake bread. With Frank, I was desirable, smart and witty. He made no unseemly advances and always appeared on time and well-dressed when he came to pick me up. He made me feel like a princess.

After a month of wooing, though, things started to slip. One cold weekend in November Frank suggested that we go to Birling's Bar, the "other" bar in town. The one the loggers went to, the one the ladies of the night were rumoured to frequent. The one I had been to only once before, to buy my car. I hesitated, partly because of a concern about being seen there, but also because I remembered how things had changed in the evening. I wasn't sure I wanted to go at night.

I trusted Frank though, and he agreed that if I felt uncomfortable, we would leave. As it turned out, it wasn't as bad as I'd feared. We went on a Friday night, so the clientele was more diverse than the weeknight I had been there with Martin, and most of the women looked just like me. The glare from the bare light bulbs above our heads was softened by cigarette smoke, and snacks came free if you bought whiskey instead of beer. The best part was the music. No jukebox here! Birling's had its own house band, The Swingin' Bears, and they played every Friday and Saturday night. They were upbeat and enthusiastic, which didn't completely make up for their lack of talent, but they played familiar tunes that got the crowd on its feet.

When I got the giggles and fell into the arms of a drunken stranger, I sobered up enough to take stock of our situation. Even half-drunk, it wasn't hard to see that Frank was in worse shape than I was. The free food had been flowing most of the night, and it wasn't me drinking the whiskey. I suggested that we step outside for a breather, thinking we both needed a break from the bar's spell. Our breath froze in the night air as we leaned against the building in each other's arms. There was another couple similarly engaged. With a giggle, I pointed them out to Frank, which only seemed to encourage him.

I let his hands roam where they hadn't gone before, while my soggy brain tried to catch up. Mrs. Norton would not approve. My back against the building, my front pressed against Frank, I rested my head on his shoulder while he fumbled with the clasp of my bra.

It was then that I spotted a familiar shape on the far side of the street. Forgetting about Frank for a moment, I struggled to place the long stride and straight back. He was out of place here, but

I knew him from somewhere. My heart leapt at the thought that it was someone from home, but almost as soon as the idea entered my head I recognized the handsome man across the street as Brother Peter. The instant I realized who it was, he turned, and our eyes met.

I suppose my expression wasn't much different than his—eyes widening and jaw dropping as recognition dawned. While this wasn't a good place for me to be, it wasn't a good place for him either. I offered up a weak wave over Frank's shoulder, and an equally small smile. He nodded at me and kept walking. I pushed Frank off me, my bra still in place, and we went back inside. I was sober now, or at least compared to before our interlude outside. Looking around the jam-packed room, the mood felt more bawdy than boisterous. It was time to go home.

Frank didn't agree. He was ready for just one more drink, one more dance. I acquiesced, but one more wasn't enough, and my knight in shining armour fell off his horse. We stayed for another hour, although it felt like three, while he tried to get me up on the dance floor or back outside. I sat and pouted. He either didn't care or was too drunk to read me and finally got up to go dance by himself. At that point I decided to walk home. He would have made a lousy escort anyway.

If thinking that Frank was a knight in shining armour was my first mistake, then thinking that walking home alone in Bear Lake was better than walking with a drunken boyfriend was my second.

Once I stepped out of the noise, the smoke, and the heat of the bar I felt much better. It was shortly after midnight; the air was crisp and cool and the black sky was littered with stars. I took it in for a moment, then buttoned up my coat and started off. The bar area was not a good place to be at that hour, so I decided to head straight to the railway tracks for a shortcut home. I was almost at the rail line when I heard a voice behind me.

"Better not go that way, pretty little thing. It's Indiantown over them tracks, not a good place for a sweet young thing like yourself."

I clutched my coat a little tighter and kept walking. But he was not to be deterred. Coming up behind me, he grabbed my arm and turned me to face him.

"Didn't hear me little girl, or ya just don't like me?"

His breath, his whole body, stank of alcohol. His face was covered in a half-grown beard and his eyes were dark and bottomless.

"I'm fine," I said. "Thank you for your help, but I know my way home."

"I think I'd better take you there myself, little girl, for your own good. You need a gentleman at your side in these parts. You won't be safe with all them drunken Indians roaming around. Those no-good buggers would take advantage of a sweet young thing like yourself, don't you believe they wouldn't."

I let him drag me along the street a bit but when he didn't let go of my arm, even when we were well past the area close to Indiantown, my fear grew.

When he turned a corner to walk down an alley, I started to panic.

"I need to get back home," I said. "It's not this way."

"That's all right, little girl. I'm takin' you a different way so's we don't meet nobody that don't like me. There's some nasty people in this town who'll pick a fight for no good reason. I oughta know, I've been beat up more times than you'd believe. Those stupid buggers, pardon my French, they just decide they don't like you, then whammo, it's a sucker punch to the gut and you're down on the ground and you ain't got a chance. I've learned to watch my back in this town, I can tell you."

"I want to go home, please." It felt like the wrong thing to say, but I was scared and I hoped the "little girl" plea might convince him.

"Ya sure didn't look like you was headed home when I saw ya. Got some Indian boyfriend have ya? They got big dicks, those redskins? Eh?"

He turned to grin at me, any pretence about his intentions out the window. He grabbed my arm a little tighter.

"Time you learned what a real man can show you, little girl. You won't want no more Indian dick after you've had a taste of a real man."

"I haven't got any Indian boyfriend, and I need to go home. People will be worried about me by now."

"Don't give me that bullshit, little sister. You don't want to make me mad, and nothin' makes me madder than lies. There ain't no one waitin' on you. You got time on your hands and I'll show you how to use it. We're almost there, so don't give me no more trouble and you'll be on your way before you can say Jiminy Cricket." He chuckled at his own wit and picked up his pace.

It was then that I saw him. My saviour. A man was walking towards us. He was weaving, a bit drunk, but then so was the one with my arm in his fist.

"Shit," my escort muttered, and put his arm around my shoulders. "Hey there, Kenny." He waved at the weaver. "How's it going?"

Kenny looked up warily. "Hey there Burt. Just goin' home, not feelin' too steady, y' know?"

"Yeah, I know the feelin'. See ya 'round."

Kenny wove on past, and Burt turned to face me. He planted a kiss on my lips, forcing my mouth open with his disgusting tongue.

"There now, little lady, that wasn't so bad was it? There's more and better where that comes from."

I don't know why I didn't say anything when Kenny wove past, or where I finally got the nerve after he was gone, but I remembered a trick my brother had taught me. Still clenched in his suffocating embrace, I kneed him in his crotch as hard as I could, and then brought my foot back down with all my might on his instep. He stared at me in disbelief, his grip initially tightening until he bent over in pain, my arm still clutched in his hand. It wasn't hard to break free at that point. I pushed him to the ground and ran.

After a couple of blocks, out of breath but still too scared to stop, I gave a quick glance over my shoulder. He was nowhere in sight. It took another fifteen minutes to get to the door of 54 Nipigon Street, and one more to drop my coat and boots and get up to my room where I lay on the bed and wept from relief, anger and fear.

November 11, 1947

We had our Remembrance Day ceremonies today. This is our second since the end of the war, and a particularly moving one for most of us. It is hard to find anyone who was not affected, even here in our isolated corner of the North. Despite its staid solemnity, many of the children had tears in their eyes. Poor Mary wept openly at one point. I'm glad my father didn't live long enough to see another war. We are stupid creatures to believe that any war will end all wars, but even stupider to engage in another so soon after the first. With all that blood and destruction so recently cleaned up, it's hard to believe that we went at it again. I sometimes wonder if Hitler thought we'd all just roll over and play dead and he'd be able to keep marching through Europe. How those intelligent Germans ever let a man like Hitler take charge is beyond me. It serves as fair warning though. If it can happen there, it can happen anywhere.

But enough depressing talk. Winter is coming on and I've moved the horseshoes to inside the hay barn. With the exception of that big snowfall in October, we've had a mild autumn so far. But the change is coming and with it some rest. I like this time of hibernation. With my only worries being warmth and food for the animals I see the increasing dark and cold as harbingers of quiet and relaxation.

Simon was by after the service yesterday. He said his uncle died in the war. He and his uncle used to go fishing in the summer. There's something different about Simon this year. It often happens. The teenage years are never simple. But he's not so much angry, as withdrawn. He used to tell me everything, to the point I barely listened to half of it. Now he speaks in short sentences and often just sits on the bench looking on while the others play. I'm not sure if I should try to draw him out, or if it's just a phase I should let him explore on his own. I don't even know why it troubles me. If there's one thing I've learned here, it's that I can't change the world. I haven't learned not to try though!

THE PENCIL

I had thought that straps and wet bedsheets were the worst this place had to offer. Then one day I kept Susan after school.

Susan rarely spoke above a whisper, and this, only when she had to. Occasionally, I would see her talk to another student, but usually she was in her own world, sometimes working half-heartedly on an assignment but often just staring absently into space.

She was a new arrival to the school. Most of the students came at the age of seven, some even earlier. By the time they were in grade five, this place was a second home to them. Susan had been living in Winnipeg and going to school there before she came here. I wasn't told why she had come, only that I was not to worry about her reticence. I was told that it was common behaviour when children first arrived and she would eventually grow out of it.

Residential school was a sea change for these children. I don't know how much was true, how much was hearsay, but I was told that they ran wild, without even a bedtime, before coming to Bear Lake. There was nothing they could not touch, no question they could not ask, no place they could not go. I couldn't imagine such a growing up, and the child in me envied their freedom. How lovely to be completely untethered by anyone else's belief in what you are capable of, to make mistakes without being told you're doing it wrong, and to learn the hows and whys of the world by experimenting with it yourself.

The nuns expressed no such envy. They thought it was shameful for children to be raised this way. The adult part of me could see their side of it too. It would be anarchy if we all grew up without rules, feeling that the world should fit us instead of the other way around. But Bear Lake, with a schedule to fit almost every minute of the day, was at the opposite end of the spectrum. The school's rule-bound world must have been a terrible shock to new students. I could understand that it would be a difficult transition.

Still, Susan worried me. It was now close to Christmas and she continued to sit in her little self-imposed bubble. Did she have any friends? Any family that was here too?

One day I asked her to stay behind after class. The children had been assigned a two-page history essay and she had not written a single word. I knew she was capable of something and I wanted to draw her out with some one-on-one time. The essay seemed like a good place to start.

"Why don't you write a story about your family?" I asked. "I'd like to learn more about them, and it would be an easy thing for you to write."

She looked at me blankly.

"Tell me about your family—your brothers and sisters, uncles and aunts. Tell me about your mom and dad. What did you do before you came here? Did you go to school somewhere else? Were you living on the trap line?"

She stared at me as though I had asked her to describe the trees that grow on the moon.

"Can you do that?"

I tried to be understanding. I was wading into unknown waters here. I knew next to nothing about this little girl. Perhaps her whole family had died in some terrible catastrophe and I was simply dredging up memories that were too horrible to contemplate.

I had left her alone the first few months after her arrival, hoping that she would warm to me and adjust to the system once she had been here a while. But I was getting impatient. Today, I was determined to make a connection. She seemed equally determined not to. She sat with her chin pressed to her chest, her arms crossed over her rough uniform, her elbows cupped in her hands—a posture that managed to be defensive but not defiant. I squatted down beside her desk and gently put my fingers under her chin to tilt her head up and force her to look me in the eye. I wanted to see her, to know what was going on behind those black orbs. What I saw made me reach out to hug her. When I did, she drew back. So instead, I picked up her pencil and wrote in her book.

"I will be kind to you."

She looked at me, said something in her native tongue, picked up the pencil and drew a big X through my words. She put the pencil down—her hand stayed on the desk beside it.

I took a breath, and exhaled slowly. She was a little bird; the wrong move would send her flying. This was the most communication I had had with her in the four months since she had first sat down in row two, seat four. My foot was in the door, and I was afraid it would be closed and locked for good if I did the wrong thing today.

I picked up the pencil again, a million possibilities running through my head. It had to be simple; it had to be clear. Her eyes were glued to my hand.

"I promise," I wrote, and put the pencil down beside her hand.

When I dared to look at her again, her gaze was still locked on the notebook, which lay waiting for her response. Our hands were now side by side on the desk, the yellow pencil between them, as formidable as a stone wall. When she didn't move to pick it up, I lifted my hand and placed it gently over hers. She let it lie there. I waited. The next move was up to her.

I felt, rather than saw, that next move. She lifted her head for a quick glance at me and I saw wet eyes, full to bursting, her tears about to spill. Such chubby, childish cheeks she had, such deep, sad, adult eyes. She slipped her hand out from under mine and stood up.

"My parents are at winter camp," she said. "Two brothers are here. My brother and sister, young ones, are at winter camp with Mother and Father, Grandfather and many family. The small ones, I hope they never come here."

She stared at the front of the classroom as she said this, then straightened her small shoulders and walked out the door.

I let her go, grateful for that one short burst of confidence and hopeful it would not be the last.

Anyway, I was unable to move. My beside-the-desk squat, which usually lasts a few minutes at most, was not a comfortable position. As soon as Susan was out the door, I sank gratefully to the floor to stretch my legs and let some blood flow back into my feet.

Such a simple decision.

"In here." The voice came from the hall just outside my classroom. It was a male voice, older, vaguely familiar. I strained to hear more so I could recognize it, while I wondered whether the pins and needles in my feet would let me stand.

Footsteps entered my classroom. It sounded like two, maybe three people. The male voice said something more, but quietly enough that I couldn't make it out. He didn't want to be discovered, that much was clear. As the door creaked shut I felt my heart pounding, and I no longer wondered if I could stand up, but rather, if I could stay concealed.

"No, please." These few words were delivered quietly, mindlessly, like a poorly performed line in a play. I recognized this voice. I had heard it just a few moments before—Susan.

"I'm not going to hurt you." Now they were inside the classroom with the door closed, the male speaker made no effort to keep quiet and I recognized his voice too. It was Brother Jerome, the high school maths teacher who had been tasked with taking over Jonathan's classes.

I didn't think. I stood up. Brave? Righteous? I wish.

"Brother Jerome, I thought I recognized your voice. Is there a problem with Susan? If she's late for anything I'm afraid it's my fault. I kept her after class for a little one-on-one. I hope that wasn't a problem."

Yes, that was all I said. No accusations. No threats of exposure. I gave Brother Jerome an out and I gave Susan nothing but a reprieve.

Despite my inadequate and feeble response, Susan looked at me gratefully while Brother Jerome struggled to regain his composure and come up with some plausible reply.

"She told me you had kept her, so I brought her back to verify her story. The sisters in her dorm were worried about her." His shoulders squared as his bluster shifted to authority, he was, after all, the senior teacher. "In the future, if you are going to keep a student after class, please ask one of the others to let the dorm sister know. It can be very disruptive if we need to go looking for someone."

"I do apologize, Brother Jerome. I'll escort her back myself and apologize to the dorm sister." I couldn't believe I had found myself apologizing to this man, but I wanted to keep Susan in my sights until he was well out of the way.

"No need," he said. "I'll see that she gets there."

"I'm sure they won't want a man up in the girls' dorm. It won't be a problem. We'll go right away so there isn't any more worry."

I hoped that I looked angry and authoritative, but as we swept past him, he looked anything but humiliated.

RUNAWAYS

The first time anyone ran away when I was at the school, I didn't find out about it until two days later, when the boys were brought back. There were three of them, two thirteen year olds and one fourteen year old. They managed to get all the way back to their home community near Kenora before they were picked up by the police. Upon their return to the school, they had their heads shaved, were given the strap, and for three days ate only bread and water at mealtime.

Humiliation and physical punishment were not enough to stop one boy though. The next runaway was a month later. Tommy, the eldest of the first three, took off a second time. A search party went out, the police were called and the people at his home were notified. Although rumours flew for weeks about his possible whereabouts, we never saw him again. After a while, it was almost as though he had never existed. No one spoke of him, and if Brother Peter or any of his other teachers worried about him, they didn't do so out loud.

It was mid-November when Tommy ran. It's cold in mid-November, and it gets dark early. It's also hunting season. Throughout the woods there are people with loaded guns. People who have often had too much to drink, who are hunting for everything from geese to moose and ready to shoot at anything that moves.

Brother Richard was always the first one sent out to search for runaways. He was the high school history teacher and the school's hunter. In the classroom, his patience was short, but in the woods he could sit for hours in the cold, waiting for an animal he was sure would come. He could spot the barest indentation in the earth, or a strand of hair caught on a branch, with almost instinctive accuracy. He was a good shot, too. If a boy got to grade nine and Brother Richard felt he showed the right aptitude he might be selected as a protégée. Brother Richard's protégées, like Brother Thomas's milking boys, would have been called prefects in the schools I went to. They were the elite.

One day, about two weeks after Tommy disappeared, I saw Brother Richard coming up the walkway from the woods, his rifle in hand. Belinda had just left to go to her music lesson with Brother Peter, and I was finishing up some marking. Brother Richard gave me a wave as he walked past my classroom window and a few minutes later he was standing at my door.

I had only seen Brother Richard at staff meetings, and he attended as few of those as possible. Like Brother Thomas, he tended to keep to himself. Unlike Brother Thomas, who was short and stocky, Brother Richard's head almost skimmed the top of the doorframe. With his broad shoulders and square jaw, he looked like the children's textbook drawing of Atlas, only without the world on his back. I don't know what life was like in monasteries or other places where monks live out their lives, but the school allowed space for men who needed a physical life. Their rugged skills were appreciated and their individuality given room to breathe.

"Hello, Mary," he said. "Am I disturbing you?"

"Not at all, Brother Richard. I could use a distraction right now. Come on in."

He leaned his rifle against the wall, and I pulled up a chair for him while he peeled off his coat, leaving it with his mitts and hat on one of the desks. He still wore his heavy weatherproof pants and the suspenders holding them up cut a wide swath down his flannel shirt.

When he sat down, he looked like a high school student sitting on a kindergarten chair.

"Well," he said, "I know this is a little odd, me coming in like this, but I saw your light and I thought I'd run something by you."

"I'm honoured," I said. And I was. I couldn't imagine what Brother Richard would want to run by me, but I was all ears.

"I grew up in the bush," he said, looking down at his hands. "It wasn't an easy life, but I loved it. It's my true church, my spiritual home."

He looked up at me for a moment, his weathered face daring me to find fault with this admission.

"When I was young," he continued, "my heroes were the men, and the women too, who didn't need a roof over their heads. The ones who knew how to find food and shelter with their bare hands, no matter the weather or the state of their own body. My parents taught us early, my two brothers, my sister and me. They taught us how to hunt, what plants are good for you and which ones aren't. I remember the first time I snared a rabbit," he grinned and sat up straight to face me again. "You would have thought I'd climbed Everest."

His shoulders spread out and back, his body squaring into an assured, confident posture. I could easily imagine a younger version proudly bringing home his contribution to the family pot.

"What do you think of bush skills?" he asked.

His direct look made me pause. While I knew what the wrong answer was, I wasn't sure about the right one. I had no idea what this story, or my answer, might have to do with whatever it was he really wanted to talk about, and I didn't want to put him off. I was also sure he would spot a dishonest answer as easily as a footprint in the snow.

"I admire anyone who can survive in the woods," I said. "I'd die the first day if I had to be out there, especially in this weather."

This seemed to satisfy him. He relaxed back into the chair, one booted foot slung over his knee, the melting snow forming a puddle on the wood floor.

"Let me tell you a story.

"One winter's day a few years back, I was out late. Darkness was coming on and I needed at least an hour for my return trip. I'd been tracking a moose, and I don't like coming back empty handed, so before I left, I walked a wide circle. I might not get anything today, I thought, but at least I could get a better lay of the land for the next time.

"I was about done my reconnaissance when I felt it. There was something wrong, something amiss. I stopped to stand awhile and assess the situation. It took me a minute or so to figure it out. I listened. Nothing. I looked around. Nothing. I relaxed a bit and waited some more. Nothing. That was when I figured it. There was nothing. No sound, no movement. No bird singing, or moving from one branch to another. No scurrying of some small animal running up a tree or into the snow. It's always quieter in the winter; there's less of everything. Fewer animals and birds, no leaves to let you know the wind is passing, no fish jumping, and no mosquitoes testing your sanity. But there's always something. An animal running away at the sound of footsteps, a bird or squirrel scolding from a tree top. Nothing wasn't right.

"I stood for a while longer, but the light was getting low and soon it would be too dark to see anything at all. So I took note of where I was and headed back to the school.

"I wasn't able to return to the spot until two weeks later. I went straight to the place where I'd noticed the strange silence, feeling a little foolish in broad daylight. There were lots of reasons the place might have been quiet, even simply my presence. I expected to find that it was just as noisy as everywhere else.

"It was. The intense feeling I'd had was nothing but a memory. When I stood in the same spot to listen and watch, a small bird fluttered from one tree branch to another, and a mouse skittered over the surface snow near my feet to the safety of another hole.

"But my instincts are good. I'm sure there'd been something that day. I let it go, and seeing deer tracks in the snow, I followed them for a couple of miles until I finally saw the animal in a thicket ahead of me. I stopped for a minute, as always, to say a quick prayer to St. Hubert before taking my shot." He glanced up at me and added, "St. Hubert's the patron saint of hunters. Not sure if I need a prayer, but it gives the animal a chance to run. It also gives me a chance to line up my shot, and it's better for both of us if my shot is clean and quick. He stayed, and my shot was clean. So I headed back to where I'd left my sled.

"I was almost there when I saw the prints. Human feet, clear as day in the snow. They weren't mine, and there are very few people who spend time in that part of the woods. They looked to be native prints, animal hide boots, and not too deep. But this was nobody's trap line, and most Indians around here use snowshoes in the winter. It was a curious thing, and I'm a curious man, especially when, as I have to admit, I consider this my bush. Who was here and why? And was this the reason for such quiet the last time? Had this unknown person been hiding a few feet from me while I stood in the cold? It was an unsettling thought. Vanity is a sin, but I must admit to some vanity when it comes to knowing my way around in the forest. If someone had bested me, I wanted to know who it was and why they'd felt it necessary to hide themselves.

"But again, I was hampered by my immediate responsibilities: there was a deer to bleed, gut and haul back to the school. Much as I would have loved to follow the prints to see where they led, I couldn't afford the luxury. I did, however, follow them a half mile or so to where they crossed the lake. There was nothing to see on the other shore, and there was no way I could cross the ice unseen, so I left it at that. I'd allow some time for a search my next trip out.

"The search for this mystery man became something of an obsession for me. Every time I went out I looked for him and when I wasn't out, I was plotting my next move. There's nothing like a challenge to make a man feel like a man. I never did find him and it wasn't long before any hint of his appearance disappeared. I think my snooping got him nervous and he left.

"Did you know we had a POW camp near here during the war?"

His question startled me. I was deep in the woods with his mystery man.

I shook my head. "No, I knew we had some in Ontario, but never where."

"The exact locations of most Canadian camps were kept quiet. But the people around here all knew. Some of the prisoners worked in the lumber camps, and it would have been easy for them to take off, but very few did. And if you ask anyone who worked with them, they didn't find them a bad lot at all. Worked hard, respected the rules. Still, every once in a while someone would escape, usually in the summer, and usually they were found and returned pretty quick. Even in summer it's not easy to survive in the bush, and those fellas didn't have much in the way of bush skills.

"Thing is, I figured that's probably who this was. A POW escapee. There'd been an escape a month before the day I felt that strange silence. Four guys had taken off. It was rare for anyone to try it in the winter. The cold makes it hard to survive and the snow makes tracking easy. Three of them were rounded up within a day, but the last one was never found. I think that's who my mystery man was. I never told anyone of my suspicions though."

He paused and shifted in his chair, planting both booted feet on the floor, his hands on his knees.

"What do you think of that? Would you have told someone?"

I didn't have to ponder this answer. "They're our enemy. Of course you should have told!" I couldn't believe he even questioned it. The lines were clear in my mind. This man might even have raised a gun against my brothers.

"Well," he said, standing up. "That's one way of looking at it. It was my first reaction too. I changed my mind, obviously. Might be you'll change yours. Think on it some. Like you, I admire a man who can live by his wits in the woods. He earned my respect, this fellow did. Yep, he knew his way around the bush."

He reached for his jacket and smiled down at me.

"I see it's time for vespers," he said, nodding at my big wall clock. "I hope my long-winded stories haven't taken up too much of your time. Let me know if you change your mind about the German. I find puzzling over moral dilemmas an interesting way to pass the time."

I walked Brother Richard to the door and watched him leave, as much of an enigma as when he'd arrived. His big boots slapped the linoleum floor of the hallway as he walked off, his jacket slung over one shoulder, his rifle over the other. Someone was on the piano in the gym; the classical notes a counterpoint to his rough and primitive appearance. How could bush skills be more important than loyalty to your country? How could a man of God hold such views?

The music filled the quiet hallway and drew me towards it. Whoever it was, they were very late tonight. Everyone else was at vespers or getting dinner ready. In spite of Brother Peter's admonitions, I often stood, unobserved, by the open door to listen. Like going to the symphony instead of listening to it on a record player, watching him play gave the music more power. Today, the door to the gym was closed, so I took a peek through the door's window. The piano was off to the left and I was surprised to see that Belinda was still at it. From my vantage point, I could just see her back and a sliver of her face. The tall form of Brother Peter stood a little to her left, behind her.

He moved his right hand as though to correct her fingering, but instead ran his hand down her arm and leaned in to kiss her neck. Or at least that's what it looked like to me. She stopped playing and sat stock still. Then, with his arms on either side of her, he played the piece himself. The notes sounded flat and monotone to my astonished ear. He picked up Belinda's hands and she resumed playing while he continued to run his hands along her arms and shoulders. Then he sat beside her on the bench, one hand on her lap, talking earnestly to her while she continued to play and I stared dumb struck through the glass.

When he turned and looked in my direction, I ducked, then slipped back to my classroom, closing the door behind me. What had I just seen? Was it really what it looked like? I didn't like Brother Peter, but I respected him. There must be some innocent explanation. And why did I feel like I'd just been caught with my hand in the cookie jar when he was one who needed to explain himself? I was torn between turning off my lights and pretending I wasn't even there, and walking into the gym to interrupt whatever was going on. I opted to close up my classroom and leave, but not at a run. As I walked towards the big front doors, the music filled the empty hallway, it's plaintive harmonies sitting uncomfortably on my shoulders.

What would Brother Richard think of this moral dilemma, I thought.

I didn't see Belinda again before her scheduled time with me on Monday. Although I watched her carefully, I didn't see anything different about her that afternoon. Perhaps I had just imagined what

I'd seen, misinterpreted some friendly gestures. Anyway, I wasn't sure this was something I wanted to get involved in. Belinda was no child after all. It might even be mutual, I thought. Although I knew I was only fooling myself with such possibilities.

The following Thursday, before her lesson, I asked her how things were going with Brother Peter.

"Wonderful," she enthused. "He's very talented. I'm learning a lot."

"I hear you practising quite late sometimes," I said meaningfully, watching her for some reaction. "You work hard at it."

"Oh yes, but playing the piano is so much easier than peeling potatoes! I'd much sooner be practising than doing kitchen duty." She smiled guilelessly at me and moved on. I left it at that.

November 21, 1947

B. Richard stopped by this evening. He doesn't stop by very often, but it's usually interesting when he does. Tonight was no exception. He thinks he's found signs of Tommy. He's seen some tracks in the snow, and yesterday he found a rabbit snare. He's going to leave some food out for him. He doesn't think the boy will survive the winter by himself. He thinks he'll find Tommy soon and he's hoping I'll help get him back to his family. We didn't even entertain the idea of returning him to the school. His plan is for me to feign some problem with the tractor to get Silas out here and then Silas can get Tommy home. Although what happens after that I don't know. They can't hide the boy forever.

He's a big man B. Richard. When he's in my little room I feel there's hardly enough space left over for him to turn around. He's got big opinions too. Views that don't always align with the church or the school, however moral they may be in his mind. I'm not sure I want to be a party to his deceit. On the other hand, if Tommy comes back, I'm afraid he'll wind up as another body in the backyard. I was going to get him on my milking team next year, but I guess he couldn't wait that long. I'll see what I can break on the tractor. At least then I won't have to lie about needing a mechanic.

B. Richard had another interesting little tidbit to pass on. Seems he spent some time talking to Mary and he's decided she's a good egg. Since she knows Silas, he thought she might be included in the plot if we need her. I'd prefer to keep Mary out of this, good egg or not.

Simon spent some time in my office this afternoon. He came by after the milking and just sat playing solitaire. He gets lonelier by the day. Hockey will be starting soon and I'm going to talk to B. David and see if we can't get him on the team. He badly needs an outlet other than a lonely game of cards.

November 27, 1947

Well, we did it. B. Richard found Tommy's shelter. I got Silas here and he and B. Richard went out together. They left well after dark, so I trust they made it undetected. When Silas came back he didn't have Tommy, but he said that it looked like the boy was doing well, and not to worry, he would take over from here. He seemed genuinely grateful for what we had done. I wonder how that balances the anger he must feel for all that we did first to make Tommy so desperate to leave.

DECEMBER
1947

THE PAGEANT

December took me by surprise. Back in October, after Jonathan left, and before Frank came into my life, each day crawled past. But as my personal life became more exciting, and as I got into the rhythm of the school, the time flew by.

December at Bear Lake Indian Residential School was consumed with preparations for the Christmas pageant. I was told that "The Pageant," as everyone called it, was the highlight of the school year. The audience included parents as well as special guests from town. Each class at school had some role to play, but top billing was given to the nativity play. The play was performed by the best students, who were, unfortunately, not necessarily the best actors. However, those in the nativity play went to town for a performance at Our Lady of Peace Catholic Church: a privilege worth working for.

Except for Shirley, who was invited to play a shepherd in the nativity play, our part in the pageant was limited to the singing of "Silent Night" and "Away in a Manager." My voice was never going to win any prizes, but if my childhood piano lessons hadn't made me into a musician, they had at least given me a tolerable ear. I knew a flat from a sharp, and when we started, we were terribly flat. But I had a secret weapon in my class, and once Belinda stepped in, we never looked back. In the classroom, the threat of not being allowed to go with her to practise brought everyone into line immediately. In the gym, the threat of being sent back to the classroom gave Belinda the ammunition she needed to manage the energy level.

One unexpected treat for me, as a result of the pageant, was meeting some of my students' parents. Silas, and one set of parents came from Bear Lake, two other sets came all the way from Kenora. Two fathers also came from a reserve near Red Lake, a two-day trip for them. They apologized that their wives couldn't come, but it was the reason they couldn't come that disturbed me.

They couldn't get a pass.

"A pass? What kind of a pass do you need?"

"To leave the reserve, you need a pass." Donald's father told me.

"How do you get a pass?"

"The Indian Agent gives it to you."

"The Indian Agent? Who's the Indian Agent?"

"He's the guy who runs the reserve. I gotta find Donald. Nice meeting you." And he was gone.

It wasn't until the concert was over and school finished for the term that I got a chance to pursue the question of the Indian Agent.

According to Brother Thomas, the Indian Agent, despite his title, was not an Indian. He was a government representative who administered the reserves in his area. He was also responsible for enforcing the rules of the Indian Act on the reserves. One of his responsibilities included making sure that no one left their reserve without permission—proof of which was a written pass from the agent. The pass stated how long you would be gone and why you were leaving. It seemed that humiliation and punishment as a method of control was not confined to the residential schools.

In the flurry and excitement of pageants and holidays I didn't realize that Belinda wasn't going home for Christmas until the day after the students had left and we were tidying up the classroom together.

"What will you be doing this time next week, Belinda?" I asked her.

"I'm not sure, Miss Brock. Probably getting dinner ready."

"Do you have any young ones in your family? I love Christmas with the little ones. They get so excited about everything. I love it when there's someone who believes that Santa comes in his sled."

Belinda looked at me quizzically, her head tilted.

"There's no Santa here," she said.

"What do you mean?" I asked. I was sure I'd made a terrible faux pas. Her family was too poor for presents or her family's traditions didn't include Santa.

"Well, some of the nuns try to make it feel like a regular Christmas. Sister Maureen puts up a tree. The music is wonderful, and the food is the best we'll eat all year. But it's kind of a sad day. When I leave this school, I intend to make Christmas as grand as I possibly can!"

The last bit went right past me. "You're not going home for Christmas? Why ever not?"

"My community is on the Bay. It's too expensive to go back and forth. They only provide transportation at the beginning and at the end of the school year."

"Oh Belinda," I said, "that's terrible!"

"Oh don't worry, Miss Brock. It happens every year. I get through it."

When I heard that Belinda was going to have to stay at the school for Christmas, I decided to ask my parents if she could come home with me. My parents could afford the train fare, and we had the space.

But they refused.

They gave all kinds of reasons. Christmas was family time, she'd feel out of place, what about all the other kids left behind, it would create jealousy and problems for her when she came back, she'd be embarrassed not being able to provide presents and so on. Their objections dismayed me.

I've been told that the best way to find out about someone is to see how they behave when they have a choice between the high road and the easy road. My parents failed the test. I was expecting something different. So I didn't invite Belinda to come, and she stayed at school. Perhaps everything would have turned out differently if she had come with me, perhaps not.

At any rate, there was no sentimental journey for Belinda that Christmas.

December 20, 1947

Well, it's done. There are still a few students here, but most have gone home for the holidays. I love this time. No farm work, no children, just time to catch up, time to reflect and time to pray. My troubled Simon has gone home. I hope it gives him some relief from whatever is ailing him. Roger is staying, so at least I have one milker and I won't have to do it all myself. The tractor needs some repairs and Silas has promised he'll come by and teach me some of the basics. I never thought farming would mean learning to be a mechanic. I'm glad we still have the horses, and some need of my old skills.

Our Lady of Peace is having a movie night after Christmas and we've been invited. Mother Magdalene and I have decided that we're going to bring the children that are here with us into town with the hay wagon and the horses. They'll love it. So will I!

B. Richard stopped in just before dinner. Silas has Tommy. He's lost some weight but is none the worse for his adventure. Silas will try to get him home during the holidays. I think everyone has stopped looking for him, so he'll be safe until September anyway. B. Richard says there may be some relatives in Winnipeg he can live with. Then he'll be able to go to a regular day school. I hope he doesn't stay out of school altogether. Although I can't say I'd blame him if he did.

The train schedule denied me a quick get-away. School finished on Friday but the next train south wasn't until late Sunday, so I used the weekend to visit Annie and Silas.

Walking to Silas's house, I felt anxious about breaking my agreement with Mrs. Norton. Silas and I would often meet at the restaurant for a cup of tea on Friday after he finished work, and initially Mrs. Norton made a point of telling me every time someone saw the two of us together. But she hadn't mentioned his name for a while, so I took this to be an easing of her misgivings about our relationship. Besides, after all my trips to Annie's, I knew how to get there without being seen by her busybody friends. With all the work on the pageant I hadn't seen Silas for a couple of weeks and I was looking forward to catching up before I went home to Toronto.

When he opened the door, I expected to see delight. Instead, he looked a little put out. I hesitated, but he invited me in. When I went to hang up my coat I was startled to see a small coat on one of the hooks, and below it, a small pair of boots.

"My nephew is visiting," Silas said. "He's out of school for the holidays."

I looked at him; there was something he wasn't telling me, but I didn't know why he would feel the need to lie. I couldn't help it. I pushed. His coat and boots were here, so this mystery boy must be as well.

"Another nephew? Is he Mark's cousin? Where is he? I'd love to meet him."

"He's asleep. He had a long night last night. Nightmares. Kept us both up until early morning."

I wanted to ask why he was doing this, but I didn't have the nerve. Silas moved to put on some tea and we had an awkward, short visit, his mysterious "nephew" clouding the air between us.

I left shortly before lunch and went straight on to Annie's. The going was slower in the snow, but I loved every step, taking in the beauty of the forest's winter transformation. No partridge warned of my arrival, but Annie had freshly made apple bread cooling on the table. She said she had a "feeling" that someone was going to visit. I was delighted with this enthusiastic welcome after my uncomfortable visit with Silas.

This time she taught me a lesson just by being who she was. When I was making the tea I dropped her little brown teapot, the one her handsome Henry had given her. I watched in dismay as brown pieces of pottery scattered in all directions, the larger ones landing at my feet. The tea made a dark stain across the floor as I stared in mute horror.

She looked at me and said, "The broom's in the corner, the dustpan is with it."

When I tried to apologize she cut me off. "The teapot held memories. But it's a thing. Things go. Memories don't."

After breaking her teapot, my hurt feelings over Silas's secret visitor felt like a petty indulgence, but I told her about it anyway. She asked me why I felt I had to know the story of the mystery nephew. It was a good question. She always had good questions for me.

"Because friends share things. They don't hide things from each other."

"So," she smiled, "you've never kept something from a friend?"

"No!" was my immediate answer. She didn't say anything, just looked at me with a barely suppressed grin. "Well, yes. I suppose so, but only if I thought the information might hurt their feelings."

"Do you trust Silas as a friend?"

"Yes! Of course! That's why I can't understand this. Why doesn't he trust me?"

"Maybe it's you who needs to trust him, Mary."

It wasn't until my walk home, when I had some time to reflect, that I understood what she meant. It made Silas's behaviour a bit easier to accept, but not much. I had no idea what he felt he was protecting me from, or even if that was what he was doing.

Ironically, I had knitted a tea cozy for Annie as a Christmas present. Before I left, I gave it to her with a promise to get her another teapot when I returned. She laughed at that and we talked a bit about holidays, traditions, and gifts. She walked me out onto the porch as I was leaving and asked me what gifts I had received that day.

I felt proud to be able to list off a few: a free day to visit her, apple bread, the beauty of the woods, lessons about the value of things and memories and friendship. Her eyes twinkled behind her wire-framed glasses, "Those are wonderful gifts. Now, how will you give your thanks?" That was the thing about Annie, just when you thought you had the lesson learned, it turned out there was more.

CHRISTMAS
IN TORONTO

Belinda was the last thing on my mind when I stepped off the train in Toronto. I was home! My parents and brothers were there to greet me under the high, vaulted ceiling of Union Station. The walls echoed with the sounds of a band playing Christmas carols and families reuniting for the holidays.

Toronto took Christmas seriously. Shop windows were emptied of manikins dressed in the latest fashions, and replaced with elves and reindeers. Toy trains ran on tracks through idyllic winter scenes, snowmen bowed and wooden Santas ho-ho-ho-ed. At the major department stores the "real" Santa took present requests and posed for pictures, to the delight of adults and bright-eyed children. The cold gave everyone rosy cheeks and decorations were everywhere. Coloured lights hung on trees in public places and festooned houses and front yards. Salvation Army bells rang on every corner and stores were crowded with shoppers. There was an energy and excitement that only a big city can create.

At home, my old life welcomed me back with open arms. Our tree was in its corner by the window where it had been every December as long as I could remember. Boxes of decorations sat beside it, awaiting my arrival. Sparky gave me a hero's greeting, barking and leaping with joy as soon as I crossed the threshold. Walking into my bedroom of muted browns and greens was like finding a budding forest in January. My mother had my favourite beef-barley soup simmering on the stove and the aroma opened up warm memories as it drifted through the house. I was home.

The holidays were filled with friends and family. At first, the familiar food and treasured traditions gave me a gratifying sense of security and happiness. I was comfortable in this world. I fit in here. But as my need was sated, I found that some, as yet undefinable part of me, had changed, and a gnawing discomfort began to grow.

Conversations with my friends centred around boys. The boy conversation was different for our generation. There were many boys who never returned home from the war, and many of those who did came back with things missing: arms, legs, sight, hearing. And then there were those who returned with things added: alcoholism, nightmares, hair trigger tempers, moodiness, depression. As hard as it was for the young veterans, for young women it was also a trying time. The pool of eligible men had shrunk and the quality of those left in the pool was diminished. The boy conversations were needed and important, but they seemed endless. When I tried to talk about my experiences in Bear Lake, beyond an initial curiosity, nobody really cared. I was wasting my time if I hoped to engage my friends in the issues of residential schools. They had other things on their minds.

Christmas passed, then came a lonely New Year's Eve. I missed Frank. He may not have been perfect, but he understood me a lot better than the frivolous girls and mixed-up boys I had returned to in Toronto. My parents tried to understand. They indulged in my diatribes about the need for change in residential schools but they showed no interest in helping me do anything to challenge the status quo.

As for me, I found it difficult to articulate the profound dissonance between what I believed was the way to raise a child to become a confident and contributing adult and the way the children were being raised at the school. I could talk about wet bedsheets and straps, but I didn't know how to make my friends and family see the burden of being told, over and over again, that who you were, your culture and your history, the very foundation of your sense of self was useless, or worse, evil. I could find no way to impress upon my skeptical audience that what these children were given to replace their parents and family was a sense of hopelessness.

This was the first time that I had even tried to put into words the intangible nature of the issue. The complete lack of experience that anyone in my circle had of being on the other side of mainstream made it difficult for even the most interested and understanding to comprehend the damage done by the insidious worm of bigotry and superiority.

Imagine if even one percent of the people who crossed your path did not think much of you—and let you know it. What if, once or twice a week, someone said something demeaning to you? What if it happened once a day? What impact would that have on you? What kind of an adult would you be if, almost every day of your growing up, you had someone tell you, implicitly or explicitly, that you didn't make the grade? The fact that some of the children under my care grew to be responsible, caring adults is nothing short of astounding.

I had hoped, that with the support of my family and their influential circle of friends, I could affect some change from the outside, since it seemed impossible to do anything from the inside. My Christmas trip home made me realize how hard that was going to be, and how truly isolated Bear Lake Indian Residential School was. By the time I got on the train in Union Station for my return trip, leaving my fancy boots and coat behind, I was more determined than ever that, if nowhere else, at least in my classroom, things were going to be different.

JANUARY
1948

JANIE

The new year began with a bang. Well, not a bang really, more of a gentle but unstoppable wave. Like the first snowfall in October that left me with my car in the ditch, this quiet storm was pleasant and unassuming, but persistent. Beautiful snowflakes fell, and fell, and fell.

It started soon after lunch on our first Monday back in class.

I barely noticed it, as arithmetic, then art, filled my afternoon. By the time the children had left and I had done my marking and prep work for the next day, it was dusk and the path to my car was covered with a load of fresh fluffy snow.

I considered my options. I could drive home, but I knew that the roads would be in no better shape than the driveway before me—too much for my car or my winter driving skills. I could walk home, or I could spend the night here.

I walked back to the big school building to check out the third option.

Mother Magdalene found me a nightgown and a toothbrush, and told me to talk to Sister Irene in the infirmary. There would be beds there.

The infirmary was a long room on the third floor, past the nuns' bedrooms. At the entrance to the infirmary, a consulting room had been partitioned off. It had barely enough space for a patient and the nurse, crowded as it was with a bed, a small desk and a large cabinet for supplies. In the infirmary itself, five beds lined each wall. White curtains that could be pulled around each bed hung limply from the ceiling.

At the far end of the room three big windows would normally have offered a view of the barn and the woods beyond, but when I arrived, the barest outline of the barn roof was all that I could see. The thick curtain of falling snow had laid a white blanket over the muddy paddock and dark woods beyond, leaving the world devoid of colour.

Two beds were already occupied. In one, by the windows, a young girl lay on her stomach, her head turned to stare out at the snow covered landscape. An older boy lay in the bed closest to the nurse's room. The nurse, Sister Irene, was at his side, wiping his face with a damp cloth. He was talking, but not in English. As I put my borrowed nightclothes on a bed, the boy began to writhe in convulsions. I stopped to see if I could help, but Sister Irene just shook her head, so intent on her task that she didn't even look up at me. After assuring her that I would bring her some food, I slipped out and headed for the dining room.

The silent meal was lightened by the unexpected treat of fruitcake for dessert. It wasn't until I had eaten almost all of mine that I noticed none of the children had any. The lump in my throat made the last few bites more difficult to swallow, but the rest of the staff ate on, seemingly unperturbed.

When I returned to the infirmary, bringing some food for Sister Irene, the boy seemed to be better. He was sleeping, and she was at her desk where she could keep an eye on him. The little girl was sitting up and staring out the window into the dark.

"Thank you," said Sister Irene. She looked exhausted.

"Is he better?" I asked.

"Sleep is one of the best remedies for any illness," she said. "I think he'll be fine. You never know how someone will react to a high fever. Sometimes it looks scarier than it really is."

"Why is the little girl here?"

"She has a bad burn on her back. Hot water was spilt on it while she was working in the kitchen. It's quite serious and I don't want her out running around until it gets better."

"She looks very lonely."

"She has an older brother at school. He visits when he can. Last night he snuck in during the night and I woke to find him fast asleep beside her. Fortunately, I'm always up early so I made sure he got back to his dorm before the wake-up bells. It's better for both of us if he avoids detection!" She smiled fondly at the small shape at the end of the room. "Her brother sometimes works in the barn, so she likes being close to the window to see him come and go. She adores him. It reminds me of my own admiration for my sister."

She stopped to look up at me, "My name was Elizabeth before I became a nun. The practice seems to be changing, but when I took my vows we were expected to take on a religious name. I took Irene, my sister's name. It warms me to see the affection between this little girl and her brother."

It warmed me to find someone who was willing to bend the rules. I left her with her meal and her charges, and went to help with study hall and bedtime. I didn't often get to see my students outside the classroom, so I was looking forward to this unexpected opportunity. Study hall was as silent as dinner time, but things changed when I went with the girls to their dorm to help with bedtime.

The time between study hall and lights out was short, but the children, under Sister Maureen's relaxed vigilance, came alive. The school discouraged siblings from connecting with one another, but here in the dormitory, sisters had a chance to spend some time together. It was interesting for me to see the students I knew well in this environment. Belinda was one of a tightly knit group who talked earnestly among themselves. Janice was bubbly and almost loud with her circle of friends and loud-mouthed Ruth was entirely captivated by a Nancy Drew mystery. Sister Maureen let them socialize for a while, then gathered the younger ones for a story. The older girls were allowed to stay up a half hour longer. I left after the little ones went to bed.

Back in the infirmary, the girl looked as though she hadn't moved, and the boy was still asleep. Sister Irene got up from her desk to say hello.

"How is he?" I whispered. Nodding to the bed where the boy lay.

"Better. He hasn't vomited for a few hours now and there haven't been any convulsions either. He seems to be on the mend."

"You must have a constant stream of patients here, with so many children at the school."

"It's not too bad. Most of the illnesses here are minor ailments like colds that can be dealt with in the dorms. They only come here when the nuns or brothers can't cope. Sometimes there's nobody here at all."

"How's the little girl?"

"The only time I've heard her talk is when she's with her brother. She never complains, never a moan or a tear. I've tried to draw her out, but she's new and I'm not sure how much she understands. I've often thought of trying to learn Ojibwa. It would be useful. When children are sick they need something familiar."

She looked pensively at the little one who was sitting like a statue on her bed.

"May I?" I asked, nodding at the small figure.

"Be my guest."

She smiled, a tight lipped, not-quite-a-smile smile, with a tilt to her head as though she were thinking of offering a different answer.

"Her name is Janie."

When I sat on Janie's bed, the only acknowledgement was a slight drawing in of her shoulders. At close quarters she looked familiar but I couldn't place her.

"Would you like me to tell you a story?"

I didn't expect a response, and got none, so I just started in. The first story that came to mind was "Little Red Riding Hood" which I related with great relish and to which I received no reaction from my captive audience.

When Little Red Riding Hood and her grandmother were safely home with Mommy and Daddy, Sister Irene came over to tell us it was time for lights out. While she checked the dressing on Janie's back I went into Sister Irene's cramped office to change into the flannel nightgown Mother Magdalene had found for me.

On the desk, a letter lay open. Despite my misgivings, I found it impossible to leave it unread. The lives of the nuns and the brothers outside the school were a mystery to me. Where had they come from? What drew them to a religious life? Why here? My curiosity got the better of me.

"Dear Elizabeth," it read. "Mother is getting worse, I'm not sure she'll last until spring. Surely you can request a few days off! She asks for you constantly and it breaks my heart to tell her you can't come. Theodore has come from Saskatoon, and of course Suzanne has been a saint. So it is the lost sheep she longs for now. Please, do what you can.

"Your loving sister,

"Irene"

A gentle tap at the door brought me up with a start. I dropped the paper back on the desk and opened the door.

"Sorry," Sister Irene said, "I don't mean to rush you, I need some ointment for Janie."

As she moved past the desk to the medicine cabinet, she slipped the letter into a drawer.

I don't usually say prayers before bed, but it was customary here, so before I got under the covers I knelt and prayed for stoic little Janie and for the boy who was recovering under Sister Irene's care. I added another prayer for Sister Irene and her mother, and with a twinge of guilt, a plea for forgiveness for me.

The snow fell all night, and was still falling when I woke again to the sound of a very loud bell.

I sat up, startled, thinking it was the fire alarm, but it stopped as my feet hit the cold floor and I remembered—wake-up bell. Both beds were quiet, and there was no sign of Sister Irene.

I padded down the hall to the washroom and changed in one of the stalls, shivering in my bare feet and squirming to find room to dress in the tiny space. From the toilet seat to the taps, everything I touched was icy cold. I was grateful to finally put on my shoes and get down to the dining room for some warm breakfast.

Thankfully there was no one with a wet bed sheet that morning, but once again, there was a discrepancy between food offered to the staff and what the children ate. Everyone was given oatmeal porridge but each of us at the staff table got an egg: none of the students did. Neither the students nor the teachers gave any indication that this was an issue, and it was the students who served us our food.

The snow continued to fall throughout the morning in a constant curtain of white. It muffled any song a chickadee might have been brave enough to sing, and turned trees and fences into objects of wonder, as tall and taller piles of snow balanced precariously on branches and fence posts.

By mid-afternoon the first patch of blue sky made an appearance. With only an hour left in the school day, I risked the wrath of Mother Magdalene and bundled up my students to go outside to enjoy the delights of the fresh snow. Perhaps Sister Bea thought I had permission, because about fifteen minutes later she and her class appeared. Within a half hour, just about all the elementary school students were out in the playground. Boys and girls together, laughing as they tried to make snowballs out of the fluffy snow, competing to see who could make the biggest snow angel, and playing tag in the deep powder. In one group, the children were enchanted by simply throwing handfuls of snow over their heads. When the bell rang to signal the end of the school day, we lined them up to go back inside and start their chores. It was then that I noticed Mother Magdalene standing at her window.

She was smiling.

The roads remained impassable, so I spent a second night in the infirmary, and had a second silent supper.

In the infirmary, the young boy had gone but Sister Irene was worried about Janie. Her wounds had turned a deep red, and the colour was spreading across her back. She needed to go into town and see a doctor, which wouldn't be possible until the next day at the earliest. Sister Irene fretted over the best way to keep her stable, doctoring her as best she could. The silent girl of the previous night now writhed and moaned, unable to find a comfortable position. Janie was cold without covers, but in unbearable agony when anything touched her back. We tried to bathe her, but that was painful too.

I spent the early part of the night waking intermittently to her moans. Sister Irene sat on her bed, and at some point in the night I noticed that her brother had arrived.

I awoke the next morning before the wake-up bell and realized I'd had a few hours of uninterrupted sleep. Sister Irene was no longer at Janie's bedside but I could see the form of her brother lying beside her. Glancing at my watch I was relieved to see that it was still a half hour before the wake-up bell so I went down to Janie's bed to wake him and get him back to his dorm.

He wasn't asleep, and I was surprised to see that Janie's brother was my Bobby. That was why Janie looked so familiar. She was the little girl that Bobby waited for by the fence at recess.

Bobby lay with one arm slung protectively across his sister's frail body. His eyes were red with tears.

"Bobby," I whispered, "you have to go back now. The bell will be ringing soon."

"No," he said. "I'm staying here."

I heard Sister Irene's soft footsteps behind me and turned to her for support.

"It's all right," she said. "He can stay."

She sat on the bed and placed a hand on Bobby's head, as though in benediction.

They were a silent threesome, Bobby, Sister Irene and the small, still form of Janie on the big bed. A horrible thought stopped me from protesting this further. It couldn't be. But when the wake-up bell rang it's loud and strident call and nobody moved I sat down beside them in despair. No! It couldn't be. It couldn't be.

But it was.

The infection that had given Janie so much pain had been too much for her small body and she had died in the early hours of the morning.

"I never thought she was that badly off. I would have insisted that we find a way into town if I'd even dreamed she was that badly off." Sister Irene looked at me with eyes that asked for forgiveness, for understanding.

"Of course you would have, Sister Irene. You take wonderful care of the children. They know that too. We all would have worked to find a way to get her into town. It's not your fault. It's nobody's fault."

They may have been the right words, but they didn't help. Her face was ashen and she clutched her rosary with white-knuckled force. She turned back to Bobby, who was sitting up, his small shoulders hunched as he stared at his sister, her tiny body barely perceptible under the white cotton sheet.

We all stared. A hushed group, devastated by the unexpected horror of Janie's death.

The silence was shattered by a voice that was even more strident than the wake-up bell.

"Robert Martindale! What are you doing here? You are not allowed here at this hour!"

Sister Irene stood up to block Brother Francis in his march down the row of beds. He pushed past her, and in a breach of etiquette serious enough to stop him in his tracks, she grabbed his arm.

He stood six feet tall to her diminutive five foot two. Towering over her he glared. Two breaches of the rules already, and he had barely entered the room.

"That's his sister on the bed. She died last night."

Brother Francis had the decency to sag, just a bit, and his face softened, just a bit. But it wasn't enough.

"He has to join the others for breakfast. There's nothing he can do now."

"Nothing he can do for her. But he needs some time."

"It will do him no good to sit and stare at his dead sister. He needs to get back into his routine, especially now."

"Especially now he needs some time with his sister. He won't get another chance. You know he won't."

Brother Francis looked at Sister Irene, a moment of indecision crossing his face. But it quickly disappeared, and he returned to the resolute assurance with which he had entered the room.

"Bobby, get up off the bed and come with me. Your sister is with God and the angels now. There is nothing more you can do for her."

January 8, 1948
The new year has started off badly. A little girl died yesterday. Her parents came to get her body today. The story is that hot water was accidentally spilt on her back while she was working in the kitchen, and because of the storm she couldn't get into town for proper medical help. But if the truth is told no where else, it will be told here. The hot water that landed on her back was a punishment. It came from S. Claire. The little girl was supposed to be helping wash pots in the kitchen and she was found playing with the soap bubbles. S. Claire grabbed a pot off the stove and dumped its contents onto her. I don't know if she chose her weapon consciously or if she just took the one closest at hand. I want to give her the benefit of the doubt and assume that she didn't think before she acted. Not that that absolves her of cruelty beyond measure.

I know all this because B. Dominic was passing the kitchen and saw it. It happened on Friday. She didn't go to the infirmary until Saturday. I can't imagine S. Irene making her stay in the dormitory, but I don't know that part of the story. I didn't even know the above until today. B. Dominic hadn't thought much of it and it wasn't until he heard of her death and made the connection that he felt the need to talk to someone about it. I told him to tell Father James, but I don't know if he will. I wonder, does S. Claire feel any remorse? Does she feel the little girl deserved it? Or does she just chalk it up to bad luck? Will she do things differently next time? I wish I could confidently say yes.

FEBRUARY
1948

LOVED & LOST

The first weekend after the big snowfall I went to visit Annie. I needed to talk to her about Janie, and I was also eager to talk to her about everything I had become aware of during my time in Toronto. In my bag I carried my yellow teapot, wrapped in bright Christmas paper. I had been tempted to buy a new one, but I thought she would appreciate the sentimental value that came with this one, so like my grandmother's. The snow on the trail was untracked, so I wasn't surprised to find her cabin empty. It looked like she hadn't planned on being gone for long, though. There was plenty of wood stacked up outside, and inside it was as though she had left yesterday. The sugar bowl was on the table, there were cans of food on the shelves, her clothes were neatly folded, and her bed made. The only thing missing was Bartholomew. Disappointed, I left my package on the table with a note to say I would be back soon.

I returned twice more in January, and again in early February. The first time I added to my note; the next time I wandered the area, horrified by the thought that I might find her frozen body halfway to the outhouse. The last time, when I saw the still untouched snow leading to her cabin I almost turned around. But I kept going anyway, went inside and knelt by her bed for a quiet prayer. Maybe she would return in the spring.

Silas and I met at the restaurant for tea most Fridays. I loved my conversations with him, but despite my protestations to Annie that friends tell all, I had not told Silas about Annie. She was my special treat and I liked having her to myself. But after my last visit to her empty cabin, I needed to know more. I asked Silas if he knew her and if he knew why she wasn't at her cabin.

"You know Kookum?" he asked.

"Kookum?" I said. "Maybe we're not talking about the same person. She told me her Indian name, but it was complicated, I don't remember it but I'm pretty sure it wasn't Kookum. She said most people call her Annie, so that's what I've been calling her."

"Animikiikaa, same person," said Silas. "Kookum means grandmother. She's not my grandmother, but she's like a grandmother—to lots of us. She lived here while her granddaughter was in the school, but she started drinking and wound up in Winnipeg. We didn't see her for a long time, until she came back with some white guy in tow."

"That's her," I said. "Have you seen her lately?"

Silas didn't answer my question. Instead, he responded with one of his own. "How do you know her?"

I explained my walk in the woods and our unexpected meeting and he nodded. "I wondered if that was you," he said absently.

"What do you mean?"

"She spoke about you," he said. Then he gave me that straightforward Silas look and said, "She's dead, Mary."

I stared at him for a long time, willing him to retract his words, as though that might change the reality. My tears fell quietly, no heaving sobs, just a sudden, overwhelming sense of loss.

He handed me a napkin. "She loved you, Mary."

All I could do was nod. I didn't want to open my mouth for fear that the heaving sobs might begin.

"She told me we would meet. Maybe you spoke to her about me, I don't know, maybe she just knew, in that way she had, that we knew each other. She wouldn't tell me your name, just the way you met. She said she'd never told you that she loved you, because you knew. But, she said, it's important to hear it. She told me to tell you when I saw you."

Silas left a few coins on the table and we stood up to leave. The waitress came by, looking at me questioningly. I tried to reassure her without words, but her eyes followed us as I walked out the door, Silas holding my elbow. He asked me if I wanted to go to his place, but I needed a walk and the cold air felt good. We went down to the park where Martin and I had sat on the swings so long ago. It was deserted now, but the swings still hung, waiting for spring and the laughter of children. Silas brushed the snow off the seats, and we sat and talked as darkness fell.

A few weeks before she died, Annie had cut her foot with an axe. She bandaged it up and medicated herself with the herbs she always had on hand and the wound healed well. Well enough that, a few days before Christmas, she made a trip into town for supplies. She spent the night with friends in Indiantown and went to a Christmas party that Silas also attended. Something they ate had spoiled and all nine people went to the nursing station the next day with food poisoning. By evening, eight were back home but Annie had gotten worse. It might have been her age, it might have been a lingering infection from her foot, but she died the next day. They took her body back to her cabin Christmas Eve and buried her beside her handsome Henry. Silas took Bartholomew.

Before we parted that day, Silas promised to take me in the spring to see Annie's and Henry's graves. I had been in Bear Lake for only six months, but already I had loved and lost.

BRIDGE

Mrs. Norton had one vanity. It was the first room on the right as you came in the front door. She called it her "parlour" and used it only for special guests and Sunday teas. The afternoon light made it bright and cheerful despite its uncomfortable faux-Victorian furniture. It was dusted and polished every Saturday, and one sure way to upset her was to replace the porcelain Corgi or the crystal astray anywhere but in their designated spot. The highlight of the room was Mrs. Norton's prize possession: her record player. I had brought a few records back with me from Toronto after Christmas in the hopes that I would be able to listen to them here. But after only one attempt, with Mrs. Norton sitting uncomfortably on the sofa beside me, I gave it up. I'm not sure what she expected to happen when "modern music" filled her parlour, but her uneasiness took all the joy out of it for me. I had to be content with my little table-top radio and scratchy CBC reception in my room to satisfy my need for music—except when Mrs. Norton went out, or when I knew she would be home late.

On those occasions, I would use her special room, being careful that everything stayed in its place. With "Peg of my Heart" on the record player, I would move with slow, graceful steps, my imaginary partner holding me tight. Sometimes I would throw caution to the wind, move the furniture aside and practise swing steps with Tommy Dorsey and his band.

On Fridays, Mrs. Norton played afternoon bridge at her church then stayed on for a potluck dinner. So on Fridays, I could indulge in this guilty pleasure. It was a wonderful way to transition from the school week to the weekend. She usually left me a portion of whatever she was bringing to the potluck and I would break all the rules: eating and dancing in her fancy parlour.

So I was surprised, and disappointed, one Friday to come home and hear her call my name.

"Helloooo Mary dearest," she said, as I came in through the kitchen door.

I stuck my head into the hallway and saw her in the middle of her immaculate parlour sitting at a bridge table. The other seats were occupied by ladies a lot like her: blue coiffed hair, bright flowered dresses, warm cardigans, and thick stockings. On their feet were the crocheted slippers Mrs. Norton kept handy for winter visitors.

Mrs. Norton smiled broadly as I appeared from around the corner. "Mary, you know Mrs. Makowski," Mrs Makowski nodded solemnly. "Mrs. Williams," Mrs. Williams was looking intently at her cards, but managed a nod too. "And Mrs. Standish." Mrs. Standish smiled even more broadly than Mrs. Norton and waved a cocktail glass in my direction.

It was then that I noticed a pitcher, half full with some pink concoction, the same pink that was in Mrs. Standish's cocktail glass. The pitcher was sitting on the coffee table, which had been moved aside to make room for the bridge table. Everyone but Mrs. Makowski had a glass at her elbow.

"So nice to have young people around the house!" said Mrs. Standish. "Mrs. Norton was just telling us what a pleasure it is to have you here. Gives her a reason to get up in the morning! Isn't that true, Edna?"

Mrs. Norton looked thoughtful. "I don't think I said it quite that way, but you are right about one thing, Flora, it is nice to have a young person about the house. Don't you think so, Mabel?"

Mrs. Williams looked up from her cards, "What was that? Young people? Nothing but trouble, I say. Now, where were we? I'm bidding two hearts."

"But you can't, Mabel! It's Edna's turn," said Mrs. Standish.

Mrs. Norton giggled. "Oh let her bid, I don't mind."

"But I do," broke in Mrs. Makowski. "There is no point in playing the game if we don't play it properly."

"Quite right," said Mrs. Norton. "All right then, I'll bid." She tried to look serious and collapsed into a fit of giggles. Mrs. Williams joined her.

"Oh dear," she said, "you can't take cards seriously or life just isn't fun anymore." And she went off into more gales of laughter.

Mrs. Makowski stood up. "You make me sick. All of you. If anyone brings anything other than tea next time, don't bother inviting me."

She plucked her purse from the collection on the coffee table, stormed past me to grab her coat and boots and walked out the front door, the blue crocheted slippers, like a mute reproach, left in the middle of the front hall.

Mrs. Norton sighed. "Mary," she said, "do you play bridge?"

"Only," I said, "to music."

Fortunately for me, Mrs. Norton had drunk enough to acquiesce and so, while I didn't get to dance, I did get to try my first Pink Lady. Whenever I hear Tommy Dorsey my mind returns to Mrs. Norton's parlour: my first cocktail, grand old dames and bridge.

BIRTHDAYS

The envelope, addressed to me in my mother's familiar handwriting, sat on the kitchen table awaiting my arrival. A card has a distinctive look to it, different from a letter, and Mrs. Norton pounced on me before I even had a chance to open it.

"Now why would your parents be sending you a card in February? Are you hiding a birthday from me?"

I looked at her in surprise. Of course, I knew the date of my birth, but in the whole time I had been at the school, not a single birthday had been celebrated, or even mentioned, and I had almost forgotten mine. I certainly didn't expect it to be celebrated.

"Well, not hiding it, exactly," I said. "I just never thought about it."

Inside the card was a cheque for fifty dollars, a huge sum. I couldn't think of what I would spend it on, but it was a warm feeling to get it and to know that somewhere outside, people were thinking of me.

I brought the card with me to school the next day and set it on my desk. The children were curious but it wasn't until they left for morning recess that Donny stopped to ask what it was for.

"Look at the front of it," I said. "What does it say?"

Laboriously, Donny deciphered the fancy script across the front of the card.

"Happy Birthday to a special girl," he read. "Who's the special girl?" he asked. "Whose birthday is it?"

"Me! It's my birthday."

"Oh."

"You sound confused Donny. What's confusing about that?"

"But—you're not a girl!"

I tried to meet his seriousness with equal gravity.

"Well, have you ever heard your grandfather call your father a boy?"

Donny gave this some thought.

"No."

"Well, often, to parents, you're always thought of as a boy or girl, even when you feel all grown up yourself."

"Oh."

"This card is from my parents, to wish me a happy birthday."

"Oh."

"When is your birthday Donny?"

"I don't know. In the summer sometime."

"Do you know how old you are?"

"Yes! I'm ten."

"But you don't remember when you turned ten."

"No. I think it must have been in the summer because when I came back I was in grade five and you're ten in grade five."

"Don't you have a party on your birthday?"

"A party? For my birthday? No. Do people have parties on their birthdays? How do you know when your birthday is? You're just a baby when it happens."

"Other people remember it for you, and when you grow older you remember it for yourself. For me, it's important to remember my birthday. Then I know when I am old enough to drive, or vote."

Donny looked at me in confusion. This was a lot to take in.

"Are you going to have a party?"

"I don't know. I suppose I could. Maybe we should have my party in the classroom."

I had no idea what problems this spontaneous idea would generate. At that point, all I knew was that it sparked Donny's interest, as little else had during his time with me.

"Will they let you?"

Would they let me have a party in my classroom? Why ever not? But this little boy was more in tune with the processes of the school than I was. Despite the constant constraints thrown my way, I still didn't get it, as was obvious by my next comment.

"I don't see why not, Donny. It would be fun."

Donny looked up at me, his eyes sparkling. If I was willing to take on the powers that be, he was willing to join me.

"I'm going out for recess now, Miss Brock."

And away he went, kicking off his shoes and practically jumping into his boots. He was in too much of a hurry to put on his coat before heading out the classroom door.

I was going to celebrate my birthday. It didn't seem like such a terrible idea.

When the children filed back in after recess the excitement was palpable. Even the girls knew about the birthday party we were going to have. So we spent a few minutes talking about birthdays. Only a few children in the class celebrated them, although at least half knew the date of their birthday. Some remembered parties before they came to the school. It was a struggle to keep them focused on lessons until lunch liberated them. I made them promise not to talk about the party until we had made our preparations, although I knew that, while they would try, it would be an impossible promise to keep. I needed some advice fast, before I got in over my head.

Brother Thomas had his head bent over a bowl of soup when I knocked on the door of his sanctuary.

"Mary Brock! I sense trouble when you come in the middle of the day."

"I brought my lunch, I hope you don't mind."

"As you can see I'm enjoying mine, so munch away. But before you fill your mouth with food, tell me what you're up to. We don't have much time."

I got right to the point. "I told the children that we'd have a birthday party in my class."

"Did you now?" he said, smiling. "You told the children that before you talked to anyone else? And whose birthday are you celebrating anyway?"

"Mine," I said.

"Well, first, allow me to wish you a happy birthday."

"Thank you."

"You're welcome." He paused, spoon in hand, while I took a bite of my sandwich. "Mary, when are you going to learn to think before you speak?" His spoon pointed to the ceiling. Was he imploring God to answer this conundrum? "This won't be allowed. I'm sure you know us well enough by now to figure that for one out for yourself. You tell me you want to gain some credibility here, but then you do things like this that only serve to undermine your goal."

He sounded frustrated, well, so was I.

"And what will be the excuses this time?" I asked.

"You've been here long enough. You tell me."

"Well," I said, "first there's the money. But the the children can make the decorations and I can bring a cake, so it wouldn't cost much."

He nodded. "Go on."

"I suppose if I had a party, then everyone would want a party and that could create problems."

"Good, Mary, you have learned our ways somewhat. What else?"

"I don't know, Brother Thomas. What else wouldn't they like? Aren't we supposed to be training them for the real world? The real world celebrates birthdays."

"We celebrate Jesus's birthday."

"Is that why they'd object?"

"I don't think so. It's mainly that it would create a whole new set of expectations and open up a can of worms that would be hard to close. We celebrate collective things here, like hockey wins, good harvests, Confirmation, Christmas, Easter, that sort of thing. Not individual accomplishments."

"I have an idea."

Brother Thomas smiled. "As we've discussed, your ideas are usually not the kind that are entertained here."

"How about we have one party to celebrate everybody's birthday?"

"Mary, what kind of discipline do you think you could maintain with a highly unusual birthday party going on?"

"It wouldn't be good."

"No, it most certainly would not. I don't hold out much hope for your idea, I'm afraid."

"You're probably right."

"I hear a 'but' coming."

"But I'm going to ask anyway."

"Asking first is always a good idea." He looked at me meaningfully, then bent to his soup.

That much was true. It never would have occurred to me when I first arrived that I would need permission to have a party in my classroom.

When I got back to the classroom after lunch I knew the word was out and I'd better get to Mother Magdalene's office before she showed up at my door. I tried to stem the children's enthusiasm by telling them that we needed to get permission first, and I had no idea what Mother Magdalene would think of the idea. This seemed to settle them a little, but I think they had more confidence in my salesmanship than I did.

"Aha," Mother Magdalene said when I walked into her office. "I thought you'd be showing up here. All right, tell me why you think you should have a birthday party when no one else celebrates them."

"Well," I said, taken aback by her forthrightness and glad I had thought of a few good arguments before showing up, "although it's not common practise, they do have parties in the rec room every once in a while. And, well, I don't know how much you've heard, so maybe I'll just start at the beginning."

I told her about the card and my idea of celebrating everyone's birthday at one party. She listened, which surprised me, I had come prepared to do battle. She asked a few questions, most of which I was prepared for, then she asked the one I was afraid would be my party's death knell.

"Mary, this is a small community. If I let this go ahead, what do suppose the impact will be on the other students who aren't getting a party?"

It's true. It was a small community. If my class got a party and no one else's did, it could create an undercurrent of discontent. Not because my class was getting something special—there were definitely favourites here. But by and large the community as a whole played by the same rules: a few parties a year—for Christmas, Easter and Queen Victoria's birthday—were the norm. Would the students start to feel that things were changing? Would I be opening Pandora's box with a birthday party?

"I thought you might bring that up and I've given it some thought," I said. "In grade ten they get to go to town once a term; in grade two they have a day with the students at Bear Lake Elementary. Perhaps this could be the special thing for grade five."

"An interesting idea, Mary. I'll think about it and let you know tomorrow."

The fact that she was even considering the idea surprised me. When I knocked on her office door after school the next day, I tried to keep my expectations low.

"Mary, I think your idea of a birthday party has some merit." My heart sank a little, I could hear the "but." "But I don't think a classroom party is a good precedent to set. I don't like the idea of using academic time for a party either. That said, I do like the idea. The students have very little here in the way of fun, and every child needs fun."

Mother Magdalene never ceased to surprise me.

"I've spoken to the church in town and they're willing to organize a party here, with a birthday cake for the students to enjoy. But, instead of doing it with just your class, we'll have two parties: one for the elementary school and one for the high school"

She sat back and smiled at me, waiting for me to smile back. I tried to.

"You don't look pleased, Mary. Why not?"

"I guess I was hoping for something a little more personal, smaller, so that each child could have a special moment. I don't see how you can do that with such a large group."

"It's true, you won't be able to. But this was the best compromise I could come up with. Do you have a better idea?"

Yes, I thought, you could force each teacher to have a party for their students. How horrible would that be? I'm forced to do things I don't like to do in my classroom all the time.

Instead, I said, "I don't want to sound difficult, but could we have an extra party for the elementary? One for the younger ones and another for the older ones? They have very different maturity levels, and that way there would be fewer children at one time."

"Mary, I'm asking a lot of the church ladies already with two parties. One more would be asking too much. They're going to bring a cake and some sodas to each—a very generous contribution on their part. To say nothing of taking up two of their Saturday afternoons."

Mother Magdalene had a way of making me feel like I was asking the sun to go backwards with what I felt were perfectly reasonable requests.

"I could make a cake for the older children. I could bring the sodas too." Then I got an inspiration. "I go to the Anglican church. I could ask them if they'd take on one of the parties."

"I don't think it's appropriate to ask the Anglicans to come to a Catholic school."

"I'm sure they wouldn't mind."

"If—and it's a big if—I decide to have two elementary parties, we will find a way to host them ourselves. It won't be necessary to involve the Anglicans."

I was disappointed, but the children were thrilled. Mother Magdalene appointed me organizer of the event and I passed this task on to the class. It was one of the most rewarding teaching experiences of my time there. Making decisions—over what games to play, or when we were going to sing "Happy Birthday"—became an opportunity for me to teach the art of debate. My arithmetic lessons were given real world applications when Mother Magdalene gave us a small budget. Even science took on more relevance, as we discussed what makes a cake rise.

A few days before the big event I got another surprise. We were going to be able to have two parties after all. The reason for this was that the church ladies no longer had to do a birthday party for the high school. They were going to have a St. Valentine's Day dance! This, in a place where the boys and girls were barely allowed to look at each other most of the year. Rumour had it that it was Brother Thomas's doing, but I didn't believe it. Maybe Brother David, or that rat Brother Peter. I couldn't think of a single nun who would be comfortable with it, and Mother Magdalene didn't even want a birthday party. She would never have endorsed a St. Valentine's Day dance! Not only that, but St. Valentine's Day fell on a Saturday that year, so it would be like a real Saturday night high school sock-hop!

February 9, 1948
Mary, Mary what have you done to me? I must have too much time on my hands these days.

Mary came by yesterday to talk about the birthday party and moaning that her beloved Frank wasn't going to be able to get to town for St. Valentine's Day. It's her first without a beau since she was thirteen! Well, it got me thinking and I talked to B. Peter, who surprisingly, thought it was an idea worth thinking about. A St. Valentine's Day DANCE. Yes, in big capital letters! We approached Mother Magdalene, because we wanted to hear her logic behind the birthday party. The hardest person to convince was Father James and it was Mother Magdalene who persuaded him. Once she's made a decision, she can be very persuasive. You'd never know she ever had any hesitations. The final argument, according to what she told me later, was that while it was possible that it might encourage romantic relationships, being a teenager meant that there were most likely crushes between students already. The dance would enable us to get a better idea of who seemed sweet on whom and to make sure that it didn't get out of hand.

So now the high school rec room is buzzing with the making of paper hearts and meetings about music and food. The older students are organizing it, and you can be sure it will be very well chaperoned. I hope that we are finally taking a small step into the modern world and out of the drudgery of wartime restraint. If nothing else, it gives us all a lift to see the students so happily engaged in something, especially at this dark and dreary time of year.

SOCK HOP

Mother Magdalene liked to see well-behaved children in her class-rooms. But, although she did her best to hide it, she had a soft spot. She liked to see happy children too. Those two criteria seldom come together at the same time, but with two separate birthday parties, keeping happy children from misbehaving was a lot easier, and I was able to indulge a little in making each child feel special. We spent part of our small budget on birthday candles so that each child got a piece of cake with his or her own candle. In addition, each child made a card for someone else, so everyone got their own birthday card too. I was delighted to be able spend two Saturdays playing Pin the Tail on the Donkey, and Duck, Duck, Goose. The only time the children weren't smiling was when their mouths were busy eating cake. The church ladies had brought special birthday napkins and I saw more than a few students wrap their precious candle in their napkin and tuck it surreptitiously into a pocket. My class got special mention at both parties for the work they had done in organizing and they were thrilled with the recognition.

There was some discussion as to whether or not I would be allowed to attend the high school dance. When I first heard about it, I went straight to Mother Magdalene to volunteer my assistance. The answer was a resounding, "No." I was told that this was a high school affair. But, despite their reservations, I was finally allowed to take part. My best guess is that I gained some level of trust with the success of our birthday parties. I was also very persistent. And, I could bring records.

I arrived early on the big day, hoping to be able to help the girls get ready and risking my delicate position by bringing some make-up with me. I was disappointed when I walked into the dorm to find the girls so completely engrossed in their own preparations they didn't even notice me. Despite their limited wardrobe—each student had two uniforms and one or two outfits from home—there was much decision-making going on as they swapped skirts and blouses, trying on and critiquing different combinations. In the bathroom, I saw some of the girls surreptitiously passing something that looked remarkably like lipstick. Their caution confirmed my suspicion that it was contraband, so I kept my own supply in my bag and went down to the recreation room to see if I could be of some help there.

The students had decorated as best they could with the resources they had, and the stark room looked festive. Red and white crepe paper streamers were strung around the room. Paper hearts of various sizes fluttered on the walls and a big banner over the basement windows proclaimed, "Happy St. Valentine's Day." There were a few tables decorated with paper flowers and placemats and on another, a bowl of punch was surrounded by small paper bags filled with popcorn. The punch was a deep red, with slices of orange floating on top—an extravagance in this place, especially in winter. The bowl itself was a utilitarian one from the kitchen, probably last used to mix bread. But, as befit its new assignment, the students had wrapped it in an old flowered tablecloth, the ends of which were tied in an enormous, jaunty bow.

Everyone arrived at exactly seven o'clock. The girls came in first and sat on the chairs that had been lined up around the perimeter of the room. They were followed by the boys who stood awkwardly, bunched up in two corners. It seemed that the organizers, while they had done a wonderful job of decoration, food and drink, had not given much thought as to how the evening was going to unfold.

Mother Magdalene, who had been standing along the wall behind the punch bowl took charge.

"Good evening boys and girls. This is a very special night. Our first dance here at Bear Lake Indian Residential School. Miss Brock has been kind enough to bring some of her records along, so we'll be able to enjoy some modern music." She let her gaze travel along the line of girls, and into the corners where the silent boys stood. "We want you to have fun, but I expect all of you to behave appropriately." She let another pause hang in the air before adding, "I'm sure I don't need to explain to you what that means."

Quiet nods greeted this inauspicious start to the big event.

"Miss Brock, would you be so kind as to put a record on the phonograph so we can get this dance started?"

I rushed to accomplish this unexpected task, and chose one that was neither too fast nor too slow, "Sioux City Sue," sung by Bing Crosby. It had been a record chart favourite a few years ago, so it wasn't too new either.

Nothing happened.

The boys stared at their newly shined shoes, and the girls looked at each other. Nobody moved. I couldn't blame them. How could they dance in front of the nuns and brothers who looked askance at brothers and sisters communicating? It was Brother Thomas, of all people, who saved the day. He whispered something to Sister Maureen who went over to the pile of records and pulled one out. When my choice ended, she put hers on the turntable and Brother Thomas clapped his hands for attention.

"Does anybody here know how to square dance?" he asked.

A few of the students put up tentative hands and Brother Thomas shook his head.

"Not enough of you," he said. "Here's what we're going to do. It's called the Virginia Reel. I need two lines: boys on one side, girls on the other, facing each other."

Once the students had themselves lined up, Brother Thomas explained the dance. Finally, Sister Maureen put the needle down on "Turkey in the Straw" and the Bear Lake Indian Residential School St. Valentine's Day dance got off the ground. Other than Sister Rachel, who spent her time with a yardstick, separating couples that she felt were getting too close, the rest of the evening went well, with one notable exception.

There were two doors to the recreation room, each with a staff monitor to make sure that no one went in or out without permission. Despite this precaution, two boys managed to get into the hall at the same time. No one noticed it until we heard the crash of a body slamming against the lockers which lined the hallway. Sister Agnes, a steely-eyed woman who was one of the door monitors, and Father James, went out to see what was going on. The rest of us tried, rather unsuccessfully, to keep everyone else dancing. When Sister Agnes came back in, she made a short announcement that there had been an altercation and the boys were being dealt with by Father James.

We decided to have the break at that point and the students were soon diverted from their whispered conversations about the fight by some surprises organized by the staff. Sister Maria, the head of the kitchen, arrived with a heart shaped cake decorated with cinnamon candy kisses and, once everyone was settled with their food and drink, Sister Irene and Brother Paul did a tap dance routine that had obviously been well practised.

By the time the last dance was announced the wooden embarrassment of the first song had been forgotten. For the grand finale, "Turkey in the Straw" went back on the turntable and everyone went back onto the dance floor, even Mother Magdalene.

THE MAN IN THE
PLAID JACKET

Despite my uncomfortable experience at Birling's Bar, I kept going back. In part, I suppose, because it's true that familiarity breeds contempt. The idea of coming face to face with a prostitute wasn't so frightening once I had done it a few times, and bad-boy loggers usually kept their hands to themselves and their mouths clean when they were around me. During the winter months, other than private parties, the two bars in town were the only places to go for entertainment, and both were crowded on the weekends. The "right" bar had good food and an atmosphere that allowed for quiet conversation. If you wanted anything else, you were bound to be disappointed.

Birling's Bar did not lend itself to quiet conversation. This was especially true when they had a live band. It was raucous and fun—and I had gotten much better at knowing when it was time to leave. If Frank was getting into his cups early, I was happy for him to escort me home and then return to drink to his heart's content. Once off his horse, my knight in shining armour never made it back up. But now that I was realistic about him, our relationship was easier.

Mrs. Norton didn't approve of my outings to Birling's, but when I asked for alternatives she couldn't come up with any. So, other than the occasional scowl when we went out, she took it in stride. Besides, she liked Frank a lot, and kept hinting at tying the knot. As far as she was concerned, at twenty-one, spinsterhood was just around the corner.

On cold winter nights, the bar was like a big, cozy living room. Cigarette smoke hung from the rafters and mixed with the smell of sawdust underfoot. Before the music started, the hum of conversation filled the room, punctuated by the click of billiard balls. If you got there before eight, you could have your first beer with a meal of stew or chili and a slab of home-baked bread. Occasionally an already-drunk and belligerent logger would cause a disturbance, but usually, in those early evening hours, it was a relaxed, friendly atmosphere.

The Saturday after St. Valentine's Day, I was there with Frank and some of his friends when things got uncomfortable. But it wasn't a logger, or even belligerence, that charged the atmosphere. We were sitting in a booth with a few of Frank's logger friends, our stew and beer on the table in front of us. The conversation was lively, then things went quiet. I was almost the last to be aware of it, chatting away until it seemed that my voice was the only one in the room. I looked over my shoulder to see what had caused the unexpected silence, and there stood Silas.

People stepped off the sidewalk to let Silas pass; men put protective arms around their wives when they saw his truck drive by. But I'd never seen him shut down a room before. I moved to stand up and greet him, but he had his eyes on someone else. I sat back down.

I had never seen Silas angry before. He took up more space in this mood, as though his pent-up rage had swollen him. The only person who hadn't turned to look at him was a man in a plaid jacket at the bar.

This man, his back a silent challenge, slurped his beer, then wiped his mouth on his sleeve, while staring vacantly at the row of bottles lined up along the wall across from him.

Silas waited.

We all waited.

The man at the bar slurped some more.

Whispers started, then voices. Gradually, people returned to their own conversations.

Silas became the tobacco shop Indian again. People walked around him to get in and out. The bartender ignored him

It took half an hour for the man to finish his drink and pay up.

When he turned to get off his stool, he nodded at the giant blocking his path and walked out the door. Silas followed.

I wanted to run outside to see what was going to happen, and I wanted to sit in my cozy corner and pretend that nothing was going to happen. No one offered to help the man in the plaid jacket. Was he a stranger? Was he someone no one liked? Or did Silas scare everyone so completely that they were all too afraid to step up?

Silence engulfed the bar at their departure. Soon after, I could hear the unmistakable sound of Silas's truck as it started up. When we heard the crunch of his chains as he pulled out of the parking lot, I was one of a rush of people who ran to the door to see what had happened.

There was nothing to see. The man in the plaid jacket was gone. Silas and his truck were gone. We all straggled back to our seats and the conjectures started.

By morning the story around town was that someone was soon going to find the body of the stranger with the plaid jacket, it was only a matter of time. There was talk of arresting Silas, but until there was a body, or a missing person's report, there was nothing the police could do.

Mrs. Norton was both horrified and thrilled that I could provide a first person account of the story. I was dying to ask Silas himself about it, but he stayed clear of me for a few weeks. When we finally met for tea, he said nothing beyond the fact that he had had a private matter to settle with the man, and all was now well. No body was ever found, and eventually the story faded away. Silas returned to his familiar place in town lore, with one more reason for people to keep their distance.

MARCH
1947

THE HAYLOFT

March 10, 1948

One week until St. Patty's Day. Around here there's not a bit of green to be seen on anything but our endless spruce trees. We haven't had many snowfalls since the January storm. But, except on the shovelled paths, we're still walking at least a foot off the ground. The sun feels a lot warmer though, and I pray for a few days of spring temperatures so that the cows can forage for food on their own. Our feed pile is getting low, and it will be hard to scrape together money for more.

This time of year always brings back sugarbush memories. St. Patty's Day was the height of the season. Daddy always let us have a sip of whiskey to celebrate, especially if it was a good year. No sugar bushing up here though—how I'd love some maple toffee. I guess I'll have to make do with a sip!

Above my head, the low, grey sky mirrored the grey snow underfoot. March was cold and damp, and even the idea of spring seemed overly optimistic. But on my way to the barn for a visit with Brother

Thomas, the clouds parted and for the first time in weeks the sun broke through.

After months of frigid temperatures, threatening clouds and arctic winds, there is nothing as welcome as spring sunshine. The winter sun can brighten a December day, but it has little impact on the cold air. A spring sun is different. When the warmth of spring sunshine touches your cheeks, it's like stepping into a hot bath. The promise of green grass and flowers lifted my mood immeasurably, despite the snow all around me, and I was excited to tell Brother Thomas about it. The noises coming from the milking shed made it obvious that milking hadn't finished yet, and I knew better than to disturb him there. Still, I was too happy not to share my joy, so I decided to leave him a note before going home.

As I approached the barn, I saw Brother Peter leaving, a few stalks of yellow straw dangling tenuously from his immaculate black trousers. He gave me a curt nod as our paths crossed, just outside the barn's big double doors. Crossing the threshold I saw, at the top of the ladder to the hayloft, Belinda Whitestorm.

Since the time I had seen Belinda and Brother Peter at their late piano lesson, I had kept an eye out for any other indications he was taking advantage of her. I had not seen or heard anything that could be construed as inappropriate, until now.

It's hard to climb down a ladder with dignity, but Belinda tried. She paused for a moment when she got to the bottom, brushing her school tunic free of straw. There was only one way out, and she walked resolutely to where I stood, rooted to a spot just inside the wide doorway.

In the short time it took her to cross the barn and reach the door, a memory I had kept locked away came rushing back. It hit my consciousness with such force it was as though I was living it all over again. That wonderful fort of my childhood in Uncle Floyd's barn was also the place where my innocence was lost.

One sunny August afternoon, when I was a fourteen, my cousin's friend asked me to show him the fort we had built in the barn. He was sixteen and handsome and I was thrilled by his interest in me. I set out immediately, worried that someone else might join us and spoil the fun of having him all to myself. We climbed the ladder up to the loft and walked over to the fort, side by side. He marvelled at how well hidden it was, but I hardly heard. His nearness made my whole body tremble. I felt light-headed and would have tripped had he not grabbed my arm to steady me. Instead of letting go once I was balanced, he took my hand and we went inside the fort together. On the one hand, this was better than I had expected; on the other, I could feel my stomach clenching. I had never been alone with a boy before and I knew I was out of my depth. Once inside the fort, he lifted my chin for a kiss and shocked me by putting his tongue in my mouth.

At the time, I knew almost nothing about sex. My most carnal experience with a boy had been at a school dance when my partner pulled me tight against his bulging pants and I had run to hide in the girl's washroom. Most dates involved holding hands in the movies, followed by a chaste goodnight kiss, lips closed.

I was much more educated when I left that barn. If I had been out of my depth with a French kiss, when he pushed me onto the ground and reached his hand up my summer skirt to pull my panties down, I was drowning. His voice was deep and slow as he assured me that he wasn't going to hurt me; this was what men and women do. It was perfectly natural. His body held a tension that made it impossible for me to believe him and his fumbling quickly grew desperate. When he pushed himself inside me, it was with such force that he had to put his hand over my mouth to stop the screech that involuntarily left it. When he was done, he stood up, buttoned his fly and dusted himself off. He reached down to help me up and I recoiled. I didn't want his touch anywhere near me.

He looked at me and shook his head in disgust. "Get up yourself, then. Just trying to be a gentleman." He ran his fingers through his hair and picked a stray piece of straw off his shirt. "And if you're thinking of telling anyone about this, I'd think again. No one's going believe a word from you. They all saw how you were mooning after me all day."

With that, he gave me the same curt nod that Brother Peter had just given, and left. I stayed behind and cried myself hoarse, until I heard my mother calling me for supper. Then I brushed myself off too. I thought everyone would know what had happened just by looking at me. Part of me desperately wanted everyone to know, and part of me desperately wanted no one to know. All anyone said was that I seemed unusually quiet. I never told anyone, and after a while I began to believe my lie of omission myself, until finally, the omission wasn't a lie any more.

As Belinda drew closer and my own long suppressed drama replayed itself, I felt I had to do something. Should I give her a hug? Grab her, and make her tell me everything? Reassure her that I wouldn't tell? Reassure her that I would tell?

With each step she took, the crunch of straw charged the empty space between us. I wanted to fill it with just the right word or movement. Instead, I froze in indecision and helplessness.

As she passed me by she nodded. "Hello Miss Brock," she said. Then she stepped out of the barn and into the late afternoon sunlight.

Her nod to me, so akin to Brother Peter's, as well as my own tormentor's, made my stomach churn and I came to understand the term "gut reaction." If she saw or heard me throwing up on the hay she made no move to show it, continuing on her even-paced way to the main building, following the same path as the man before her.

All the suspicions I had harboured about Brother Peter had not prepared me for the knowledge that they were true, and especially the extent to which they were true. I went home that afternoon in a state of shock and spent a sleepless night pondering my options. I was under no illusion that anyone would believe me over anything Brother Peter might say. I realized, with another stomach churn, that Brother Thomas must be in on the events. It would be naïve to assume that his absence was coincidental.

It was two days before I saw Belinda again, when she came, as she did every week, for an afternoon in my classroom. She arrived just as class was beginning, gave me a smile and a bright, "Good afternoon, Miss Brock," and went to the back of the class where she waited until she was needed. The rest of the afternoon was the same. Belinda was calm and pleasant, looking me in the eye and helping the children with her usual quiet efficiency. She left when they did, giving me a cheery goodbye and no opportunity to talk.

Six days after seeing her in the barn I resorted to subterfuge in order to get her alone. I told Mother Magdalene that I needed Belinda to help me after school.

"Mother Magdalene said you needed me for something?" She stayed just inside my doorway, hoping for a quick exit.

"Come in, Belinda," I said. "And please close the door behind you."

She did as she was told, coming to stand beside my desk with her hands clasped behind her. She held her shoulders back and looked at me directly, and coldly. From my seat behind the big teacher's desk I saw a frightened girl who was not going to cry before the firing squad. My prepared speech dissolved. She was not going to hear anything I had to say.

It was an unseasonably warm day and a movement outside my window made me look that way. Although there was still snow on the ground, it was melting fast. The sun was shining and the younger children were outside playing.

"Perhaps we should go for a walk," I suggested.

Again, that nod. She wasn't going to give me any excuse to punish her, but she wasn't going to be compliant either.

I grabbed my sweater from the back of my chair for Belinda, my jacket from the cupboard for me. We walked in silence, me in the lead, towards the little waterfall I had first seen in the fall. I prayed that no one would be there and that I wasn't breaking any rules by bringing Belinda.

When we reached the falls and the little bench beside it, I invited her to sit down. She perched on the edge of the seat, her hands between her knees and her eyes on the ground. She didn't want anything from me, not even the sweater, which was now lying across my lap. She looked like she was facing an inquisitor instead of a sympathetic advocate.

I decided that the best way to deal with it was head on. But it was not an easy conversation.

"Has Brother Peter been with you before?" I asked.

Silence.

"Does anyone else know about this?"

Silence.

"No one is blaming you."

Again, silence.

This was not going well.

"I want to try to help you, but I need to know what you want first," I said.

I waited again for something , anything. Didn't she realize I was on her side?

"If you can't, or won't, tell me, then I'll just have to do what I think best."

She stared at the slushy ground between her feet. Her shoes were wet from the walk and looked too small for her feet. Her bare legs had goose bumps from the breeze blowing across the cold water. Once again, I offered her the sweater, but she shook her head.

"Belinda, please, talk to me. This can't continue. It's not fair to you and it's not something he should be allowed to get away with. He's supposed to uphold moral values."

She mumbled something to her feet and I felt a leap of gratitude. Finally, a response.

"Sorry, Belinda. I didn't hear you."

She looked up at me. "You can't stop it. They won't stop."

"Yes," I said. "We can stop it. We must stop it. We just have to find the right person to talk to."

"You can't stop it, Miss Brock. You just can't. If you try, they'll make you leave. It's better if you just ignore it."

"What's better about staying if nothing changes?"

"Then there's someone at school who cares about us. You can't change it. No one can."

That was all she was willing to give me. At every other attempt I made to persuade her to let me speak out she simply shook her head. I gave up and we headed back. But when she finally accepted the sweater I offered, I felt I had made some inroad.

When she left me to return to the dorms, she stopped after a few steps and turned. "You're a good person, Miss Brock. But you don't understand this school. Maybe one day things will change. But for now, the children are happy in your classroom and that means a lot. It's better if you don't say anything and stay teaching. I'll be leaving soon, but the others will need you. Don't tell and then you won't have to leave."

But I had to tell someone. Surely in an institution that was supposed to be based on Christian values, there was someone with authority who would tell Brother Peter to leave instead of me.

Believing that Brother Thomas was complicit in what was going on, I hadn't been to visit him since seeing Belinda in the barn. But as difficult as the conversation was sure to be, he was the only one I could think of who could offer me some realistic advice. So, despite my misgivings, I walked over to the barn to find him. He met me on the path from the milking shed. He was delighted to see me.

"Mary Brock! You're a sight for sore eyes! Where have you been? I've missed you!"

Now it was my turn to be silent. Where to start?

"Ah, but you're looking very serious. Come into my humble abode. We'll have a chat and solve the problems of the world. It can't be as bad as all that."

I followed him into the room that had been such a refuge for me. It was still the same: the dirty armchair, the old student desk littered with his journal, account books and piles of receipts. This tiny space had always been big enough to allow me to speak my heart and let my inhibitions go. Now the walls crowded in, and I couldn't bear to look at Brother Thomas's expression of concern and kindness. How could such a warm-hearted person be party to such cruelty?

The big armchair enfolded me and I looked into the bright blue eyes I had once trusted so completely. "Last Monday I came to visit you. You weren't here, but as I arrived, I saw Brother Peter leave. Belinda Whitestorm was right behind him."

There was a long pause. He didn't take his eyes off me as he leaned back to cross his arms.

"I'm sorry, Mary."

No lies at least, no protestations of innocence.

"How can you let it happen? How can you just... let him do that?"

He raised his hand, not in protest, but to try to calm me, my voice was rising. The anger that I had kept in check was breaching the wall of restraint I had needed for Belinda.

"Let's go for a walk, Mary. This is a long conversation and not the place to have it."

He wore a soft look of concern, and I wondered if I had looked the same to Belinda. How could he possibly explain this situation in a way that would make it acceptable? Even to him. I felt unbearably sad, and tired. If Brother Thomas couldn't help, then it appeared that perhaps Belinda was right after all.

And I didn't want another walk. I had exhausted my store of civility.

When I left, he didn't try to stop me or to follow. As I trudged to my car, I wondered if, like Sister Bea, his true loyalties were to the church above all else. If that were true, perhaps he would pre-empt anything I might try to do, telling Mother Magdalene some story to make me look the fool before I had a chance to harm anyone's precious reputation. It seemed that there was no one I could trust.

March 21, 1948

I came face to face with my own hypocrisy today, and I don't like the look of it at all. Mary came into the barn when B. Peter and Belinda were there. The only thing I'm proud of is that I didn't try to pretend I knew nothing about it. Although I didn't tell her directly that I knew all about it either. Nor did I tell her about all the other liaisons I keep quiet about.

It's almost five years to the day that B. Peter found B. Mark and me in that same loft. At least we were two consenting adults. But what a tangled web has developed since then. Perhaps I should just tell all that I know and let B. Peter tell all that he knows. B. Mark is long gone. But I feel that this farm, and especially the animals, would be lost without me. In truth, though I hate to admit it, I know there are others who are perfectly capable of learning the ropes, and would probably love the opportunity.

But where would the boys go? What of Simon, who worries me more each day? What of little Alexander, who would have killed himself had he not had a place to retreat to? What of Leroy, who was bullied so relentlessly? Who would they go to if I wasn't here?

After B. Mark's departure and Father Paul's absolution, I felt I was given a clean slate. But a clean slate in heaven is different from a clean slate on earth and dark secrets are heavy burdens. Has mine become too difficult to carry? What have I accepted in order for it to remain hidden? Has the price of secrecy finally become too steep? Who would have thought the little girl from Toronto, the one

I thought wouldn't last past September, would make me ask such questions of myself?

I had to make it through two more days of school before the weekend gave me some respite. Belinda came as usual on Thursday afternoon and she was her usual pleasant self with the children, ignoring me as much as she could. She came in after recess and left when the bell rang again at the end of the school day. I had told myself to expect nothing, but I was disappointed when that was all I got. Brother Thomas did not try to see me.

In my mind it was simple: Brother Peter, masquerading as a man of God had taken advantage of—raped—a young girl. He needed to be ex-communicated, face a jury of his peers, then go to jail like the common criminal he was. Give him shifty eyes and a fedora, or give Belinda my skin colour, and jail might have been possible. I knew that Brother Peter's peers wouldn't be as sympathetic to Belinda as she deserved, but if we could convince anyone that he had done what he did, I didn't see how the church could keep him on. Over the weekend, as I replayed my conversation with Belinda, some of the things she said finally filtered through. She was not the first, nor would she be the last, and Brother Peter was not the only one.

Then I remembered. How could I have forgotten? Little Susan, only ten years old and already the object of Brother Jerome's unwanted attentions. Why hadn't I paid more attention to it then? But if it was endemic, all the more reason to stop it as soon as possible. Surely, if there were others involved in these nefarious activities, there were many more who would be as horrified as I was to know it was taking place.

I spent the weekend on a see-saw: practical and realistic one minute; fuming with moral outrage the next. I didn't want to talk to Silas; I was afraid of what his reaction might be. Frank wasn't around. Mrs. Norton was too much of a busybody, and Nancy was too close to Mrs. Norton. Going around in circles in my own head was exhausting, and by Monday, I still had no plan of action. I decided to try Brother Thomas again.

A look of relief crossed his face when I stepped into his office. I was pleased. It made me feel less like a supplicant. He stood and gestured to his easy chair. while he moved from behind his desk to his daybed, leaning his back against the wall.

"How are you, Mary? I'm sorry I haven't come to you. I wasn't sure you wanted me to."

"I need to know where you stand on this Brother Thomas," I said. "I can't believe that you condone such behaviour, yet you obviously let it go on in your barn."

He sighed. "I've been thinking of nothing else since you left here last week. It's a good question. How can I turn a blind eye to such blatantly un-Christian behaviour and still call myself a good Christian? I could bore you with how I got to this point, but I don't think that really matters. What matters is moving forward from here."

I felt a moment of elation at his words. Was he ready to join me and face the demons of the school?

"There are many times in our lives where compromise is the only acceptable avenue open to us, even when compromise comes at a steep price. How many Frenchmen during this past war had to let Germans eat at their tables, share their homes? Things are gradually coming out that would horrify most of us. But people did what they had to in order to survive and to protect the vulnerable. We are face to face with a different enemy, but like our French counterparts we have to look at the greater good, the whole picture, before we decide on a course of action and—"

"They were dealing with life or death! That's entirely different! They had no choice. We do."

"True, but the principle is the same."

"The principle is whether or not we should let someone's status stop us from doing the right thing. When your life is at stake, you can be forgiven for turning a blind eye. What do we have at stake? Our jobs? What price is too high?"

"Let me ask you this, Mary. Why do you want to expose him?"

"What is that supposed to mean? Do you think I've got some ulterior motive lurking in a twisted corner of my brain?" I was shouting now. "I want to stop him! And all the others who are taking advantage of these children!"

"And if we tell? Will it stop him? Will it stop any of them?"

I sank back into my chair. It was what I been asking myself all week.

"Remember when you had to decide about your living situation and I asked you to think about what you would have to live with afterwards? We have to think hard before we do anything, Mary. These are serious accusations. We have to look at the impact to this school in particular, to the Indian residential schools in general, and even as broadly as the reputation of the Catholic Church itself. The papers love a scandal, and if this ever got out there would be untold damage done by exaggerations and blanket assumptions that would tar us all with the same brush."

"So you're suggesting that we sit in our corner and ignore it in case Brother Peter, the school, or heaven forbid, the church, gets a bad reputation? Don't they deserve a bad reputation? If we do nothing we're complicit in this moral outrage."

"Neither of us is doing 'nothing,' Mary. Each of us, in our own way, is doing something to help the children here lead happier lives. We need to look carefully at what we do next, and try to keep our emotional reactions on the back burner. There are good people here who deserve accolades, not denunciations. Exposing this would put a black mark on every teacher here. What would happen to the rapport that the teachers try so hard to establish with their students?"

"Rapport? What rapport? Most students arrive here wanting nothing more than to go home to their parents, and they leave wanting nothing more than to be done with this place. Their 'rapport' is learning how to avoid punishments."

Looking at Brother Thomas's weathered face, I felt some of my anger subside. What would happen to him if this came to light? He was a good man, but Belinda was a good girl, a wonderful girl, and she deserved better.

"I know that not everyone here is a monster," I said. "There are people here who do try to establish rapport and do their best for the children. But when I look at the big picture I see a church and a school that aren't living up to their commitments."

I waited a moment to give him an opportunity to object. When he didn't, I went on.

"I get your point. A scandal in an isolated northern school could tarnish the reputation of the whole Catholic Church, one that could well overshadow all the good the church does. For a while. But it's like a splinter. Even when the rest of our body is working perfectly, the tiny splinter is what we notice. Once it's out, there's no scar, no pain, it's like it never happened. On the other hand, if we don't take care of it, infection can spread. Personally, I don't have a problem with ripping the masks off perverts like Brother Peter. If I were a student, especially a female student, I would feel a lot safer here if I knew that teachers like him would get what they deserved. I would trust the church a whole lot more if I knew that it was cleaning out its splinters before they infected the whole body. The fact that he has gotten this far without any repercussions means that there's already infection, there may well be a scar, and there certainly deserves to be some painful recuperation."

"An interesting allegory, Mary. In principle, I agree completely. But let's be realistic and look at what would be likely to happen if you were to tell Mother Magdalene or Father James what you saw. You saw Brother Peter leave the barn, then you saw Belinda coming down from the loft. It's easy to assume what was going on. But you didn't actually see anything untoward, and even if you had, it would be your word against his. You can be sure he isn't going to confess to anything. Who do you think the administration is likely to believe?"

"But it isn't just the barn. My conversations with her back up my assumptions, and there's the piano practise too."

Brother Thomas sighed. "Do you honestly believe that will change the tide for you, Mary?"

"Well what would then?"

"I don't know Mary, and that's my point. It would take a lot more than your conjectures to make anyone believe something so terrible of Brother Peter. And will Belinda back you up? Think of the repercussions for her if she did. We need to think it all the way through."

"You mean *I* need to think it all the way through."

"True. Because when I think it all the way through I'm not prepared to lose what I've built up here. My barn is more than just a refuge for the likes of Brother Peter. Many boys come here with secrets they can tell no one else. If I were to expose some of those secrets I would be exposing those boys, just as you would be exposing Belinda if you were to tell your story."

"Nobody is asking you to expose any other secrets! We're just talking about Belinda."

"Do you think children would be allowed to come here if this place were seen as place of assignation? And do you think my role would not be found out? My big picture includes the church, but it also includes each child who comes here for some respite. What would their lives be like without the barn for a place to throw a few horseshoes and forget about the world for a while? Do you know how I choose my milking boys? It's not the best students, or the finest milkers. It's those who need a safe place, even if it's only for a little while. My milkers know it too, and that allows others to trust me."

"What are you telling me, Brother Thomas? 'A safe place?' Is this place so terribly dangerous?"

"Those weren't the best choice of words, Mary. But in a boy's world you have to prove yourself. You're either top dog or you're at the bottom of the pile. And being at the bottom can be terrible. I value my position as mentor to these boys. I believe I am doing some good here, making some lives a little easier. I wouldn't jeopardize that for the slim chance that Brother Peter would be asked to leave. I'm sorry. I know that's not the answer you'd like, but it's my truth, and I hope that you can at least understand it."

Except for one twitching foot, he was quiet while I mulled over everything he had said. When I finally found my voice, it trembled. "Belinda has no one, Brother Thomas. Can you understand that? No one. Where is she, and girls like her, supposed to go for help, or even solace? Are you suggesting that I stay silent and take on the role of confidante to the girls? *She has no voice.* The school is against her, her parents are miles away, and I'm being told, by her as well as you, to keep this to myself. And why? So students can have one class they don't hate, or at best someone to confide in? Wouldn't you rather they had nothing to confide? It seems to me that you've given up without even trying. And please, don't tell me one more time about losing battles."

"We're back to where we started Mary. What do you suggest be done that would actually rectify this? Do you honestly believe that you can bring justice to Brother Peter or for Belinda?"

"I don't know. But doing nothing is driving me crazy."

"My advice to you would be to think carefully before you do anything else. And talk to Belinda before you do anything at all. In all probability, whatever you do will impact her more than it will impact Brother Peter."

In the days that followed my talk with Brother Thomas I tried to take his advice and speak to Belinda about what I could or should do. She didn't want to talk to me, and the few conversations she allowed me were short, but poignant.

She was adamant that I do nothing. She continued with her time in my class and with her Thursday afternoon piano lessons with Brother Peter. I made a point of staying late on Thursdays, and of saying hello to Brother Peter as he went down the hall for the lessons. I wanted him to know I was there.

He would nod curtly to me, so reminiscent of the barn nod, that my stomach lurched each time.

It seemed that nothing was the best I could do.

March 23, 1948

Mary hasn't been back since our last conversation. I'm still uncertain that I'm on the right course. If I felt it would change anything I might speak up, but with my own history who would listen to me? And it's not just B. Peter and Belinda, to root it all out seems an impossible task. But Mary's question, "Wouldn't you rather they had nothing to confide?" sticks with me. Is it possible to provide an environment where there would be nothing? Not if we don't try, certainly. But I'm not sure of the best way to try. Now, as I stick with the status quo, I feel I'm giving in, and I suppose I am. Mary called it "being complicit" which puts it in a whole new light. Still, it's the best I have to offer right now.

APRIL
1947

THE GRAVEYARD

Despite the fact that Christmas has taken over as the big Christian holiday, Easter, and Good Friday before it, are the most significant days of the Christian calendar. Most Ontario schools celebrated Easter with a one week holiday. Here, I got a four day weekend and the children had no real holiday at all. I did my duty and spent an hour in church on Good Friday. The children had to spend the full three hours of Christ's time on the cross sitting in mind-numbing boredom in the cold school chapel. Saturday's chores must have felt like a reprieve. On Sunday, while they had to spend much of the day in church, at least it was a happy celebration with cheerful hymns, alleluias and a good meal afterwards.

I got back after Easter to some disturbing news about Belinda. Unlike Christmas, when she had stayed at the school, she had been allowed home for Easter, and she hadn't returned. Rumour had it that she had gone to Winnipeg to help her ailing mother and she wasn't expected back.

The news shattered the equilibrium I had worked so hard to attain. Did she leave because she couldn't stand the tension of knowing that I knew, and the fear I might say something? Or maybe I should have said something, and she left because she couldn't stand his advances anymore. Either way, I was certain I had failed her. My only solace lay in a half-hearted attempt to believe that she was happier wherever she had gone.

I missed her, and the students missed her too. There was a tangible relaxing of the atmosphere when she was present. She understood their lives in a way I never could. Some of the older students were cold, even cruel, to the younger ones, but Belinda was always kind and approachable. The students had a protector in her, perhaps the closest they would come to having a mother at school. With her, they could make mistakes without fear of punishment and share private, inside jokes that would have been lost on me.

We were given a new student helper, a handsome young man named Sam. The girls were thrilled with this development, but I found him more of a distraction than a help. Where Belinda had been self-directed, Sam needed prompting and coaching for every little thing. Unless I asked him to wander about to see if students needed help, he sat on a chair at the back of the room staring at the backs of their heads or doodling on his ever-present pad of paper. He never volunteered to do anything, and his grammar and spelling skills were only marginally better than those of my students.

When I finally took a look at Sam's pad of paper, though, I discovered his bright spot. The pages were full of wonderful sketches — drawings of everything from the classroom in front of him, to imaginary beasts on exotic planets. With my ability to teach and his to draw, the class started to produce pieces of art we were proud to display. In addition, when I stopped resenting the fact that he wasn't Belinda and spent some time in getting to know him, I discovered another skill: arithmetic. He was very good at it, and could point out errors in method and final outcome with unerring accuracy. But he was incapable of teaching it. I once watched him try to explain how multiplication worked. It was like watching a bird try to explain how wings worked. I had him mark papers instead.

With no one to talk to about Belinda, or my own moral dilemma, the period after Easter was one of my loneliest times. I tried to broach the subject with Frank during the Easter break, testing the waters with questions about what he thought of older men with younger girls. He barely bothered to hide his impatience during our short discussion about such an unimportant social taboo. Sister Bea and I often talked about the students, but our conversations had never slipped into anything remotely personal, and she seemed to prefer it that way. Brother Thomas had made his position clear, and as much as I understood it, especially after my talks with Belinda, I still couldn't shake the feeling of betrayal when he made no effort to help.

But, despite the fact that Brother Thomas was not going to change his mind, he was ready to listen and always sympathetic. When I needed an ear or a sounding board he was happy to accommodate me. So, eventually, I found my way back to the barn.

One afternoon I was at the horseshoe pit with Brother Thomas and a few of the boys when a young boy ran into the middle of the pit, crying with complete abandon. It took me a minute to recognize him as one of my pupils, Charles Carpenter. Charles was small for his age, a good student and a quiet child. This behaviour was not like him at all. He had two older sisters at the school. Every once in a while one of them would stop by to "help" me with my class. I was pretty sure their visits were illicit, but if they could manage to get there, I wasn't about to throw them out.

A quick once-over made it clear that Charles wasn't crying from any physical injury or pain, but he was too hysterical to talk. The boys looked to Brother Thomas for what to do. Brother Thomas, in turn, looked at me, nodding towards Charles who, at that point, was throwing up in the bushes on the edge of the horseshoe pit.

I approached him cautiously. His hysteria was so intense I wasn't sure if I could, or should, break into it. When I reached out a tentative hand and placed it on his back, he twisted about and started flailing at me with his fists. Despite his small stature, the intensity of his feelings made the blows fierce. I backed up, but he kept coming for me until one of the boys grabbed him from behind and hauled him off. This seemed to break something inside him. He sat on the ground with his tiny shoulders shaking, rocking back and forth with his head in his hands.

I sat down behind him and held him. We rocked together and waited for the storm to ease. Brother Thomas came by with a hankie and most of the boys drifted off. Two or three stayed behind, sitting on the short wall of the horseshoe pit, absently throwing horseshoes towards some unknown target in front of them. The occasional clang of horseshoe hitting horseshoe was the only sound that could be heard over Charles's weeping.

When he was finally quiet, Brother Thomas picked him up and took him to his office in the barn, nodding for me to follow. Once there, he lay Charles on the daybed and told him to sleep.

"Can you find out what happened?" I asked.

"From him? Not now."

"No, not from him. From someone else."

"No. I'll wait until he decides if he wants to tell us."

"Wants to? I think it's obvious that he wants us to know, or he wouldn't have come to the horseshoe pit."

"Perhaps you're right. Or perhaps he came to the horseshoe pit because he knew it was a place where he wouldn't have to explain himself if he didn't want to."

"Is that some Indian thing? Or some man thing?"

Brother Thomas laughed. "It's a Brother Thomas thing."

April 6, 1948

Cheryl Carpenter died today. She had the flu that's been going around and succumbed. Before Mary came I would have left it at that. Now I wonder: Did we do our best? How can someone die of the flu with the medical care we have available today? Why wasn't she sent into town? There's no snowstorm this time. That's two deaths this year, and its only April.

When something as terrible as this happens I think; Mary's right, I should say something about the unspeakable behaviour I'm privy to. Changes need to be made. But her brother, Charles, came running to the only place he felt safe. When I look at it from that angle, I'm sure that keeping quiet is the right line of action—or inaction.

We're starting to think about planting. It's been a warm spring and the cold is leaving the ground earlier than usual. It means that the older students will be back on half-days soon as we prepare the soil. I always feel a twinge of guilt when I take them away from their studies. But once we get going, I enjoy being out there with them, and I like to think that they enjoy the freedom from classes, especially as the weather improves. Certainly young boys need a physical outlet, and farming is a constructive one. As well, it teaches life-lessons of patience and persistence. Skills we all need.

April 7, 1948
It appears that it wasn't the flu that killed Cheryl. After listening to Mary rant about how old fashioned our methods are, I went to talk to S. Irene to see what she thought. She said that while Mary may have a point, there probably wasn't much they could have done for Cheryl. Apparently, she had been complaining of a headache when she went to bed, and a stiff neck. S. Agnes thought the headache was a ruse, and the stiff neck a symptom of window washing, but when they found her in the morning, she had a rash on her body as well, all symptoms of meningitis. As terrible as her death was, I do feel somewhat vindicated, knowing that there was nothing we could have done.

It was school policy that when students were sick, they were allowed to stay in bed for a day or two. After that, they were expected to return to classes and normal duties, unless the nurse decided to keep them in the infirmary. This apparently taught them the ability to keep going in adversity. I'm not sure of the value of these lessons, but the staff believed in them wholeheartedly.

Unfortunately for Charles's sister, it backfired. She was very sick, and made to go back to school after three days in the infirmary. It was believed that she was no longer contagious, and she had already overstayed her two-day rest and recuperation period. Perhaps if it had just been schoolwork she returned to, she might have managed, but she was expected to keep up with her chores too. Spring cleaning was serious business at the school, and one of Cheryl's spring jobs was window washing. Difficult work at the best of times, it was exhausting while she was still running a fever. But once again, archaic methods reigned and it was decided that the best way to cure a fever was to work it out. It may have worked for other people, but it didn't work for Cheryl. Too sick, or too afraid, to go back to the infirmary, Cheryl died in her bed, all alone.

Cheryl came from a small community with limited access, especially in spring when the winter roads across the ice are no longer safe and the waterways not yet open. Her family wasn't able to make it out to the school, and her body could not be sent home. So she was buried at school.

The graveyard lay some distance behind the school, hidden by a copse of trees. Father James led a short ceremony there after classes let out. Charles, his other sister, Jill, a few of the nuns and I were in attendance. Someone had made a small wooden cross to mark the gravesite. After everyone left, I stayed on for some quiet time to myself.

Before Cheryl's death I hadn't known that the school had a graveyard. I suppose it wasn't something anyone liked to talk about. It lay a few hundred metres behind the main building and was about the size of a tennis court. Most of the markers were close to its gated entrance and most markers bore the names of brothers or nuns. The students who had died from the Spanish flu epidemic were marked by one large stone inscribed with fourteen names. With the exception of Cheryl, the most recent death date I could find in the front section of the cemetery was ten years earlier. The back half looked unused and overgrown, with vines and bushes growing haphazardly throughout the site, but I wandered over to have a look anyway. At first glance, it looked as deserted up close as it had from a distance. But when I tripped over a concrete tablet which was half-covered in overgrowth, I started to look more carefully. Under a twisted mat of vines I found a few wooden crosses. They were lying on the ground where they had fallen, the names on them illegible. I also saw numerous small mounds without any markers. No one had to tell me which members of the community lay buried here. Was Cheryl given a proper burial because of my presence? Or had things really changed?

In the graveyard where my grandmother lies, there are large trees, manicured lawns and winding roads. People wander there on a Sunday afternoon because it's quiet, and peaceful. This place was quiet, but I felt no peace.

BRASS PLAQUES

With Belinda gone, I no longer felt any obligation to stay silent about Brother Peter. Conversely, Brother Thomas felt that, especially with Belinda gone, there was no need to raise the issue. He used Charles's abrupt arrival at his horseshoe pit as evidence that the children needed a place to go when they felt that all was lost. But I couldn't help thinking that we wouldn't reduce the number of children who felt that all was lost if we didn't try to change the circumstances that created their despair. The real question was— would speaking out change the circumstances?

Whether or not Brother Thomas felt it, my inaction made me feel complicit too, and the helpless guilt it created overwhelmed everything. I had to do something. Someone in authority had to be made aware of what was going on. If nothing was said, nothing would change. Maybe telling would change nothing anyway, but I had to take that chance.

Making the decision to act quieted some small part of me. However, even with the satisfaction of my resolve, it took me three days to work up the courage to go and see Mother Magdalene. For three days, when I left my classroom at day's end, I made a sharp left at the crucifix and went out the heavy front doors, without even so much as a glance of hesitation in the direction of Mother Magdalene's office farther down the hall.

It was only fifty paces from the school's front door to the familiar door of my classroom. My classroom number, 10, was on a brass plaque just below the door's window. Above the number was my name, written on a white piece of paper and slipped into the slot prepared for it. Normally, when I arrived in the morning and saw my name on the door, it gave me a thrilling sense of proprietorship. Walking into my classroom was like stepping onto a winner's podium. But each day that I slunk out of school instead of heading to Mother Magdalene's office, that white slip of paper would greet me the next morning with a reminder that I was a coward. And each morning, I decided that today would be the day.

Mother Magdalene and I were not friends, but I thought that perhaps she could make a difference. I had no illusions about who would be believed, if it came to a clash of stories. But I did hope that, being a woman, Mother Magdalene might have a more sympathetic response than Brother Thomas. At the very least, telling Belinda's story might open her eyes to the possibility that this was going on and make it harder for the perpetrators to continue. I knew I also ran the very real risk that I would be fired. This was the only outcome that gave me pause. I was torn between my responsibility to my students and what I believed to be my responsibility to Belinda.

Just like me, Mother Magdalene's name was on a piece of paper in a slot on her door, but her office didn't have a number. Instead, below her name the word "PRINCIPAL" was written in big brass letters. Even with the stimulus of my overwhelming shame, when I finally walked past the big double doors to continue down the hall to her office, it took me another two days to knock on her door. I would stare at those brass letters and wonder if the risk of telling was worth the torture of staying quiet.

Those two days were the hardest. I was ashamed I had done nothing to help Belinda, even though nothing seemed to be what everyone thought was best. I had talked to anyone I felt would listen,

I had even tried prayer. But either God wasn't listening, or He wasn't talking, or maybe I simply couldn't hear Him.

That week of indecision, I barely ate or slept. Mrs. Norton was worried. I think she was waiting for me to grow a belly. I snapped at my students and avoided any contact with the staff. People were starting to notice.

Sister Bea asked what was troubling me. The children were abnormally quiet, as though afraid to test my wrath. But the day my self-absorbed Sam asked me if anything was wrong was the day I finally went through Mother Magdalene's door.

If I spoke up, the worst they could do was to fire me. I struggled with whether or not that would be worse than the way I was feeling now. Perhaps when I spoke up, other voices would join in and we could right a wrong. It was a desperate hope, but I had to believe it was possible.

When I lifted my hand to knock I knew that this was a defining moment in my life. We don't get many opportunities to watch defining moments. Usually they just happen, and only in retrospect do we understand how important they were. Trust me, it's better that way.

It was a Friday afternoon and the halls were quiet. The children were doing chores or burning off energy in the playground outside. Brother Antoine, in charge of janitorial services, passed by with a smile as I stood outside Mother Magdalene's door. When he turned the corner, I raised my hand. The sound of my fist on the wood was unnaturally loud. On the other hand, Mother Magdalene's muffled, "Come in!" was quiet enough that I was tempted to pretend I hadn't heard. This was the point of no return and I was learning, sadly, that I was no hero.

I'd like to say that crossing the threshold made me brave. I'd like to say that the butterflies flitting about my stomach came to rest, that I became fierce with resolve and steadfast in the knowledge that I was following the right and moral line of action.

It would have been wonderful if that had been the case. But it wasn't. Stepping into Mother Magdalene's inner sanctum, my stomach continued to betray me, making the difficult ever so much worse, and my angry speech became a poorly delivered monologue.

I remember very little of my time in her office. I was there for almost an hour, an eternity of humiliation and discouragement. She questioned me, in her straight-backed no-nonsense fashion, not only about the facts I presented, but any possible motive I might have had for presenting them.

As Brother Thomas had predicted, my word against Brother Peter's was not going to get me very far. And because Belinda was no longer with us, Mother Magdalene made it clear that there was even less incentive to pursue what would only create problems for the school and the church. The fact that the school and the church had created the problem didn't enter into the conversation, and I lacked both the nerve and the debating skills to bring it up.

I left feeling defeated, and elated. I had done it! I had spoken up! I had made an effort to right a wrong. That the effort had come to naught was unmistakably depressing. That my own value as an honest and upright teacher, a respected member of this community, was not enough to warrant an investigation was discouraging at best, humiliating at worst.

I didn't tell Brother Thomas. I was happy to have finally said something, despite the outcome, and I didn't want to hear him say, "I told you so." The weekend felt like a holiday. I slept in late and I could carry on a conversation with Mrs. Norton without my mind wandering. When I got back to school on Monday, I felt some measure of joy at seeing my name on the door. I can live with this, I thought. At the very least, I've planted a seed. Who knows when, or how, it will grow.

Then, at the end of the day, Sister Abigail came by my classroom to tell me that Mother Magdalene wanted to see me. I was naïve enough to be surprised. I thought it was all over. As I walked to her office I worried that the worst had come to pass.

When I opened her door, I came face to face with Brother Peter. He was sitting in one of the two wing chairs Mother Magdalene had set up around a coffee table in a corner of her office. Mother Magdalene sat in the other wing chair and a wooden student's chair had been pulled up for me. Mother Magdalene offered a tight-lipped hello and gestured to the empty seat. Despite its obvious status, I was grateful for it. I don't know how long I could have stayed upright.

I waited. I wasn't about to start this conversation. Neither, apparently, was Brother Peter.

With a slow and deliberate delivery, as though she were talking to a difficult student, Mother Magdalene began. "Mary, I take accusations such as the one you presented me with on Friday very seriously. We pride ourselves at Bear Lake in taking care of our students and giving them the best education, both academic and spiritual, that we can. Your concerns about Brother Peter's behaviour could have serious consequences, some of which we discussed on Friday. I have always felt that the best way to solve a problem is to go to the source. Brother Peter and I have had talked at length over the weekend."

Up to this point my gaze had stayed on my hands, which were clenched in my lap as though in prayer. Mother Magdalene paused here, which made me feel that she expected some response. I managed to lift my head, face her, and nod.

"Brother Peter has denied any wrongdoing, and has expressed, not only shock and horror, but a great disappointment that you would think him capable of such unconscionable behaviour. I have asked you to come here today because I think it is vitally important that we nip this story in the bud, and give you the opportunity to offer him both an apology and an explanation."

I thought it would be impossible to look Brother Peter in the eye again after seeing him in the barn that day. Making sure he knew I was in my classroom on Belinda's piano lesson days was about all I could manage. I never thought I'd be asked to apologize. Mother Magdalene's roomy office felt cramped as I turned to face him.

Brother Peter smiled benignly at me, his beautiful green eyes limpid, waiting to hear my apology. I looked back at him while inside me anger fought with frustration, resignation, and disgust. Brother Thomas, bless his cowardly heart, had warned me. This was nothing but a he-said-she-said situation, with Brother Peter holding the advantage.

But when you know you are right, when every fibre of your being tells you that the situation is wrong, it's hard to pretend otherwise, even when you know the battle is lost. For the first time in this whole contemptible affair, I felt righteous anger give me the courage to do, if not the right thing, at least the righteous thing.

"Brother Peter, while I respect your position and your talents, especially because I respect your position and your talents, you can appreciate that I would not make an accusation such as this without a lot of thought and without believing it to be true." As I spoke my fear dissipated. Facing the enemy felt good. I was not going to win the war, but neither was I going to lie down and play dead.

"Miss Brock." His voice sounded rough, as though the silence he had been keeping since I came into the room, had been hard to maintain. "I cannot imagine why you would take a coincidental meeting in the barn to be proof that I am carrying on an illicit affair. It goes against my highest principles, both as a member of the church and as a man."

That's all it took. I knew there was no point in describing my conversations with Belinda, Brother Thomas's silence, the creeping hands at music practice. I didn't want to hear his innocent explanations. It was too easy for him and I didn't want to squirm. I was not going to be humiliated any further by this man for whom I had no respect whatsoever. Mother Magdalene may have believed his lies, but I wanted him to be sure that I did not. I stood, and looked down into his smug face and alluring eyes.

"Well then, Brother Peter, if it is true that I misread the situation, then I apologize." My anger made me strong, my voice was clear and unhesitant as I turned to Mother Magdalene, whose brown eyes regarded me with a look I can only describe as curious. "I apologize to you as well, Mother Magdalene, for having drawn you into this sordid mess. Thank you for going to the source and straightening the matter out."

Then I left.

April 12, 1948

Mary has told Mother Magdalene. She came skipping, yes skipping, into my office today. Then she sat down and burst into tears. I closed the door and let her cry for a while. When she told me what she had done, I was flabbergasted.

It was Friday when she talked to Mother Magdalene and today she had to face B. Peter. When she told me the conversation I had to applaud. Not literally, although I was tempted. Bravo Mary! She gave them the apology they wanted. But, if her recounting of the conversation is accurate, it would appear that when she left the room, she also left them with no doubt as to what she thought of B. Peter's innocence. I can't imagine what the ramifications will be, but I can't help but be proud of her. I hear vespers ringing. I'm going to prayer today!

GOLDILOCKS

After my brief visit with Brother Thomas I went straight home to Mrs. Norton's. For the rest of the week I went to school and back home again without engaging with anyone unless it was necessary. I did my best with my students, but that was it. I was sure that I would soon get another summons to Mother Magdalene's office, to let me know that I was no longer needed at the school.

As Friday neared and no one came to get me, I began to hope that maybe I was going to be allowed to stay. I had no hope that I would be asked to come back in September, but maybe, just maybe, they needed me. In those first few days after facing Brother Peter, the weeks until the last day of school at the end of June had stretched out before me like a bed of nails. At that point, I imagined that getting fired might be easier than seeing his smug face, even one more time. But despite my dips into hopelessness, I knew I wanted to stay more than I wanted to leave. I owed my students that much.

I had grown up with the firm belief that the good guys always won, that we were a fair and just society. I had also grown up believing that the leaders of the church represented the best we were to strive for. These men and women were the ones helping the poor and the downtrodden. They were the ones who resisted temptation and kept to the straight and narrow. At the very least, they were the ones who tried their best not to do wrong, recognized it when they did, then asked for forgiveness and made an effort not to do it again.

For my generation, the war and the patriotic fervour it had generated had strengthened that belief in good guys and bad guys. We believed that the good guys, while they may take a beating now and then, would eventually triumph. But now, although I knew I was on the right side, I was on the losing side, and I couldn't see any way to win. If this truth were to triumph, it needed more allies than I knew how to muster. It was a rude awakening for me.

My initial relief at having spoken up proved to be short lived. With my failure to effect any change at school, I couldn't let go of the feeling that I had to do something. The thought that Brother Peter was going to get away with this gnawed at me. With each step I had taken, I believed that I would find an answer, an ally, a way to make things right. With Belinda gone, and no help coming from any of my superiors, the only allies I could think of were outside—the newspapers or the church in town. But as each of these ideas surfaced, so too did my visit with Mother Magdalene and Brother Peter. Who would believe me without someone from the school to back me up?

I thought of trying to find Belinda, but I had no idea how. Annie and Silas were the only people I could think of to ask, but Annie was gone, and Silas was the last person I wanted to confide in. I was certain he would believe me, but I was terrified of what his reaction might be.

As time passed, the weight of my secret grew. My fear that I would let something slip made me quiet again, which drew questions, which in turn deepened my fear of an inadvertent slip of the tongue. A quote from Benjamin Franklin kept running through my head, "Three people can keep a secret, if two of them are dead." Apparently, that would be true only if I wasn't the one left alive.

As the week drew to an end, I could think of no one to share my burden with, except Silas. I convinced myself that he would be receptive, that he would understand that all I needed was to unload some of my guilt and frustration. I didn't expect, or want him to do anything. I hoped that talking it out with him would help me find some peace of mind. So, on Sunday, I made the trek into Indiantown.

The spring melt had left the unpaved roads muddy and potholed. Front yards were strewn with stranded shovels and sleds. Mittens sat in puddles, and old beer bottles and the odd boot could be seen half-buried in mud. The wood piles had shrunk, and in some cases were non-existent, even though night-time temperatures still hovered around freezing. As I made my way to Silas's house, I worried that the depressing landscape was an omen for what was to come.

When I got to his house, smoke was billowing from the chimney, but his truck was gone, so I wasn't surprised when no one answered my knock. I decided to go inside and wait for him.

The familiar smell of tobacco, sweat and stew welcomed me the moment I opened his door. Hungry, I took a bowl down from the shelf and helped myself to a ladle of the savoury concoction that always seemed to be simmering on top of his stove. Sitting at the table in what must have been Silas's regular seat, I saw an open book lying face down on the table. I flipped it over and read as I ate, soon becoming engrossed in a story about animals taking over a farm. But the meal, the cabin's warmth, and the fatigue of carrying my secret overcame me. By the time Silas got home I was comfortably curled up and asleep in his big easy chair, the book on the floor.

The slamming of the metal door to the wood stove woke me up with a start. I opened my eyes to see Silas, in stocking feet but still wearing his heavy coat, looking down at me with a weary expression. I glanced over at the table, where evidence of the meal I had eaten still sat, and attempted a small laugh. "I feel a bit like Goldilocks," I said. "I didn't think you'd mind."

He continued his silent stare. I hoped it wasn't my uninvited arrival that had upset him. I stood up and, still silent, he reached for my coat, taking it from its hook by the door. Before handing it to me, he stopped and asked me a question.

"Mary, why didn't you tell me Belinda had left the school?"

"Belinda? How do you know about Belinda? That's why I came. I wanted to talk to you about her. How do you know her?"

Silas looked at me, his dark eyes suspicious. "She said you knew everything."

I sat on the arm of his big easy chair. "You spoke to her? Where is she? What's happened to her? She said I knew everything?"

"What do you know, Mary? And why the hell didn't you tell me?"

So I told him. I told him what I knew and why I hadn't told him. I reminded him about the man in the plaid jacket and how I thought his brand of justice would only make things worse. Then I cried and apologized. Obviously, my brand of justice hadn't worked either.

Silas was unimpressed by my tears or my apologies. When I was done he handed me my coat, then took his own off and hung it up on its peg. He put my dirty bowl and spoon into the sink and put the kettle on while I reluctantly prepared to leave.

"Tomorrow, Mary. We'll talk tomorrow."

I spent the next day at school anxiously scanning the halls and taking any chance I could to wander by the offices. I was sure Silas would come barging through the big oak doors full of his own righteous anger. But he never showed up.

When I crossed the tracks the next day, the muddy pathways and garbage-strewn front lawns took on the sheen of fond memories, as I wondered if this might be my last walk through Indiantown. I paused at Silas's house to gather what courage remained to me before turning down his path. There might as well have been "PRINCIPAL" in big brass letters on his front door. When he opened the door to let me in my tentative smile was met with a blank stare. He was woodenly polite, hanging up my coat, then pouring a cup of tea while I took off my muddy boots. I could hardly wait for this interview to be over.

I sat in my customary seat, and once he had handed me my mug, he sat opposite, no tea for him. His looked out the window behind me. I looked at the floor.

"If you'd trusted me, Mary, things might be different." I had no answer for this accusation, but I looked up at his words, hoping to catch his eye. He continued to stare out the window, his expression unreadable. I waited for more.

Finally, he spoke again.

"I know that dealing with a man in a bar is different from dealing with the school."

I opened my mouth to speak but he held up his hand. "You had your talk last night." So again, I waited.

"Belinda is with her mother. She's safe, for now. And for now, safe will have to be good enough. Her mother, her father too, thought her life would be different, better than theirs, better than this. Nobody's given up hope, but it's going to be harder now. There's not much I can do against this system that holds us hostage. Still, I wish you had trusted me."

His eyes moved from the view outside the window to stare at me. Was he blaming me for all this?

Once again he held up his hand as I opened my mouth to protest. I had no illusions about what I meant to Silas. I knew that as much as he enjoyed my company, our get-togethers were also a way for him to gather information about the goings on at the school. Our friendship meant much more to me than it ever would to him. I could, and did, talk to him about anything. He would indulge in my rants about Mother Magdalene and listen to me enthuse about some student who could finally write a proper sentence. My ignorance about anything from living without your children to how to ice fish, was always handled with equanimity. But I had crossed a line this time and I wasn't sure if I was ever going to be allowed back.

"Belinda is fine. She says to tell you that she knows you did your best. I don't know if I could've changed anything, Mary. Probably not, but I certainly can't change anything now. You, and Belinda too, you have ..." He hesitated, searching for the right word. "You've, you've been cowards." He stared at me to drive the point home. "You think Belinda is the only one? You think this isn't happening right now—to who knows how many girls, or boys? You think that Brother Peter is the only one?"

He stood up, his voice rising. "These people," he spat out the word, "they think they can do whatever they want with us. They don't care about our education, or our souls. They think we're garbage, to be thrown out when we come of age. Sent back to the reserve or the back streets of some city to die drunk or beat up or both. They don't give a shit about us."

Silas sat down. Deep shadows darkened his eyes. His weathered face looked twenty years older. The hands that rested on his knees were clenched with unspent rage while his shoulders sagged in exhaustion.

"Every time I see a child go through those gates, a part of me breaks."

I sat and stared at him in mute horror. There was nothing I could say, even if he'd wanted me to.

AS EQUALS

There was nothing intuitive or psychic about my sense that someone was at my door. It's hard to miss the black shape of a nun filling an open doorway. And to further demonstrate my decided lack of intuition, when I looked up to greet the guest who seemed too uncertain to knock, I was shocked to see Mother Magdalene observing me. One seldom needs to guess what Mother Magdalene is thinking, it's written all over her face. For most of us that might be a disadvantage, but for Mother Magdalene it added to her ability to project. Today, she looked like she had something difficult to say.

I wondered how long she had been watching me before I'd noticed her. It would have been a boring pastime, as I had been sitting at my desk marking papers for the previous hour. Despite that, my first response was a sense of panic, not at what might come, but at what secrets she may have uncovered during her silent observations.

It took me a moment to recover and invite her in.

She shut the door behind her. And took command immediately.

"Come and sit with me at the students' desks," she said. "I'd like to have this conversation as equals."

We both sat sideways in the pull-down seats, our knees almost touching in the narrow aisle between us. As usual, her perfect posture made me acutely aware of my own rounded shoulders. Even "sitting as equals" I felt anything but.

"Some things have come to my attention, which I would normally have discounted as common gossip. But because of your accusation against Brother Peter, I feel the need to give it some credence and look into it further."

I waited. If I had learned anything from my time at Bear Lake, it was to keep my mouth closed unless I was sure of what was going to come out. I tried my best to appear neutral, to hide the surge of curiosity her statement had sparked.

"I admire your strength of character, Mary. It will take you far." She offered me a rueful smile. "Probably far into areas you wish you hadn't ventured. But far, too, into those areas that will serve you well. When I saw you in my office with Brother Peter, I saw a different girl from the one I met last August. You managed to leave with dignity and with no doubt as to what you thought of Brother Peter's explanation. You can imagine his reaction. You are in this classroom on very shaky ground, despite the fact that you have managed to stabilize your position somewhat over this past month."

A slight shift in her shoulders, as though to make herself more comfortable, made me extremely uncomfortable.

"Mary, do you have any contact with Belinda?"

"No!" Did she? "I heard that her mother's sick and Belinda went to Winnipeg to help her. Have you heard anything else?"

"I hear many things, Mary, most of which are not worth my time. But I know that Belinda was special to you."

"Belinda was simply special. She was bright, and kind. She *is* bright and kind. She brought warmth into this classroom. The children loved her and she loved them back. We miss her, a lot."

Mother Magdalene looked at me sympathetically. I took that as an opportunity to continue.

"Can you imagine, Mother Magdalene, living as they do? No parents for most of your childhood? However wonderful you may believe their upbringing is here, it can never replace the security a loving parent offers. Belinda was the next best thing for my students."

"Loving parents are a wonderful asset, Mary, I agree. But many of these children do not have loving parents, and even for those who do, loving parents are not enough to prepare them for life in a new world."

I looked at her in disbelief. Did she really believe those sanctimonious platitudes?

"You know, Mother Magdalene, I used to believe many of the things I'd heard about the Indians. They're drunks. They live off the government. They don't care about themselves or their children. It's true, some of them are like that. There's a part of Toronto that I don't go into because many of the white people who live there are like that too. But we don't take those children from their parents and send them off to boarding schools far from home."

"Not always, and perhaps it would be better if we did," she said. "And too, with deprived children in our cities, we don't have the difference in culture we deal with here. We can, and do, try to help them in their own homes."

"Have you ever been into Indiantown, Mother Magdalene?"

"Not here," she said. "But I've been to many of the reserves these children come from."

"Well," I said, "I've never been to any of the reserves, but I've been to Indiantown many times. I've met some people there, Indian people, who aren't drunks, who don't live off the government. People who care a lot about their children. Who care enough to leave their homes and move here, just to be close to them. Not only that, one day I realized that my best friends in Bear Lake were not my landlady's daughter and her circle, but Annie, who lived and died on her own terms in the bush, and Silas, who listens with less judgement and more wisdom than most people in my life. There are wonderful people and horrible people on both sides of the tracks."

I was expecting another rebuke, but Mother Magdalene stayed quiet, watching me intently.

"There is one difference between Indiantown and the white side of Bear Lake." I said. "And it's not the condition of people's houses or the colour of their skin. It's the silence—a particular kind of silence. I was walking back to my house on Nipigon Street the day I first noticed it. To get home from Indiantown I walk through the poorer and into the wealthier neighbourhoods of Bear Lake. Every time I take that walk there's noise, the noise of children. Children playing games, children building snow forts, children racing their bikes. They're everywhere. Can you imagine living in a world without the noise that children bring, their honest laughter and irrepressible shouts of frustration or joy? I haven't had any children of my own yet, but when I do, I'll want them close."

I stopped. I had been speaking as though I had nothing to lose. But I did. I had a lot to lose.

The months which had felt so unbearably long when I left Mother Magdalene's office a few weeks ago, now seemed far too short. I desperately wanted to stay on with the class full of children I had come to think of as "mine." We had been talking about Belinda, the childless communities left behind were not Mother Magdalene's concern.

"And what would you suggest we do Mary? It sounds like your solution would be to close the schools and send everyone home. Is that what you're suggesting?"

"Honestly?" I said.

She nodded.

"How many of your graduating students have made their lives work once they leave? Has anyone gotten into university or a college program? Do any come back to visit and reminisce with their old teachers? As much as I think that teaching children the skills they will need to function in the modern world is a laudable goal, I don't think this school is the way to reach that goal."

Well, I thought to myself, whatever stability I had put into the ground was probably shaken loose now. At least if I was asked to leave I could do so knowing I had said what I needed to say, and into the ears of someone who was in a position to do something about it.

Mother Magdalene regarded me with the same look of curiosity I had seen when I left her office after meeting with Brother Peter.

"Most of us here have thought, at one time or another, that there must be a better way. Perhaps this system is now becoming old-fashioned, but having a place where everyone and everything works towards a common goal is helpful. The children are getting the same message from everyone, and if we want to achieve real change, then that's the best way to do it."

"That sounds very plausible," I said. "But what change has this school created? I don't know what things were like before these schools began. Maybe you're right, maybe things are better. But it doesn't look that way to me. I came here believing in those common goals. I came to help these children move into the future, develop skills that would make them contributing members of modern society, lead self-sufficient lives. But I don't see that happening. Oh, we teach them how to read and write, how to add and subtract, and how to say mass. But we also teach them that speaking their language is a crime, that close family ties are unnecessary, that following the rules is more important than following their dreams. So what, really, is the message we're sending?"

"That's a very negative way of looking at our system Mary. We teach them English, an invaluable asset. The less they speak their own languages, the faster they'll learn English, which also makes their regular education that much more effective. How can anyone follow a dream without a good education? Our rules also teach them a discipline of mind and body, something they can apply to anything they do, including their dreams. It will take a few generations before they have the qualities that will make them good candidates for university or college. Right now, graduating high school is hard enough."

"Graduating high school is not hard enough," I said.

I leaned in towards Mother Magdalene. I wanted to shake her. "My students are not stupid. They're perfectly capable of anything I was capable of at their age. Why don't they graduate? The parents of most of these children went to residential schools themselves. How many generations do you think it will take for them to develop these qualities you speak of? Belinda is a perfect example. Where is she now? She was one of the shining stars from here—a bright, capable young woman who was probably one of the few likely to go on to college or university. Why did she leave? What is her future now?"

Then it dawned on me. Of course she would have had to leave. I sat back on the wooden seat. "She's pregnant, isn't she? That's what you've heard, isn't it?"

Well, she wanted to talk as equals. I knew my days were numbered, and I was more desperate for news than I realized.

Mother Magdalene regarded me coolly, as though trying to judge if I could cope with her information.

"Yes, that's what I've heard. But Mary, it doesn't necessarily follow that Brother Peter had anything to do with it."

April 29, 1948

Sometimes living this far north can try my patience. We spent last week getting the garden beds ready for planting, and yesterday we had snow. It won't last, but the warm weather leading up to it had fooled me into thinking that winter was behind us. I believed that we could actually start planting this weekend. You would think that after so many years I wouldn't be fooled so easily. We will put in some of the hardier plants, the root vegetables and cabbage. We'll get started anyway once this snow melts. And hopefully it will warm up properly soon. Then we can start planting the rest. Next week will be back-breaking, with lots of soap needed before dinner. Kitchen duty won't seem so terrible!

Mary has been keeping her distance lately, but she stopped by today with news that Mother Magdalene says Belinda is pregnant. Poor Mary. She was depressed about it. It's what happens to women, though. Belinda would have wound up pregnant sooner or later. Which isn't to say that I don't understand Mary's point, and I know that in the coming days it will make me think again about what I've been closing my eyes to, but is it really so terrible? I'm too tired tonight to ponder moral values.

Justin needs new shoes, but the farrier isn't available for a week, so we'll have to use him as is. I'm off to feed, first the horses, then me.

I couldn't believe that Silas hadn't told me that Belinda was pregnant.

After dinner that night I made a trip into Indiantown to confront him. I had seen him only once since his angry tirade. We had had a quick cup of tea, and arrived at a detente of sorts, an attempt on both our parts to bring something of our friendship back. I hoped my anger wasn't going to undo this fragile reconnection.

When Silas opened his door, he didn't look too pleased to see me, but I didn't care. I started in as soon as the door had closed.

"Why didn't you tell me that Belinda was pregnant?"

He looked confused. "I assumed you knew. Why else would she leave?"

The anger I carried with me dropped from my shoulders like a heavy pack. Why else indeed? How could I have been so blind? Deflated, I looked at Silas. "I'm sorry," I said.

"I'm not really sure what you're sorry for, Mary, and I'm tired of the whole thing."

"I have one more question." I looked at him for reassurance that he was going to keep his calm. He waved his hand in a "go ahead" gesture and I plunged in.

"How is it that you know Belinda?"

He took a moment before answering, staring at some distant point over my right shoulder. I clasped my hands in front of me. I was sure that I had, once again, crossed some invisible social line.

"Belinda's mother, Rose, and I are," he paused, "like husband and wife."

"Really!" was all I could come up with. This new information made me smile. So Belinda's mother was the one he had referred to when he had said that he was as good as married. I had a million more questions but his look made me reconsider.

Instead I asked, "Can we talk?"

"What about?" he said, looking directly at me this time.

"Not about Belinda's mother," I said. "But I'd love to know more about Belinda."

"On one condition," he said.

"What's that?"

"After this, no more," he said. "If Belinda wants me to tell you anything, I'll tell you. Otherwise, no more questions."

I agreed. In return I learned more about Belinda, but also about the system under which Belinda had grown up.

When a child went to a residential school the parents lost not only their child, but their rights as legal guardians. Principals were the legal guardians of their students. In most cases this made little practical difference because parents had no control over whether or not their children attended a residential school anyway. Officials could, and did, search homes and communities if they believed anyone was trying to keep their young ones at home. Parents who refused to give up their children could be jailed for doing so.

By the time Belinda started school her parents had separated and she was living with her mother in Winnipeg. Her father, who had remarried, still lived in the small community on James Bay where Belinda had been born. During Belinda's first year at the school her mother contracted tuberculosis and had to live in a sanatorium. Because of this, Belinda's mother lost the right to have her at home during school holidays so she had to live at the school full time. When she was ten, the school began allowing her to stay with her father during the summer. When she was thirteen, her father reunited Belinda with her mother. The school was aware of this, but despite the fact that her mother lived in Winnipeg and was no longer sick, the old rules still held. Belinda was still not allowed to stay with her mother, even on those holidays when her father's community was inaccessible.

Silas met Belinda's mother when he worked in Winnipeg and they had lived together there for a few years. She supported his decision to move to Bear Lake, especially as he could keep an eye on Belinda along with his own children.

Before I left, Silas gave me Belinda's address. I wrote to her immediately and was grateful when her first letter arrived a week later. She told me she had a job helping her mother as a seamstress and her pregnancy was going well. She said she was excited at the thought of being a mother. I looked forward to each letter from her, but I always felt unsatisfied after reading them. It was like having a meal that doesn't quite fill you up. I don't know what I expected; some miracle that would turn her life around, I suppose. But she sounded content and so, once again, I found myself with nothing being the best I could do. At least she had her mother, and Silas too. I suppose she was luckier than some.

MAY
1948

BLUE EYES

Something happened one spring day at recess that created a shift in the relationship between the students and their teachers—at least in the elementary school. The day was sunny, with a warmth that promises summer, and a few hardy insects were already out testing the air. The tree buds were full to bursting, and in sunny corners green shoots of early spring flowers dotted the dark earth. In the midst of this glorious optimism, the swing set sat empty and still. Usually it was full of children, but someone had spotted something of interest off in one corner of the playground and everyone was huddled around it, trying to see.

Until high school, when it wasn't fitting for a young lady to be seen doing childish things, I used the swings every chance I got. We had a playground near our house in Toronto and often, even in high school, I would head over to swing and dream. But I hadn't been on a swing for a very long time.

When the children returned from their corner investigation they found their teacher with skirts flying and legs pumping as I thrilled to the feel of the wind in my hair and the weightless drop and rise of the swing. At the sight of me, Sister Bea laughed and hopped on the swing beside me. Then Sister Maureen put down the child she was holding and got on another. By the time a disapproving Sister Rachel came by, it was too late to stop. The children loved it, and soon there was a circle of girls holding hands and dancing around the swing set while their teachers laughed and pumped, higher and higher. When Sister Rachel rang the bell for class, we were dishevelled and happy, especially because there was nothing she could say in the face of such unabashed joy.

After that, everyone wanted to swing: teachers and students. Even those teachers who had initially held back under Sister Rachel's censure joined in on the fun. The little ones sat on our laps and the older ones competed with us to see who could go the highest or lean back the farthest. Mother Magdalene stepped in to ensure that only one teacher was on the swings at a time, but for a week we had a recess we could all enjoy.

I guess Mother Magdalene decided that one week was enough. At our staff meeting she made a quiet, but authoritative, ruling that the playground equipment was for children only. Most of it wasn't strong enough, she said, to sustain constant use by adults.

The swinging ended, but the damage had been done, and the result was a discernible shift in the children's relationship with us. The younger ones had always adored Sister Maureen, but for the most part, the connections between the students and teachers were a lot like what I had seen with Sister Bea: both sides observing a cautious, studiously polite, distance. As for me, I had always been the outsider, not fully trusted by anyone, except perhaps some of the students in my own class. After the swinging, children would come and hold my hand, or ask me to join them in their games. One day I was sitting with some of the younger ones, playing a hand game, when one little girl asked me, "Miss Brock, how can I make my eyes blue like yours?"

The circle of girls all stopped to look expectantly at me. What magic potion was there? Could they do it too?

"But you can't!" I said. "God made your eyes a beautiful brown. They're perfect the way they are."

"Brown is an ugly colour," she said. "It's the colour of dirt. Your eyes are like the sky."

"Brown is a wonderful colour," I said. "Trees are brown, and look!" I pointed to my arm, "My favourite sweater is brown. There's no such thing as an ugly colour."

"Yes, there is. Your sweater is nice, but most brown things are ugly. Dirt is brown, rust is brown, my skin is brown, my eyes are brown. I want to have white skin like you and blue eyes. I'll never be pretty."

"Of course you're pretty. I sit in the sun every summer trying to get lovely brown skin just like yours."

"You do?" She looked at me, shocked.

"I do. Every summer one of my goals is to get a beautiful brown tan. You already have it. You're the lucky one!"

"Sister Agnes says brown skin is a sign of sin. She says that I'll never be able to hide my heathen bones from God. He'll see it in my skin. She says I could wash as much as I wanted and I'd never be able to wash away my brown."

Another one piped up. "Sister Agnes tried to wash off my brown skin. She made me scrub and scrub and scrub and I never got one bit lighter."

There were nods around the circle. It seemed that Sister Agnes had made more than a few girls suffer this ritual.

"Sister Agnes is mistaken," I said. "God made each one of you, and God doesn't make mistakes. I'm sure there are other teachers here who would disagree with Sister Agnes. Ask Sister Maureen or Sister Irene, and see what they have to say."

"Am I going to hell?" another girl asked. "All the good people have white skin. The nuns, the priests, even you." She paused. "I hate my body!"

Eight years old and she hated her body. Not because of something she could change, like the bulge of a muscle or stomach, but because she wasn't the "right" colour. How many others had left this place with that horrible belief fixed in their heads?

"Your body is beautiful," I said. "Look at how fast you can run. You can do handstands. I'm even afraid to try them! And you beat me at tic-tac-toe every time!"

They looked disappointed at my platitudes. They weren't talking about muscles and sinew, or how well their brains could work. They were eight years old and a beautiful body meant white skin and blue eyes. Blond hair would make it perfect, thank you very much. I knew many women with those attributes who couldn't have held a candle to the sweet young children sitting with me that day.

The bell rang and we headed back to class. I was disappointed that I hadn't found a way to reach them, and angry that I needed to. They never talked to me about beauty again. I hope they found their own when they grew up.

SIMON

May 10, 1948
I'll bet everyone is sleeping well these days! The planting is full on now, with the corn starting this weekend. I'm glad for the tractor when we do the big fields. I'm also glad for the longer daylight hours. The winter wheat is poking up and the potatoes, turnips and onions are all done. The boys hardly have any energy for horseshoes these days. We plant, eat and go to bed.

May 22, 1948
I found Simon in the barn a few days ago with another boy. It was a relief in a way, now I know why he's been behaving so oddly this year. He came to see me the next day but he didn't talk about what happened and I didn't ask. We talked about the cows and how he'd like to start milking next year. I told him I'd think about it. Maybe he was just trying to feel me out. I'm not sure if I met his needs or not, but it sure didn't feel like it. Between Simon and B. Peter and Mary, I'm starting to wonder: Should I stay on here? The problem is, I'm not sure I'd fit in anywhere else, and

I do believe what I told Mary. What would Simon do if I wasn't here for him to talk to? Even if he doesn't want to talk about what happened, at least he knows I can be trusted to keep a secret.

Then today, my worst fears were realized. I was out checking on the onion fields, to see if we needed to do any weeding. On my way back, I stopped by the woodshed to see if I'd left my good knife there. It's been missing from its hook on the wall for a few days now. Stepping into the semi-darkness my foot landed in something wet and slimy. I looked down to see what it was, but I couldn't really tell. It was just a dark, wet puddle. I wondered if some animal with bad digestion had left something behind. As I moved inside I heard noises in a corner. There's my critter I thought, I hope it's not a skunk. I moved farther in to have a look.

The shed is practically empty this time of year. The trees we dropped over the winter are waiting to be cut into smaller pieces, and last winter's wood is mostly gone, so there are only a few dark corners left in which to hide. When I got to where I expected to find a frightened animal, I found instead, a frightened boy.

Simon had an axe in one hand and my knife in the other, his wrists were bleeding and blood was streaming down his face as well.

"Leave me alone," he said.

"Not on your life," I told him.

"My life isn't worth anything," he said.

I told him I disagreed and he threatened to attack me with the axe if I came any closer. He looked weak enough that he probably couldn't have done much damage. Nevertheless, I stayed where I was and talked to him until finally, he fainted. I took the knife and axe away, did what I could for his wrists, then ran to get S. Irene. She was a Godsend—calm and practical. There is an unspoken agreement between us that this will not be mentioned outside our small circle. She stayed with me in the shed until Simon came to, then we took him to my room. After he had settled, S. Irene brought him up to the infirmary. I went to B. Peter with a story of Simon cutting himself with the axe and having to spend the night in the infirmary. God forgive me my lies. I didn't know what else to do. The last thing this boy needs is punishment.

JUNE
1948

GOODBYES

When I was a student in elementary school, the last few days of the school year were a mixture of frustration and fun. It was frustrating because we were still expected to do some schoolwork even though we knew that nothing we did really counted — our report card had already been written. A summer of freedom lay a few long days away and it was torture to sit in a hot, stuffy classroom. On the other hand, the teacher was lenient, the work was minimal, and we were allowed to fill spare time with charades or board games we had brought from home. We tidied up the classroom, put books away for the next year's class and scrubbed desks and blackboards.

The last day was one big party. We had the run of the school as we went from one classroom to another, saying goodbye to our teachers and collecting signatures from our friends for our autograph books.

At Bear Lake Indian Residential School, things were different. Report cards were done, but classroom discipline was expected to continue as usual. There were no board games from home, no autograph books, no running unsupervised from one classroom to another. The only resemblance to my schooldays was that it was still unbearably hot and stuffy, and going home was still a few long days away.

Any lingering hope that I might be asked to return the following September had been quashed a few weeks earlier when Mother Magdalene had given me a letter of recommendation to take with me when I left. So I decided to break the rules and have a party—without asking for permission. I found some decorations at the general store and borrowed Nancy's portable record player. On our last day, I arrived early to tape up crepe-paper ribbons and prepare some games for the few short hours I had left with "my children."

They arrived looking listless. Some students had already gone home, and some were staying on for an extra week or two because of transportation problems. It was a time of transition, which is never easy, but especially difficult for these children who had no secure place to call home.

It was a treat to see their eyes light up when they saw their classroom. After the last child had entered and I had closed the door, they sat in their seats looking expectantly up at me. I looked back at my sea of brown faces, knowing it was the last time, and started the speech I had polished in front of the mirror that morning.

"I came here not knowing a single one of you, but I know that when I leave I will miss each and every one of you. You have challenged me and rewarded me and made this year one that will stay with me forever. I'm very sorry to tell you that I will not be coming back next year. This is not because I don't want to. I would like nothing better. Unfortunately, there is no job for me here next year. But I don't want to end this year on a sad note. I'll be sad tomorrow. Today, I want us to have some fun—but we will have to have quiet fun. Is that understood?"

I watched their faces as I spoke and I have to admit that I was touched to see dismay on some when I said I wasn't coming back. A few even looked ready to cry. It was gratifying, that first year of my career, to see that I had reached into the hearts of some of my charges.

But the moment was brief as they returned to the present and the possibility of fun. Someone pointed to the record player I had set up on the back table and I started the first of many games. Despite my admonitions to keep things quiet, it was impossible. It wasn't until

I brought out the cookies and cake I had made, along with an orange for everyone, that silence finally reigned.

At the end of the day, as they left my classroom for the last time, a few turned to give me one last smile. My impulsive Ruth even gave me a hug. I had to work hard to keep my emotions in check. It wasn't until after the last straggler left, giving me a little wave as he ran out, that I was able to close the door and allow myself a self-indulgent cry. I was glad of the box of tissues still sitting on my desk.

When Sister Bea popped her head in my doorway, my eyes were red, but the tears had stopped. "I don't want to prolong the goodbye," she said, "but I'll miss you. Would you like to stay for dinner?"

This was just another day for Sister Bea. She would go to vespers, maybe have a sit by the waterfalls, supervise bedtime and go to bed herself. The only difference for her would be that most of the children would be gone for a few months. Come September, life would return to its usual routine with a different batch of students, most of whom she already knew well. At our last staff meeting, Father James, Brother Peter and Mother Magdalene told us what an exemplary job we'd done and how well the year had gone. There had been fewer runaways than last year and more students had been promoted— a banner year by all counts. There was no goodbye party with the staff, no end-of-year celebration with a few drinks and raucous tales of narrow misses and crazy test answers. This was it. Pack up my things, and walk out the door.

"Thank you, Sister Bea, I'll miss you too. And I also hate long goodbyes. Mrs. Norton has a big dinner planned for tonight, so this will have to be our farewell."

Sister Bea came in for a hug, our first in the time I had known her. She was a good person and an honest one. She had been kind to me and had had a patient ear for my many complaints. But, except for a thank-you note I would send when I returned to Toronto, it was unlikely that I would ever feel the need, or even the desire, to get in touch with her again. Sadly, that was true of all the staff. Brother Thomas was my closest confidante, but it was never the same after Belinda. It saddened me that after a year, there was no one I was going to miss.

Except the children. I knew I would miss the children.

June 25
Mary left today. Before she did, she came by with two baskets filled with games. She was afraid they might get thrown out. I watched her drive off in that old Ford of hers, the dust hanging in the air long after she'd gone. While she would probably disagree, she leaves a school that's changed. The barn 'field trip', birthday parties, the St. Valentine's Day dance, and teachers on the swings. There is an undercurrent of empathy towards the students that I haven't seen before. She's certainly changed me. I began by writing her off as a no-good do-gooder. Then she wormed her way into my heart. I let her down, and thought I'd lost her for good. And in a way, I did. She liked to come by for a chat, she liked to have someone to vent to. But after she found out about Belinda it was different, as much as I'd like to pretend it wasn't. She's left me her address and I'll write. But she's going to a different world now, better equipped, I hope, but far from this one and the aches and pains we fret about here. It's a good thing summer's arrived. There's too much to do to spend time wallowing. Although tonight I might just have a sip and shed a tear for my sweet, sweet Mary.

Frank left before I did. He had taken his job in the logging camp at Bear Lake in order to make enough money for a few months of travel; so now he was going to live out his dreams and head to South America. He planned to come back when his money ran out and try his luck in the lumber camps of British Columbia. He'd heard that the money was better there. By the time we went our separate ways we both knew, that although we enjoyed each other's company, neither of us wanted a lifetime together. Still, we spent our last weekend in each other's arms. We went back to the secluded beach where we had had our first romantic picnic and he produced a sturdy white mug as a present for me to remember him by. Later, we danced the night away at Birling's Bar, and Mrs. Norton said nothing when I tiptoed upstairs to my room at 2 a.m..

Frank's train left at noon on Monday, so we said our goodbyes on Sunday after a farewell turkey dinner served by Mrs. Norton in his honour. Frank was a good man, and my life in Bear Lake was vastly improved by his affection. It was a bittersweet goodbye.

Mrs. Norton was the hardest person to leave. It wasn't because I had any overwhelming affection for her—although I have to admit that by the time I left she had become a surrogate mother. She could be cranky and judgemental, but she was also wise and warm. Whether or not I agreed with her, she always had my best interests at heart. My last week of school she barely let me out of her sight, insisting on making me breakfast every morning, tea when I came home from school, and my favourite meals every night for dinner.

On the last day of school, a Friday, she hosted a big party for me, inviting practically everyone I had crossed paths with during my time in Bear Lake. Nancy and her family were invited of course, along with many I hadn't gotten to know as well; Reverend Metcalfe, the Anglican minister, even Sid from the garage and grumpy Mrs. Makowski from the bridge group. It too, was a bittersweet goodbye. I had often felt lonely and displaced in Bear Lake, but seeing all those people crowded into Mrs. Norton's kitchen and parlour made me think that perhaps my loneliness had been more self-imposed than I realized.

In May, when the snow was completely gone and the paths dry, Silas had made good on his promise and we visited Annie's cabin and her grave. From our entry point just inside the glade, her cabin looked untouched. The pail hung, shiny and clean, on its hook by the door, empty hoops still waited for furs on the back wall and the woodpile stood ready to be used. The bright cushion on the front porch had been chewed up by some animal, and the windows had lost their sparkle, but otherwise the cabin looked as it had when I first saw it. We paid our respects at her gravesite, swept the porch and path clear of forest debris and went for a short walk up to the beaver pond. Surprisingly, it wasn't sad. As we shared our Annie stories by the pond, it felt as though she were sitting there with us.

I had hoped that the intimacy of that visit would carry over into our friendship. But once we stepped back into Indiantown it was as though a curtain had been pulled on our shared connection. We still met, but sporadically, and as my time grew short, I worried that each visit with Silas would be my last.

So I was honoured when he invited me to have a farewell lunch at his place on my last day in Bear Lake.

"We'll have a Northern meal of fresh trout and bannock," he said. "You won't get that in Toronto."

I wanted to offer him something in return, but he was a hard man to buy a present for. So when he told me, that in anticipation of his children visiting over the summer, he had bought a record player, I knew what I would do. When I walked over to his place for our final rendezvous, I had my Tommy Dorsey record under my arm.

Silas answered my knock with a broad smile, and then, instead of inviting me in, stepped out onto his cramped porch.

"I thought we'd eat at Annie's cabin," he said. "It seems a fitting place for our last meal."

He had a knapsack on his back, and without waiting for me to agree, he led the way down the steps and towards the woods. I followed, disappointed. I felt I had said my goodbyes to Annie already, and I was looking forward to playing the record for him before I left. But he seemed oblivious to my parcel, or my dismay.

It was a beautiful summer's day, however, and I didn't stay in my slump for long. Silas's ebullient mood was infectious and his pace was quick. "Got enough fish to feed a family," he said. "I hope you're hungry!"

When we broke into the clearing, I noticed that the cabin door was open and the path newly swept. Silas marched on ahead of me, apparently undisturbed by these signs that someone was using the place. When we were almost to the porch, I heard women's voices. Silas stopped then, and turned to grin at me. I had no idea what he was so ridiculously happy about.

It didn't take long to find out.

A woman I didn't know walked onto the porch, smiling almost as broadly as Silas.

"Hello, Miss Brock," she said, holding out her hand. "My name is Rose Whitestorm."

My jaw dropped. I looked from her to Silas and back again.

"Silas's Rose?" I asked. "Belinda's mother?"

"Yes," came an unmistakable voice. "My mother."

I practically pushed Rose aside in my headlong rush to reach Belinda. The record dropped to the ground and I flew up the step to where she was standing just outside the door. Belinda! Big pregnant Belinda. Her belly surprised me, but did nothing to mar the delight I felt at seeing her standing there with her own wide grin.

It was a fitting end to my time at Bear Lake. To see Belinda surrounded by the love and support of Silas and her mother was reassuring. We had lunch at the beaver pond, where Silas built a fire and cooked his fish. The fish was decorated with wild strawberries that Belinda and her mother had collected, and beside it lay freshly cooked bannock, slathered in butter. We all waddled back to the cabin later that afternoon.

Before we left, Silas and Rose went to do some spring cleaning of the gravesite and Belinda and I went inside to chat. We sat at Annie's table, where my brightly wrapped Christmas present, brought those many months ago to an empty cabin, still waited. When Belinda heard the story behind it, she insisted that we unwrap it and make some tea. She had grown up a lot since I'd last seen her. Pouring each of us a cup of tea, with some canned milk that she guaranteed had survived the winter, she looked like any expectant young mother. She assured me she was going to do her best to continue with her education. We talked about the love she already felt for her unborn child, despite the circumstances of its conception. She was confident that she would be a good mother. I was sure she would be too.

When Silas and Rose returned, all four of us headed back to Bear Lake and our very different lives. At Rose's insistence, I carried my yellow teapot, and Silas had my record, thankfully still in one piece after being dropped in my sprint onto Annie's porch.

Leaving them at Silas's place, I made my final walk through Indiantown. I imagined that the howling dogs I passed, their faces raised to the heavens, were sympathizing with me and lamenting my departure. I was so caught up in this fantasy that it took a moment for a different sound to register. I turned around, and through Silas's open window I got my last view of that small family that meant so much to me. Silas had one hand in Belinda's and the other in Rose's. As Tommy Dorsey's trombone filled the room and spilled out onto the streets, they danced around the wood stove, Bartholomew watching from his post on the big easy chair. The uplifting melody of Opus No. 1 got my feet moving too, and I left Indiantown dancing.

ACKOWLEDGEMENTS

As much as writing often feels like a solitary pursuit, no one writes a book alone.

First and foremost, I want to thank those people who have so honestly and thoughtfully told their residential school stories. Some stories I heard privately, some publicly. The last residential school closed in 1996, and most were closed much earlier. But the legacy of the schools, and the ideals that made them possible, are still an integral part of Canadian society. We must each do our part to make the future different.

Without my husband, Ray Kohut, and his heartfelt belief in this book, along with my ability to write it, it would never have seen the light of day. He was supported in his cheerleading by family members and friends both near and far, as each encouraged, read and critiqued drafts, and encouraged some more.

My writing group has been of invaluable support. We have met for many years and their love of the craft, their honest feedback and true friendship have sustained me in keeping the dream alive.

My editors, Mary-Lynn Hammond and Colette Stoeber, offered up gently worded pearls of wisdom; of which you, dear readers, are the lucky recipients.

My proofreading friends, Nicola Jennings and Gerri McManus, gave of their time and talents to fine tune the manuscript - any errors you may find are mine entirely!

And finally, this book could not have been put together without the skills of the people at Tellwell.

Chi Meegwetch. Thank you all!

1920: Duncan Campbell Scott, Superintendent General of Indian Affairs, makes attendance at residential school compulsory.

1920s: The government buys and takes over many church owned schools. The churches continue to operate them.

1931: Peak period of residential schools, 80 across Canada.

1940 Government policy changes to encourage day schools and integration with provincial public schools.

1948: End of compulsory attendance at residential schools.

1969: The Canadian Government takes over the residential schools from the churches.

1970: First residential school to be run by a band.

1980s: Small groups of residential school survivors start court cases against the government and churches.

1996: Gordon Indian Residential School, the last residential school, closes.

1996: Royal Commission on Aboriginal Peoples. A report to develop strategies to improve the relationships between Aboriginal Peoples, the federal government and Canada as a whole.

2006: Indian Residential Schools Settlement Agreement. A federal financial compensation package for residential school survivors.

2008: Truth and Reconciliation Commission begins it's work.

2015: Truth and Reconciliation Commission presents its report.

Apologies
1986: United Church
1993: Anglican Church
1994: Presbyterian Church
2008: Canada
2015: Alberta, Manitoba
2016: Ontario

A BRIEF CHRONOLOGICAL HISTORY OF INDIAN RESIDENTIAL SCHOOLS

Early 1600s: The earliest 'residential schools' run by missionaries in New France. They were poorly attended and run independently.

Early 1800s: Church schools, run by various denominations.

1831: The first Indian residential school opens in Brantford, Ontario. It closed in 1970.

1842: The Bagot Commission recommends that residential schools should teach agriculture, proposing that assimilation would be best achieved if children were separated from their parents.

1847: Report on Native Education – Ryerson recommends industrial and agricultural schools to be run by the government and churches. He supports Bagot's proposal that keeping children from their parents would promote assimilation.

1857: The Gradual Civilization Act – This act sought to encourage assimilation of Aboriginal people through enfranchisement. It was altered to become the Gradual Enfranchisement Act in 1869.

1867: Confederation of Canada, BNA Act

1876: The Indian Act – This act defines who is and who is not a status Indian. It also outlines federal roles and responsibilities for status Indians and the lands set aside for them.

1879: The Davin Report recommends setting up industrial boarding schools for "Indians and half-breeds" with church support.

1884: School attendance (not necessarily residential school) becomes compulsory for status Indian children.

1892: The federal government and churches partner to operate residential schools.

sexual abuse, it's hard to believe that anyone who spent their childhood at an Indian residential school could leave with enough belief in themselves to create a meaningful life—for themselves, and especially for their children.

Intergenerational trauma is something we have only recently given a name to, but it has been around as long as there have been generations. How is it possible to raise a healthy child when you have never watched someone else do it? When you, and most of the people around you, are struggling: mentally, physically, spiritually and emotionally? It's simply not possible.

And yet.

And yet here is Belinda's great-granddaughter, Emily. And she is not alone. There are thousands of Emilys across this country. Against all the odds, she walks tall and strong. She is not a white person with brown skin. She knows and loves her Anishinabe heritage. Somewhere along the line, her people, given horrendous circumstances, chose the heroic. For many, life was, and continues to be, a struggle against persuasive voices that live in their heads and in their communities. Voices that tell them they are unworthy, that there is no hope. Voices that are only quieted by alcohol, drugs or suicide.

Yet, someone, many someones, found the courage to rise up against those voices and claim their birthright as beautiful, whole, and valuable souls. Their lives serve as a lesson to us all.

All my relations.

But I am old enough now to know that few things really end. A wretched ending is really nothing more than an uncomfortable bump in the road.

So now, let me bring you back to the present: my sweet granddaughter and her lovely friend. You remember them, from the prologue? They are the new "end" of this story, the new bump in the road. But this bump is not one to trip us up, rather a hilltop from which we can see grand and beautiful vistas.

When I went to teach at Bear Lake, I thought I was doing a good thing. I believed the myth that there was only one way to live a fulfilling life and it was the way I had been taught. It was as though democracy, Christianity, capitalism, upward mobility and flush toilets were indistinguishable one from the other. I went to Bear Lake having grown up in a white monoculture that prided itself on its moral, intellectual and physical superiority. This was easily demonstrated by our ability to turn a forest into a flourishing city and build an army that could prevail over the Germans twice in thirty years. We were proud, prosperous and full of promise in 1947. I too, was proud, prosperous and full of promise in 1947. I was twenty-one and there was nothing I couldn't do.

The world had been good to me, and I wanted to give something back.

So I applied for and got the job to teach at Bear Lake Indian Residential School. The prevailing sentiment was that if we couldn't make the Indians white, we could at least prepare them for a life in the white world. After all, that was the new reality. There was some truth to that; there is always some truth in good propaganda. The old way of life was dying, not only on reserves, but on farms, in the bush and in small towns everywhere. In big cities too, life was changing, and I was excited to be a part of the new generation. I was ready to save the world, and I was going to start at home.

Instead, I was saved.

The people I met at Bear Lake were unlike any I had known before. From Annie to Mrs. Norton, Silas to Brother Thomas, no one fit neatly into any of the black and white categories I had arrived with. I learned that there is no one who can be labelled good or bad. Each of us, given the right circumstances, is capable of doing horrendous things, and each of us is capable of doing heroic things.

What separates the cowardly from the courageous is when, given horrendous circumstances, we choose to be heroes.

I was humbled there. Humbled and humiliated by my inability to change the system. But more importantly, as I began to understand what the students and their families had to endure, I was humbled by the grace and courage, with which those who were affected managed to maintain their integrity, and their dignity.

When I poked my ineffectual sword at the feudal culture of Bear Lake Indian Residential School, I was met with a wall of arrogance. I hated that wall and all the people and institutional frameworks that kept it impenetrable. Later, as time and reflection gave me some perspective, I came to realize that I was just as much a part of that wall as Mother Magdalene or Brother Peter, and that it was not unique to Bear Lake Indian Residential School. It was everywhere, and it was built by our collective arrogance. We honestly believed that given the alternatives, any thinking person would choose our way of life, a model of democracy, individuality and upward mobility that represented our noblest ideals. It was literally unthinkable that any other model of community might be preferred or, heaven forbid, thought to be better. In addition, there was an unequivocal notion that only white-skinned people could claim this advanced culture. The realization of my own collusion with, and inherent belief in, this notion of cultural superiority surprised me, bewildered me, dismayed me. It seemed an impossible task to clean up the mess we had created.

Then one day Emily, Belinda's great-granddaughter, showed up on my doorstep.

Emily was not a mess. She was a delightful, confident young woman.

It hit me then that maybe we, who had made this mess, weren't the best people to clean it up. That thinking we are is just more arrogance, best left behind along with all the other tools of persuasion and coercion that hadn't worked the first time around.

There were good and kind people at Bear Lake Indian Residential School. I'm sure there were good and kind people at every Indian residential school. But goodness and kindness can only go so far when your role is to make someone believe their history, culture and very DNA are something shameful. Even without any physical or

SEPTEMBER 2010

My dear reader, I will not leave you there. Although, truth be told, I was left there for longer than I care to remember. Belinda had a little girl, born on August 27, 1948, ironically, a year to the day that I first arrived at Bear Lake. We continued to write, although as the years passed and both our responsibilities grew, we had less time for letters, until finally, without my even being aware of it, there were no more. The last time I heard from her she had moved to Bear Lake. It was her turn to sit at home while her children lived a few miles away at the residential school. By the time the school closed, in 1968, our correspondence had already ended.

When I left Bear Lake, I thought I had failed. Belinda was pregnant, Brother Peter was still principal of the high school, and I was not going back. I felt deeply ashamed that I had not done anything to improve the lives of the children there. Reading Brother Thomas's pages helped me to see that things had shifted more than I realized. But at the time, my departure felt like a wretched ending.

EPILOGUE